P9-ARG-733

a/k/a

also by Ruthann Robson

Fiction

Another Mother
Cecile
Eye of a Hurricane

Nonfiction

Legal Issues for Lesbians and Gay Men
Lesbian (Out)Law: Survival Under the Rule of Law

a/k/a

Ruthann Robson

St. Martin's Press
New York

CARVER PUBLIC LIBRARY
P.O. BOX 328 MAIN STREET
CARVER, MA 02330

This is a work of fiction. Names, characters, places, and incidents either are the product of the author's imagination or are used fictitiously, and any resemblance to actual persons, living or dead, events, or locales, is entirely coincidental.

a/k/a. Copyright © 1997 by Ruthann Robson. All rights reserved. Printed in the United States of America. No part of this book may be used or reproduced in any manner whatsoever without written permission except in the case of brief quotations embodied in critical articles or reviews. For information, address St. Martin's Press, 175 Fifth Avenue, New York, N.Y. 10010.

A version of Chapter 4 appeared in *Close Calls: New Lesbian Fiction*, edited by Susan Fox Rogers (St.Martin's Press, 1996).

Design by Nancy Resnick

Library of Congress Cataloging-in-Publication Data

Robson, Ruthann.
    a/k/a : a novel / Ruthann Robson.
      p. cm.
    ISBN 0-312-15469-0
    1. Lesbians—New York (State)—New York—Fiction. I. Title.
    PS3568.03187A8 1997
    813'.54—dc21   97-7200
                                 CIP

First Edition: September 1997

10 9 8 7 6 5 4 3 2 1

acknowledgments

For critical support throughout various projects including this novel, I am grateful to my editor, Keith Kahla, my agent, Laurie Liss, my friend, Victoria Brownworth, and my lover, S. E. Valentine.

For incisive comments on the manuscript, in addition to the foregoing, I am indebted to Sima Rabinowitz, Margaret McIntyre, and Steve Scott.

For generosities important to the creative process, I would like to thank David Nadvorney (for his apartment), Steve McNaghten (for his candor about his career), Kathy Kennedy and Chris Weizel (for allowing me access to the production of daytime dramas), Denise Holzka (for glass), and several women who wish to remain anonymous (for free-ranging and detailed discussions about their personal lives).

contents

Part One: Prelude
Chapter One   *3*
Chapter Two   *7*
Chapter Three   *10*

Part Two: Margaret
Chapter Four   *15*
Chapter Five   *31*
Chapter Six   *51*

Part Three: BJ
Chapter Seven   *67*
Chapter Eight   *86*
Chapter Nine   *101*

Part Four: Episode
Chapter Ten   *121*
Chapter Eleven   *131*
Chapter Twelve   *134*

Part Five: Margaret
Chapter Thirteen   *141*
Chapter Fourteen   *153*
Chapter Fifteen   *156*

Part Six: BJ

    Chapter Sixteen   *171*

    Chapter Seventeen   *183*

    Chapter Eighteen   *187*

Part Seven: Margaret

    Chapter Nineteen   *203*

    Chapter Twenty   *215*

    Chapter Twenty-one   *223*

Part Eight: BJ

    Chapter Twenty-two   *233*

    Chapter Twenty-three   *241*

    Chapter Twenty-four   *245*

Part Nine: Coda

    Chapter Twenty-five   *259*

    Chapter Twenty-six   *272*

    Chapter Twenty-seven   *276*

part one

Prelude

one

The name on the door, etched on a flaking gold-colored plate, is PROFESSOR GERTRUDE YARNES. Two women hover in the hallway; neither of them Professor Gertrude Yarnes; both of them glancing at the nameplate on the door as if to summon the professor to her ten o'clock appointment.

There are other names etched on other plates on the doors of the other offices in the hallway. Each woman walks a little one way and then the other, reading other nameplates on other office doors, pacing the narrow hallway that continues for an equally moderate distance in both directions until it right-angles into stairwells that only go down. Each woman guesses that the other is also waiting for the same professor, hoping that this is not true. Schedules are tight. And each woman is already wincing at the eventual arrival of the professor with the attendant jockeying. To be first is certainly preferred, but both women are awkward with the graciousness demanded of the position of preference. To be postponed is presumably insulting, and both women are weary of the trivial indignities of the city.

Each woman wishes she had brought something she could read. In fact, each woman has something she could be—should be—reading in the leather bag she carries.

In the black leather knapsack, purchased from a vendor on 14th Street, there is *Casebook and Materials on Criminal Procedure, 5th Edi-*

tion. It is a thick brown book, marked with yellow highlighters and annotated with black ink until about page seventy-five.

In the red leather bucket bag, purchased at Leather Loft in an upstate factory outlet mall, there is *Episode #7839*. It is a stapled sheaf of ordinary copy paper, with green stars on the top of about one-third of the pages, marking her parts in the script.

Neither woman judges her reading suitable. Too unwieldy, too revealing. So each is relegated to glancing again and again at the names on the doors, at the outdated announcements on the walls, and at each other.

One woman watches the other hoist the black knapsack from shoulder to shoulder, shifting its weight on her average frame. It is not only her frame that is average. Medium height and weight, with medium brown hair of a medium length. White skin, but neither fair nor olive. Difficult to see the eyes from this distance, but probably some shade of hazel. Nothing striking about her, nothing at all. She could play any role, except the most singular. And yet, attractive. Especially that tentative smile. Yes, attractive after a few glimpses. Or perhaps it is only the absence of obvious defects, a condition often mistaken for attractiveness.

The woman with the black knapsack feels the glances, the assessment, interspersing her own between polite pauses. The woman with the red leather bucket bag looks vaguely familiar, or perhaps she just has that familiar look about her. There is always the chance that they have met before, of course, but it is not only the size of the city that is responsible for the instant suppression of this possibility. There is also a distinctive brightness about her, unusual in the capital of fashionable black. The red bucket bag is tastefully, if inexactly, matched by bright red suede shoes, accessorizing a silkish jumpsuit of a red print. An expensive haircut, but not executive. A bit of natural-look makeup, heavy on the mascara. Well off and conventional. And yet, beguiling. The way she throws the red bag over her shoulder. Yes, beguiling even after a half hour of staring past her silhouette. Or, perhaps it is only the absence of explicit and polite interaction, a situation that enhances interest.

4

At ten-thirty, in the fluorescent corridor, one woman looks at her silver watch and announces the time, looking at the other woman for confirmation. The other woman nods ever so slightly, as if in agreement.

In another part of the building, Professor Gertrude Yarnes also looks at her watch, attempting discretion, wishing she could deftly excuse herself from this meeting with the administrative dean and vice-chancellor concerning the new budget. While the professor may believe her ten o'clock appointments, inadvertently scheduled for the same time, are more important than this discussion, she knows that the administrative dean and vice-chancellor would not concur. In her more bureaucratic moments, she agrees with the administrative dean and vice-chancellor, even as she positions herself against them, advocating the preservation of certain "expensive" portions of the academic program. So she resigns herself to apologies and rescheduling, refusing both guilt and self-pity.

The professor allows herself to think that perhaps the two waiting women will simply assume she has been detained and invite each other for coffee in the downstairs lounge, amusing themselves with witty conversation which would gradually—or at least by the second cup—evolve into a more substantive exchange. They would be perfect for each other, Gertrude Yarnes muses, although she does not know either the law student or the soap opera actress particularly well, does not even know anything for certain about their sexual preferences. Still, she thinks, they both seem so lesbian, as well as serious and smart, albeit in very different ways. In the Criminal Procedure class that Gertrude teaches, she has observed the law student take notes with an attentiveness that even the student's studied casualness cannot disguise. On the soap opera for which Gertrude is a consultant, she has noticed the actress interpret a crucial legal scene with a subtlety that even an actress's professional training cannot explain. Yes, Gertrude thinks, both women so extraordinary in ways difficult to articulate. And both so deserving of the kind of love that makes life worth living, that makes life more than scrutinizing the numbers floating on the piece of paper that the vice-chancellor slides toward her, that makes life more than the hope she will find some carefully crafted deception masquerading as a mistake. Gertrude Yarnes suppresses her imagination of the two women sipping coffee and concentrates on the calculations.

It does not occur to either woman in the hallway to introduce herself and obligate the other to respond with a name. Each woman avoids such interactions, especially in unstructured situations. For each woman has more than one name and changes names more often than she changes her leather bag.

It does occur to each woman to suggest coffee—or something—to prolong their contact. Some temporary insulation from the complicated life that awaits beyond this hallway. Some possibility of simplicity that is not superficial.

But neither woman speaks.

And if asked at this moment whether she believes in love at first sight, each would laugh the light tinkle of denial. And if asked at this moment whether she believes in love at all, each would laugh again, only with much shorter and shallower sounds, echoing as the two women shadow each other down the stairs and out to the street, fading into the city, beyond each other's horizon.

two

*M*argaret, a proper and protective name. Like the precise pigment of a blanket a mother might choose for her day-old infant, admiring the shade against the baby's skin, both mother and daughter innocent of the color's cloying consequences. As if inevitable, the irritating pink of Margaret becomes the salmon of Peggy, the tea rose of Rita, the coral of Maggie, and even the shocking fluorescence of Marbalo. Each foster parent, however temporary, seems to desire a unique identity, an alteration of aura. The caseworker does not make a notation of this parade of nicknames; her notes only reflect average weight and average height, competent school work, and a "chameleon personality."

Margaret would take this judgment and bend it into necessary talents. Her talent: to control the perceptions of her, to control her own perceptions. Perhaps a minor talent, but perhaps not.

Developed beyond pink. The red of Melanie. The green of Colette. The yellow of Ursula. Violet. Olive. The subdued brown of Tamara. The blue of sky and ocean and salty promises birthed in colonies of criminals who changed their lives and their names.

For each client she chooses her name. She uses lists of names from a little book, *Les Guérillères,* that Dominique had left behind. But some of those names are too exotic, meaning they are both too easily forgotten and too easily remembered. Alienor, for example. The more suitable names have little checks. The book's spine is split from use, from having tiny pieces of paper scribbled with places and dates inserted into its weary pages.

Margaret was the name she chose for her competent school work; it was the name closest to the student she wanted to be, a name not merely from a book but also from the closest thing she had to a past. Like the public school teachers her caseworker had interviewed, her undergraduate professors had found Margaret Smyth smart, even exceptionally smart, but never brilliant. Several teachers sensed a buried potential and tried to bully and coax Margaret. But brilliance requires both risk and passion, and her professors could provoke neither. So they soon abandoned their efforts, judging Margaret as lacking in ambition and begrudging her the excellent grades she continued to earn. Some of them were surprised when they learned she was going to law school; the most cynical of them used this information to confirm their low opinion of lawyers. None of them asked Margaret why she had chosen law; none of them would have understood her one word answer—Dominique—even if she could have uttered it.

Whether she is being Margaret or Ursula or Tamara, she eschews colors other than the bright hues of her name. Black is the color she chooses to wear when she is Margaret. Even her underwear, especially her underwear. Black is inconspicuous in the city, but she had worn it when it had seemed more dramatic than modest. It makes it very easy to do the wash, although it makes her closet incredibly dark. Brightened only by Ursula and Melanie.

That long hallway of a closet, like a coffin almost, that separates her apartment from itself, that separates her life. She bolts the front door, checks the front bedroom and bathroom, looks briefly at the neat kitchen, all from habit. She sidles into the closet, pausing to hang up a black jacket on a wooden hanger, not pausing to check the contents of her tapestry-covered attaché sequestered in the darkest corner. Then she exits the other side of the closet into her back bedroom, the sunlight flickering through the three floor-to-ceiling windows she thinks of as her three graces. She looks west out the windows and into a future she is still imagining, her horizon interrupted by New Jersey. Two other walls of the large room boast tall bookshelves, on which volumes are stacked both vertically and horizontally. Biographies. Australia. Books that might tell her about her own life. The life she has; the life she wants.

She props her black leather backpack against a chair back, fishing out *Casebook and Materials on Criminal Procedure, 5th Edition.* The thick textbook joins the other thick textbooks on the table she uses as a desk. For a few hours, she looks over her notes from the previous class and reads the cases for the next class, while the afternoon sun slants lower and lower through her windows, descending to the river.

Then she takes *Les Guérillères* from her shelf, checking a yellow Post-it note with squiggles of water-based ink. Unlike a certain professor who did not show up for an appointment this morning, she is always punctual and efficient.

three

*B*J." He calls to her, motioning her to move away from the woman who has captured her attention. When she does not respond, he calls again, "BJ," allowing the last letter to be inflected with irritation. Despite himself, he smiles at his failure to break through her absorption in her conversation; he appreciates the way she nods her head sympathetically at the woman. Then he shields his mouth with his hand and yells toward her, "Hey, Jill. Jill Willis." But even his transition from familiar to professional does not attract her attention. So he cups both hands like a megaphone around his fading smile, imitating the PA systems. "Paging Mavis Paige. Paging Mavis Paige. Your presence is required immediately." She looks over at him, acknowledging their old joke, and shrugs apologetically. Returning her face to the woman's, she gestures in his direction, giving the woman a pat on the arm, amplified by a quick hug. Then she gives him her attention, following the trajectory of his head, compliantly walking toward her office.

"Again," he commands. She does not want to do it again. She is tired, having already spent time waiting for that law professor who failed to show. But neither BJ Willensky nor Jill Willis nor even Mavis Paige would ever question him, although each has different supports for the well-constructed edifices of acquiescence.

So, she opens and closes the door gingerly, both because that is what Jill Willis knows she should do to a door that hangs on a plywood frame attached to corrugated walls and because that is what Mavis Paige does when she returns to her office after a difficult day defending the downtrodden. Step one, two, three. Towards the desk. Stop. Turn.

"What?" Pause. "What are you doing here?" Startled, but not altogether displeased.

"We have a few things to talk about," the man standing in the set that is her office says very seriously. He looks very smooth and shaven, but his speech is a shade too hesitant.

He walks toward her. One. Two. She sits on the desk and looks up at him. He leans down to kiss her. She averts her face. But only slightly.

The tears stream down her cheeks. Beautifully plump tears. Tears that do not puff her eyes or mottle her pale skin or swell her sinuses. This is her talent: she can cry without the usual symptoms; she can cry and remain passably pretty. Her entire career is not built upon this singular talent, but it is certainly a weight-bearing column.

The man grabs her chin and covers her mouth with his roughly, using his tongue to separate her lips.

She does not think he is very good at his craft. Does not think her new love interest will last long; they never do. Sometimes they become someone else's lover in amicable breakups in which she bounces back to give them advice about their new girlfriends. Sometimes they just disappear, having been murdered or placed in a witness protection program.

She used to suffer all these kisses from all these men by thinking of her woman lover of the moment. Until her woman lover of the moment—of the year, of twelve years—became Lenore. She finds it difficult to use Lenore as a buffer, difficult to imagine Lenore as a predicate to pretending passion. But she has long disguised this difficulty with professionalism.

Breaking the kiss, she looks at her current love interest. Long and hard. Counting in her head, waiting for a voice to interrupt, the same voice she did not hear earlier when she was consoling the prop girl about lover troubles. But now she would hear that voice even if it were a whisper. Her whole body is attuned to that voice, the voice of the director-of-the-day, which will tell the cameras to cut and let everyone know the teaser scene is over.

"Five minutes," the director-of-the-day announces. She smiles at him and he returns the smile. They are not friends, but they have worked together for almost twenty years, for almost half of their respective lives. Friendship would be superfluous. It might mean that he would know that "Jill" forms no part of "BJ," like he assumes it does. It might mean that she would know he had wanted to be a Hollywood director, but she assumes that he once did. It might mean that they would know each other better, but it might also mean that they would know each other less.

In her closet-sized room, she routs through her red leather bucket bag, looking for today's script amid the other scripts for *In the Name of Love*. Yes, that's the one: *Episode #7839*. She worries over her costume first. The bright blue dress? Good, she knows where that is, knows how it will fit. Her mother will like this dress when she sees it; her mother says she looks stunning in royal blue. BJ smiles at the thought of her mother, then goes back to the script to review her lines while the crew runs through the other teasers. Then her parts in two scenes in two of the six acts, at the beginning and end; still the possibility of an early exit looms. If the rest of the blocking goes well. If no one is late from lunch. If the taping goes smoothly. If. If. If. Then she could drive out of the city, following the river north, toward the horizon, home to Lenore. Then she could kiss Lenore, and kiss Malcolm, their child. Then she could fix dinner, fix the glitch in Malcolm's computer like she had promised, fix it all. Then. Then. Then.

part two

Margaret

four

Ann-Marie is my rent. I am her identity, her adultery, her orgasm.
We are each other's Thursday evenings.

She tells her husband she is taking art lessons to fulfill her long-
neglected talents. She tells me this conversationally, guiltily proud
of her deceit. She tells me this, week after month after year. Sometimes we go to museums, as if we are art students, and then go to
dinner at mediocre Midtown restaurants, as if we are tourists. Other
times we go to galleries because Ann-Marie wants to see work that
is trendy. But our schedule demands we hurry back to my apartment
on Riverside Drive; Ann-Marie must leave the city by eleven P.M.
And, if she does not linger too long after sex, petting my head and
practicing her excuses, I sometimes have time to see someone else.
But usually I read; sometimes I study.

Ann-Marie is a large woman. She wears size eleven shoes and
shops at Tall-Girl. Middle age has not eroded her hesitancy about
her height. She hunches, folding her shoulders as if they are flaps
that would close the envelope of her body. Her back curves like a
question mark: the one which I answer. It is the hook by which I
hooked her.

Ann-Marie is a good woman. Balancing generosity and morality.
She is not paying for my services, she is helping me out. She is a minister's daughter, a minister's wife. She is a cheerleader's mother, a

choir director. She calls herself my lover, or my friend. She calls me Tamara. She pays cash, the first Thursday of every month.

Ann-Marie wants to be an artist, a painter perhaps. Or a even a potter. Instead of practicing those techniques, she flexes her long fingers above her head, gripping my pillows as I touch her. Her talents are evident as she arches her back, inverting her interrogatories into declarative moans; her shoulders stretch, unself-conscious, smoothed by my talents. Afterwards, I massage her broad back and watch the clock.

"Tamara," she says when she leaves, hunching into a blazer that seems too small.

"Thursday," I say. And smile at her as she shifts her long, long bones toward the place she calls home.

This Thursday she seems preoccupied. I move to soothe, but also to excite. It is a precarious balance. I suggest a museum, an important one with a new show and Thursday evening hours. She declines, shaking her head.

I swallow to allow me a second to contemplate my reaction. Compassionate or rude? What does she really want, beneath the bent wings of her shoulder blades, kindness or direction? Or some subtle combination?

"Oh," I say, "I should have known." I sound contrite.

"Known what?" Ann-Marie betrays her curiosity, but also her anxiety.

"That show would probably upset you," I say.

"It would not."

"I've heard it's very graphic."

"What does that mean?"

"Graphic, you know, like sexually explicit." I wink at Ann-Marie.

"I know what graphic means. I mean, what do you mean?"

"About what?" I lick my lips, slightly. Ann-Marie's eyes follow the edge of my tongue. She no longer seems so preoccupied.

"About that. About me being upset by some show. What do you mean?"

16

"Oh, nothing."

"I can't believe you think I'm like that."

"I don't," I say. But now Ann-Marie is riveted on me, or more precisely, on my perception of her. Ann-Marie wants me to value her artistic judgments; sometimes it seems as if she forgets I am not her art teacher.

"I've just heard that this show isn't as spectacular as its hype."

"Probably not," I agree.

She smiles.

"But it does sound fun," I tell her.

"Let's just have dinner."

It is my turn to smile, so I do.

"Some take-home."

I nod. We turn back and walk a few blocks to that most famous and most crowded of Upper West Side delicatessens, a department store of gourmet food. I always meet Ann-Marie here, near the cheeses. She usually has one of the store's distinctive white-with-orange-print bags, full of treats to bring home to her husband and child. Nothing that needs to be refrigerated. But this evening she buys a bag for us. "What would you like?" she asks me.

"You choose," I tell her. Her eyes brighten and focus, rewarding my hunch. She wants to take care of me tonight; she wants to nest; she wants to try me out as a different life but not too different from the one waiting in Connecticut. I assume that things are not going well at home. I sense her fear.

I let her unwrap the packages in my kitchen. "Roasted chicken, how wonderful!" I compliment her.

"Do you really like it?"

I kiss her neck in response and take out a bottle of wine from the cupboard. "Just a glass."

I kiss her neck again, almost chastely but certainly appreciatively.

"I hope you like potato salad." She holds up a plastic container. "It has some of that French mustard in it."

I kiss her neck again, murmuring about mustard.

After our kitchen picnic, Ann-Marie commenting several times on the smallness of my apartment, she takes out the final box from her bag. "Russian pastries," she announces.

"Would you like some coffee?" I offer, although I do not want to dilute the effect of her three glasses of Cabernet.

"Coffee?" She turns on me as if I have said something ugly.

I try to step back in the tiny kitchen.

She softens quickly, not only because she is a woman who always softens quickly, but because she must realize she is being silly. "Oh, I must not have told you. I'm giving up coffee. Have given it up, really. I think it's ruining my life. All that caffeine. You know, it just takes over your life. It's really been my major problem."

I stifle a smile, but she does not notice.

"Did you know I started drinking coffee when I was thirteen years old?" She looks at me for confirmation of this tragedy. "I mean, my parents gave it to me. My own parents! Can you believe that? That parents could be so uncaring. It was my parents who started me on coffee!"

She is nearly shrieking now, so I nod sympathetically. I suppress the urge to murder her by pouring her another glass of wine.

Your parents gave you coffee? My parents gave me up.

Of course, I do not say this.

What I say, to myself, is that it doesn't matter. It doesn't matter. Nothing matters that can't be changed. I lead her to the windowless bedroom, where I will lick the chicken grease from the side of her mouth, where her lipsticked lips meet.

Tamara browns the lamp and sits next to Ann-Marie on the bed, taking the glass of Cabernet and putting it on the shining white night table within reach. She holds Ann-Marie's hand for a moment before unbuttoning Ann-Marie's crepe blouse. Ann-Marie sighs, tilting her head back as if to offer her throat, or perhaps her still-encased breasts. Tamara accepts both, starting with simple kisses that accelerate to untoothed sucks with the pace of Ann-Marie's breaths.

* * *

Tamara is careful not to make slurping sounds, careful to remove Ann-Marie's blouse and drape it neatly on the white bedroom chair, careful not to snap the elastic as she unfastens the substantial bra, careful to modulate her motions to the blotches of excitement speckling Ann-Marie's chest. Ann-Marie shifts, stands up, slips off her shoes, and removes her skirt and stockings, tossing them toward the crepe blouse. When the clothes fall to the floor, it is Tamara who folds them neatly, arranging them more sturdily on the chair. Ann-Marie poses on the bed, imitating a Renaissance artist's model. She pats the empty space next to her, as if Tamara is a painter who will color and shape her with admiration, making her real.

Afterwards, Ann-Marie cries. Ann-Marie sobs on Tamara's still-shirted shoulder about her minister husband, the one who will not fuck her. Ann-Marie rages against Tamara's ceiling about her first lover, the woman who did fuck her—oh, did she ever—but then left her for the army. These weepy monologues are as predictable as Ann-Marie's orgasms, only more passionate and less efficient. Ann-Marie says "fuck" as if it were the ultimate release, prolonging its single syllable as long as she can. Tamara delivers the attention required of her by listening for a change in Ann-Marie's weekly narrative— a detail embellished or omitted, an insight gained or erased—but it is always the same, almost exactly.

Always ended by Ann-Marie asking curtly, "The time?" and Tamara announcing it, passing her clothes. The dressing, the bathroom, Ann-Marie gathering her things together, checking the bedroom again. Ann-Marie's polite kiss at the door with her relipsticked lips in the same pucker she uses for the elderly parishioners. And, if it is the first Thursday of the month, there will be Ann-Marie's envelope of money, a rectangle remaining on the chair where her clothes had been.

When I step out of the shower, steam still circling around the black vinyl curtain, I am no longer Tamara.

19

I slip into my closet. That long hallway of a closet, like a coffin almost, that separates my apartment from itself, that separates my life. On the other side of the closet is the back bedroom.

It is just past midnight, but the lights of the city flicker off the river and through my three windows, my three glass graces. I look west, out the windows, as if trying to see a future I could choose. But my horizon is interrupted by New Jersey.

In these moments, I am no one. Hovering. Pure. Like an angel. Like the moon or a river on another continent. Like the brightest blue.

My hair is still wet. I could wrap it in another towel, but I don't want to go back through the closet, back out there. I could check my messages from my numerous services, but I don't. I could study, but I have no classes on Fridays, so I don't. I could masturbate, read a book, get dressed and go get an ice cream or a coffee or a slice of pizza, but I don't want to do any of these.

I just look out the long narrow windows, recounting how they came to be my windows. Reciting silently how this boarded-up back bedroom came to be my room, as if examining a bolt of expensive fabric for a hole in my story. Retracing my steps, looking for the missing link whose name is Dominique.

Maybe I was fourteen, maybe a bit younger, maybe older. But definitely not twenty, not yet eighteen. I was still a ward of the state. I was illegal.

"I'm from Australia," I told her.

She laughed, tilting her chin toward the rip in my American jeans. "And I'm from France."

"Paris?" I hoped I could make a sophisticated joke, something about April in New York. But she did not answer me, only posed on the sidewalk as if allowing me to look at her. I did. She had hair that was every color human hair could be and eyes of no color that any human would remember. Her skin was beige, covered in some places by makeup or a sidewalk-colored blouse or tiger print pants that were tight only if one looked closely. I looked closely. One had to look closely at Dominique because she blended with her surroundings. And I looked closely because I knew enough to be wary of people who seemed malleable. I was one of them. We are smooth, striped snakes waiting in the grass until it is safe to strike at what we want. So, I needed to figure out what it was she wanted with me, so she'd never have the chance to strike. Unless what she wanted was what I wanted. Which meant I needed to figure out what it was that I wanted, or at least what I needed.

I figured she wanted a friend, a daughter, or even a trick.

I knew I needed a place to sleep and a bath.

But she did not want what I thought she wanted; maybe she did not know what she wanted. Except perhaps a cat, a witness to her existence. Maybe she just picked me off the streets because her elegant prewar building prohibited pets. I was something she could comb when she wanted and ignore when she didn't. Camouflage is useless without background, without danger.

After I got what I needed, some sleep and a bath, and after I got other things I needed, some French bread and Greek cheese that I folded together like a common sandwich, I did not know how to think about what I wanted.

So I watched her, since she seemed to like that. I watched her treat her hair with an artist's paint brush she dipped into different bottles she kept on an oval tray. She would stretch a strand tight as a canvas, then stare at it in the mirror until she decided where the bit of highlighter or bleach or auburn toner would go. Watched her watch me. Watched her slide the needle under her tongue, pretending I wasn't watching, pretending I didn't notice that even the inside of her mouth was beige, like a faded paper bag.

Valium was plentiful. As were Quaaludes. And beauties, those black whirls of amphetamines. Some of her clients were physicians, she told me, but that didn't explain the cocaine, the heroin. Sometimes I think that what she wanted was for me to save her. To watch her long enough and hard enough that rescue would be the only obvious option.

Instead, I organized her. Her drugs, her clients, her clothes, in her long closet that was as narrow as a coffin. I organized her back bed-room, back behind the closet-coffin which was really a hall, a secret passageway like in a European mystery. I dusted the hair-color bot-tles and the bottles of tea rose, the only cologne in the apartment. I shined the wooden floors to reflect the light from the trinity of win-dows that framed Riverside Park. When I looked out the windows, I could see trees, trees that were budding a jaundiced green against the background of the wide, almost-blue Hudson River. I straight-ened piles of papers: old newspapers, little notebooks with half the pages torn out, calendars that could fit in the palm of a hand, cock-tail napkins ripped with ballpoint pen numbers. And then I organized other papers: ones in a bag she pushed toward me. There were rent receipts and yearly leases, bank deposit slips and checkbook starter kits, bills from Con Ed, some Canadian currency, and a hospital bill from an emergency room stamped PAID.

She told me I did a good job. I waited for her to ask me how I knew how to do all these things. I was ready to smooth over my background as a foster child into something more glamorous. I was ready to shed my own sad story: the foster parents who kept me for seven years until they divorced and I was no longer the cute and adoptable tod-dler. The succession of foster mothers afterwards. The ones I can no longer remember. Except for the last one.

But Dominique never asked.

So I asked her. More for something to say, I guess. To fill up the space where her question about my past would go. I asked her if her name was really Sarah Tudor, like Con Ed and CitiBank and the Ridgeway Management company seemed to think. She laughed a raspy laugh and told me I'd better learn her rules if I was going to stay with her. "Rule one," she said, "I don't answer personal ques-tions."

I didn't ask anything else, just thought about the "if" in the possi-bility that I might stay with her. Just thought about whether it was an invitation or not. Just thought until I knew I couldn't think about it anymore.

Instead, I thought about whether that was really rule number one. And whether it was her rule or my rule. And thought about scrawled notes I'd seen in her tiny notepads: *Never trade sex for money with a woman. Plan for forty. Never pity clients. No chains.* I supposed these were other rules.

Sometimes they appeared next to numbers, like lists. Mostly they just floated on what remained of torn out pages. *No whoring for women,* she wrote. Over and over. I wondered whether it was a litany to lost opportunities. Or whether it was the way she convinced herself she had limits.

We sat in the back bedroom, which I realized must have been intended as the living room and dining room of the apartment. Someone had bricked over the entrance between the kitchen and this room; someone had transformed the hallway into a closet. She took off her shoes and I took them to the closet, placing them on the floor in line with the other pairs of shoes. I rubbed her feet, first the arches and then the heels, first with my thumbs and then with my whole hands. She sighed, sipping what I had thought was iceless water. The lemon rind refused to float, despite her prompting with a long index finger. Later on I asked her: "What's rule number two?"

She asked me why I wanted to know.

I told her I didn't know why I wanted to know, I just wanted to know.

She told me that I shouldn't ask a question if I didn't know why I wanted to know the answer, that I shouldn't want anything unless I knew why I wanted it.

I asked her if that was a rule.

She laughed.

She told me I had to find my own rules; she told me I had to make my own choices.

She told me she wasn't my mother.

I didn't ask her what she was. I didn't ask her if rules were choices. Or if choices were rules. I only rubbed her feet some more, with some cream I mixed with tea rose cologne. I took her glass through the closet and into the kitchen, pouring from the bottle of Tanqueray she kept in the freezer, and returning to her to sit on the bed next to her. I ironed her clothes and washed out her underpants. And I kept all the pills in the right bottles and all the needles clean.

Sometimes it seemed like I was her maid, sometimes her devoted lover. But sometimes her student, her apprentice. Especially when she lectured me, even explained her rules. Rules about never fantasizing about clients: the rule was they should fantasize about her. Only she said "you," "Clients should fantasize about you, not vice versa." I tried to pretend that the "you" was a metaphor, not a prediction. Or a rule that I twisted in an attempt not to fantasize about her. That she was a beautiful lady and I was her lady-in-waiting. That she was my lover and I was her beloved. That she was not a junkie, even a junkie-trying-to-get-clean. That she was not a common whore.

She never offered me drugs. They were there; I knew how to ask. And that had always been one of my rules: not asking. Still, I was alone in the apartment often enough, I could have just taken something. Or taken something for the road when she asked me to leave the apartment for a few hours because she had to "entertain." Or taken something for the boredom when she told me to stay in the hidden back bedroom because she needed the front one for a client.

Only once, in all those months. It was late in the summer, probably past August. The wafer rested in the palm of her hand, her index finger curled over it like a fern. Wafers and ferns reminded me of Betty, my last foster mother, the one who lived in the country and took me to church three times a week. I slipped the methadone under my tongue, letting it melt like Betty had taught me to take communion. Closing my eyes against the holiness.

It was raining in the city, on the statue of Joan of Arc that stood in a triangle of grass and on the river that churned brown and gray. It was raining through the trinity of windows into the back bedroom, onto the bed which we had pushed under the unscreened windows to catch the humid breezes. It was raining on my face, next to her face. I licked drops from her face; she tasted pure with the slight burn of tea rose. I stroked her tongue with mine; she seemed swollen and reluctant. I lifted my head away from her, hitting it on the bottom of the casement. She laughed, but this time her laugh seemed easier, lower in tone and longer. I thought of Betty again, how her face was flat on the floor courtesy of my swipe with a cast-iron frying pan the day I ran away; how she called me Maggie so that it sounded like maggot; how her stomach rolled up beneath her breasts then rolled back down to her crotch, then back up, like one of those change-color waves encased in a small square of acrylic, on sale for amusement. I had wanted one once, I remembered it even now, remembered the church carnival and not asking Betty about it; it was blue and pink. . . . I stopped thinking about the toy, about Betty, about the frying pan. That was my talent: I could control my mind. I could think about this but not that; about that but not this. Even stoned on a junkie's maintenance, I could refuse to think about anything unpleasant. I could refuse to think I was a killer. Or *could* be a killer, I corrected myself.

Dominique moved a pillow under my head. The pillow was wet with rain and I pushed my face into it. She pushed my hair around with her fingers; I thought my hair pushed back. She pushed my flesh with her index finger, along my neck and around my breasts. My skin did not push back, but let her sink into it, let her sink into my bones with a dampness that made them twitch. Still, I didn't push back until I couldn't help myself, until her index finger was on my clitoris and the rest of her hand was inside me. And then it began to rain inside my head, steady and comforting. Outside did not exist.

It wasn't the first time I had ever had sex. Not even a time that still had a number. I was street smart and a graduate of foster-home-sex-education classes where it was best not to count the times with foster siblings, foster parents, and even the government workers. But it was the first time I ever had an orgasm. Not just a sort of sparkly feeling that spread through my cunt, but a feeling of being folded inside out, like swallowing my own skin and surfacing inside someone else. Coming up for air inside her, swimming against a current swollen with rain.

She was laughing.

And I was crying, though I didn't know why. Drops slid down my face onto the damp bed, and finally into the flood of her cunt, fol-

CARVER PUBLIC LIBRARY

P.O. BOX 328 MAIN STREET

CARVER, MA 02330

lowed by my tongue. I felt a little shy, but soon I hit a stride we both seemed to share. I convinced myself I knew the exact moment when she shifted into her own pleasure, not an easy accomplishment given her profession, or so I flattered myself. And I convinced myself that I knew the exact moment when her orgasm rippled through her hips as I fingered her bones and my tongue dove deeper, although there were a few times I thought this was happening.

She pulled my wet face to her shoulder. I started crying again. I really didn't know why I was crying, but knew enough to be grateful in my knowledge that she wouldn't ask. I guessed it was just the orgasm; now I knew what all the fuss was about. Why everyone else had always seemed to want it so much. Although, if I'd known that was going to be my last orgasm as well as my first, I would have been able to tag a reason to my tears.

The next day, Dominique was dead.

And I had killed her, hadn't I?

Or, at least, I might as well have murdered her.

I hadn't saved her, had I?

And now she was dead. Like Betty, supine under the frying pan.

I sat in her chair, looking out the middle window and not-thinking. Waiting for her. Waiting for her to come back to me, back from her "date." But I didn't think it was a client; I thought it was a connection. Which was why I wasn't thinking. Wasn't fantasizing any longer that her methadone maintenance was working. Just watching. Watching the people on the sidewalk coming out of the park as if summer would never end. And then watching her staggering out of the park holding her hand against her mouth. Her hand remained there when she tumbled on the curb; it did not break her fall. It only moved when she was otherwise motionless, stretched across the sidewalk, and her index finger pointed back towards the park, toward the statue of Joan of Arc, riding nowhere on her huge gelded horse.

Someone stepped over Dominique, a few people gathered.

Waves swept over me, from the inside coming out, but not demanding like nausea. I recognized it as inertia, the wave that would pull me close, pull me under whenever Betty had started slapping

CARVER PUBLIC LIBRARY
P.O. BOX 328 MAIN STREET
CARVER, MA 02330

me in the face on the way home from church; whenever any foster parent veered toward violence. The wave that rocked me back and forth, trapped in the acrylic enclosure of my life. I watched the paramedics and the police. I watched them strap her to the stretcher with her face covered, no tubes dangling from her nose, her arms, her body. It was as if she sloughed off her life, like it was no longer useful. I looked down five stories and watched them drive her away. I noticed a leaf that was starting to turn red. I noticed the dark spot on the sand-colored sidewalk.

I waited for her to come back. Thinking it might be a mistake, a nightmare, some unreality. I paid the rent, electric, and phone of Sarah Tudor. Washed clothes and tried them on. Polished the bottles, then flushed the contents. Watched the rain bang against the sidewalk. Tried to read the inscription on the platform underneath Joan of Arc and her horse. Touched myself until I was raw with boredom. Tried to convince myself that maybe absence was another one of Dominique's disguises.

By the time the picture outside of the windows looked like a fire, some trees still blazing and some already burnt bare, I had slunk into beige, into black. Fit my life around some of her rules; made up my own.

Inverted the one about sex and money and women.

My weekends are successfully busy. While my classmates are occupied studying or perhaps partying or possibly even visiting the parents who are paying their tuition, I am working. Although if my classmates saw me in public, they would think I was merely socializing. Thankfully, such coincidences do not occur often. The faculty is more troublesome. I worry that this is a tiny town only disguised as a big city; I worry that it is a small world. I worry about finding work when I graduate. Not just because I do not have the right kind of references and contacts, but because I have the wrong kind.

My plan is impossible. I have come this far, to the second year of law school, but I have so much farther to go. Escape is a fantasy. Margaret Smyth is a fantasy. With her good grades and her low profile and her application to be a research assistant for a professor, Margaret Smyth lacks a certain sparkle; she does not make a compelling fantasy. Surely, I could do better.

But Margaret Smyth is my plan for forty. A lawyer somewhere simple, representing battered women or consumers. She will live in a townhouse, a house in another town, and maybe have a cat. She will not pay Sarah Tudor's rent, she will never be called Tamara, she will not wait for Dominique to come back from her messy escape, she will not wait to be prosecuted for the murder of her foster mother. I will be her, all the time.

Impossible.

Unless I pay close attention to the details. Unless I am very lucky. It is still impossible.

Although I have gotten this far. Gotten farther than I thought I could go when I was thirty. When I was going to be thirty and realized I was not yet dead. And that I hadn't planned for that.

Impossible. Forty is impossible.

Anxiety rises like steam off my body; I decide to cool off in another hot shower. I can never take too many showers it seems. I can never take enough.

To get to the bathroom I need to leave my back bedroom, to travel through the passageway of my closet. It is dark. It is always dark. Not only because there is no light, but because so many of the clothes are black. Black is inconspicuous in the city, but once it had seemed more dramatic than modest. Now Margaret always chooses black. And Tamara, brown. A somber palette, brightened by Ursula and Melanie, who are difficult to find without the flashlight, so straight and solid and lonely, among the line of paired shoes.

The shower solves nothing.

Might as well clean for the weekend, since sleep seems as if it will be elusive. The front bedroom is first. Strip the sheets. The workers at the laundry on Columbus Avenue must think I am fastidious, if they notice at all. I like a bit of starch. I like white. I like the aura of a respectable hotel.

No need to sweep. Just take the used sheet and wipe the wooden floor. There is a scrap of paper on the floor, under the white chair. A grocery coupon. Fifty cents off. SUNLIGHT. Fresh Lemon Scent. Good on any SUNLIGHT machine dishwasher detergent, GEL or POW-DER. It must have fallen from one of Ann-Marie's pockets. Or out of her purse. Did she bring her purse to the bedroom? She must have. The date is expired. The fine print is sinister, a Warning to the Con-sumer: Coupon is Void If Used to Purchase Products for Resale.

I crumple the coupon, but suddenly a sharp anger sputters and spins. Alone in the front bedroom, and no longer Tamara, there is nothing to curb my anger. Nothing which makes me modulate it. Nothing which can transform and transcend it.

Of course, hate has many hues. There is disdain, disrespect, dis-appointment. There is fear. There is jealousy, envy, and lust. I know my hate should have the shape of disdain. A minister's wife, living in suburbia, her choices limited to gel or powder, except for her Thurs-days when she can choose an art gallery or a fuck, or some potato salad made fascinating by its mustard. A minister's wife, paying for sex with a woman, who is confident that giving up coffee is going to solve her problems.

But my anger is envy, Ann-Marie. I cannot pity your wasted life, only imagine what I would do with it, would have done with it. Be-come a librarian or an art history professor at a community college. I would have fallen in love with a dyke with bigger feet than my size elevens, a woman's basketball coach with long long legs and long thick arms and a cunt that smells like sweat and peppermint liniment. And even now, waking up married to some self-righteous minister, I'd confront him quietly and get a good settlement using the threat of scandal. I'd go somewhere like Iowa, eventually moving in with a former nun I would meet at a local woman's coffee house. We would have a garden in the summer, tomatoes and peppers and corn. She would show me how to quilt in winter. I would make floor to ceil-ing bookcases, using hand tools and no nails, only wood dowels. We would feed the squirrels and the birds. I would read biographies of famous woman artists and my lover would tend the fire. We would have a bright Mexican shawl on our old couch. We would have bright blue rugs, made by a local weaver, scattered on our ceramic tile floors. I would use coupons at the local grocery store and I would use them promptly and never let them expire. I would heed all the warnings; I would not be involved with products for resale. We would have a black and white kitchen, with a beautifully black dishwasher. I would choose powder.

Yes, I would choose powder.

five

*P*atty is from Staten Island. Daughter of a dear departed father and CEO of the company he started the year she was born, Protective Products, Inc. Bullet-proof glass. Yes, then it was glass. Now it is plastic. Patty on the phone, dealing for the newest resins. Patty on the construction site of a new bank, hard hat on her hard head. Patty and her sealed bids, her computer-generated cost estimates, her cutthroat integrity. Patty's short fingers on a blueprint, pointing at a union worker, passing me money.

Patty talks business better than any of my other clients. She is not afraid of numbers, does not think dollars are impolite. She likes to negotiate, tells me I drive a hard bargain, grinning when she says it. Yet she is among my most generous clients; her bonuses do not float on promises or expectations.

It is Friday morning and her Lincoln Continental idles at the corner of 81st Street. Of course it is her car; just in case one does not recognize the custom shade of brown paint or the creamy vinyl top or the golden wheel covers, PATTY is enscripted in gold, the italic letters about three inches high, on both front doors, just under the windows that glide up and down without making a sound. I open the door, sticking my head in first to make sure Patty—the car—contains Patty—the person. To make sure she is alone.

"Hey, Melanie," she says to me, smiling.

"Hey." I smile back. I throw my knapsack in the back seat, ask her if she brought the sleeping bags.

"In the trunk," she announces. Then launches into the tale of their procurement from Barney, her cousin, who used to go hunting before he got married to Angela, the prettiest girl from his high school. Angela does not approve of hunting, Patty grimaces, as I imagine Barney grimaces, indulgently as if to confirm Angela's continuing status as a pretty girl. "You remember Barney and Angela, don't you?" Patty's grimace shifts to a full, if oblique, smile.

"Sure do." I smile back. "But I remember some of your other cousins better."

I'm talking about Patty's cousin Dominic, which Patty well knows, because it was Dominic who brought us together. He did not introduce us or anything like that, but he was the reason Patty first contacted me. Hired me. She needed an escort for the wedding, so she looked in the classifies of a local lesbian paper. She wanted what she called a "drop-dead gorgeous dyke."

We met at a bar and she looked me over. I assumed she was a bit disappointed. I considered talking to her about how very average looking men could transform themselves into the most beautiful women with enough cosmetics, cash and courage, but I assumed that discussing drag queens was not the way to convince her I would be suitable.

"You said you want gorgeous, but you need to tell me what type of gig you want an escort for," I tried to reassure her. "Perhaps I can fit the bill, perhaps not." But, of course, I thought I could.

"A wedding."

"Yours?" I laughed.

"No." Patty was serious. "My cousin's. One cousin. But I need a woman for my other cousin. Obnoxious Dominic."

"Obnoxious? Sounds charming . . ."

"That's just a nickname," Patty quickly explained.

"But a man, right? I don't escort men."

"No, no. Not to be with him. To be with *me* in front of him."

"As a date?"

"Yes."

"You want to give me some more background?"

"Why do you need it?" Patty's voice was suddenly tinged with suspicion, as if perhaps an escort was not such a good idea.

"Well, two reasons, really." I tried to soothe her sensibilities. "First, I don't like danger and so if I have some indication of the situation I can avoid putting myself—and my client—in a precarious predicament. And second, if you have a specific goal in mind, it helps if I know what it is so that we can both work to attain it."

Patty acted as if she was considering this, sipped her drink. "Well, it's not dangerous. People get a little drunk and maybe throw a few chairs, but that's about it. As for what my goal is, I guess I want Dominic to salivate over my date."

"Salivate?" I smiled. "We"—I chose the *we* with the utmost intention—"might be able to accomplish that. So tell me, what kind of women does Dominic salivate over?"

"Gorgeous women." Patty answered simply. It was clear that she did not have sophisticated notions of beauty: Women were either gorgeous or not.

"Well, there are different types of gorgeous," I attempted to explain. "Not everybody thinks alike, do they? So, does he go for the virginal type or—"

"No." Patty's interruption was vehement.

"Then what?"

"I don't know. Pinups, I guess. *Playboy* models."

"Okay. That's a start. Any particular types? White women?"

"Yes." She laughed.

"So far, so good," I said, somewhat relieved.

"Blond." She looked away from me and my brown hair.

"Easy to accomplish."

"Breasts. Big ones."

"Also easy."

"Sexy."

"Sophisticated or street?"

Patty just looked at me, blankly. "Well . . ."

"Okay. I need some pictures. Photos of women he thinks are sexy. Girlfriends or former girlfriends. Or even some centerfolds he has pinned up."

"Can do. He has thousands of centerfolds. I'm sure he won't miss a few."

"And I need to know his favorite color," I said. She looked at me quizzically. "For the dress," I explained.

"Oh. I suppose blue."

"Navy? Royal? Peacock? Sky?"

"Pale, I guess. No. Red. He likes women in red."

I thought to ask what shade of red, but decided against it, so I simply nodded. Then we talked money. I went top of the line. Half up front. Half on the day of the wedding.

"That's pretty steep."

"Second half, conditional." My instinctual barometer put Patty in the trustworthy ranges. "Only if you're satisfied."

"If Dominic's satisfied," she said.

"And how will we know that?"

"We'll know," she said.

"Will he tell me he thinks I'm gorgeous?"

"Probably." She laughed.

We shook hands. Patty paid for the drinks. I noticed her tip was generous but sensible.

On the morning of the June wedding, Patty picked me up on the corner of 81st Street and Broadway. I had told her to look for the blonde with the breasts in the crimson dress, but still she did not seem to believe it was me when I rapped on the window of her brown Continental. In fact, she just stared at me for a long moment.

"Well, do I pass the salivate test?" I asked, after I was in the car. I crossed my legs under the silk slit to the thigh, one dyed-to-match high heel resting on her floor mat and the other dangling near the console that separated us.

"Uh. Yes." Patty was obviously flustered. She had on a two-piece dark suit of some sort, with a pleated skirt that did nothing for her, even when she was sitting down. And she had applied some pale lipstick and perhaps a little mascara.

She kept glancing at me as we drove to Staten Island. "Nice necklace," she finally said. "I have a cousin who is a jeweler."

"You have a lot of cousins." I laughed. And touched her arm. Lightly. "Don't worry, it's real."

"I wasn't worried," she said too quickly.

"Oh?"

"Okay. So maybe I am."

"So, it's not only cousin Dominic that you want to impress. Are you out to everybody in your family?" I asked, looking for clues on how to act.

"How could I not be?" She smiled her oblique smile then. "I mean, it's kind of obvious, isn't it?"

"You'd be surprised." I return her smile. "So, you want devoted lover or casual date?"

"A little of both, I guess."

I held her arm, as if I needed just a bit if direction and support, as we walked into the church. Sat close to her during the ceremony. Let the numerous glances and the few bold stares slide down my body. Stood outside the church afterwards, maneuvered through her introductions. Nodded demurely at her mother. Less demurely at her uncles. Held her arm again as we walked the few blocks from the church to the banquet hall. Soon I was sitting at the table, in front of the placard that announced PATTY'S GUEST and next to cousin Dominic. I waited for Patty to introduce me to him before I looked at his eyes with mine, which I knew shimmered blue and brilliant courtesy of my DuraBright contact lenses. His were bloodshot. Next to him, the woman Patty introduced as "Dominic's wife," was wearing a red dress with an empire waist. She was chewing gum and did not return my gaze. "What did you say your name was?" I reached across Dominic and grazed his wife's hand.

"Didi," she said, as if startled.

"That's a nice name," I complimented her. "Mine is Melanie."

"Melanie." Dominic boomed. He sounded intoxicated already. "Now that, that is a nice name. Really too nice of a name to be a friend of old Patty, here. Sort of sounds like a model's name. And you look like you're a model, too. Or at least too good-looking to be with hare-lip Patty, here. You didn't tell me you had such a gorgeous friend, Patty."

Patty nodded and straightened her skirt, as if she had lost every shred of confidence. But I had enough confidence for both of us, now that Dominic had uttered the magic word "gorgeous" and insured the second half of my fee.

"Actually, I have done some modeling."

"Like high fashion? Designer clothes that cost more than even old Patty could afford, though she runs the whole damn company and is floating in money. Not that any clothes could improve her. She wouldn't look good even in the most expensive clothes. Unless a veil was included."

It was easy to understand why Patty had hired me. More difficult to understand why she still associated with the creep, or with any-body else in her family. But I knew it was all too easy for someone to be judgmental about other people's relations with their families; all too easy especially for someone like me. Besides, it seemed like a large number of the family members here were also Patty's em-ployees.

But I knew my assignment was not to defend the insults to Patty; or at least not to defend them explicitly. So I leaned close enough to Dominic to smell the Scotch on his breath. "Not exactly. No, not ex-actly clothes." I arched my back in a way that a more subtle man might have understood. But Dominic persisted.

"Then what?" He flagged down the banquet waitress for another Scotch.

I leaned even closer into him. My breasts, under- and side-wired so that they pushed out of my dress, almost touched his jacket. Patty was pressing her leg into mine under the table.

"What?"

"Centerfolds." My whisper was hoarse.

"I knew it," Dominic exclaimed. "You didn't look like one of them flat-chested girls. Most of them are just girls, don't you think? They don't even have boobs."

I nodded.

"Hey, Georgie," Dominic called out to another man walking past our table. "This girl here is a centerfold."

The man shrugged in my direction. "I see you're getting acquainted with 'Obnoxious Dominic.' "

"That's my nickname," Dominic said almost proudly. "I'm considered obnoxious because I speak my mind. But that's just my philosophy. I'm not going to die of cancer or heart disease because I keep everything I think inside me where it rots. No, not me. I just speak my mind."

"Candor does have its benefits," I agreed.

"So then, while we're being candid, I just got to ask. Are you *with* harelip Harry over here?" He nodded at his cousin Patty. "I mean, a gorgeous gal like you could have any man on the planet. Maybe even yours truly."

Patty was pushing her thick thigh into mine with even more pressure than before. She must have wanted me to stop; but I figured she also wanted me to continue.

"Oh, really." I tittered, then whispered as loudly as possible, "Like most centerfolds, I'm a lesbian."

"You're kidding me. A homo?"

"Oh. We all are."

"I'm not. All who?"

"All models. Real women models, I mean, not the girls." I twisted so that my breasts pushed out of my dress a bit more. The wires dug into my ribs.

"That's just not possible." He reached for his wife's glass and started to drink.

"Of course it's possible. What other women would pose like that? I mean, would your wife Didi pose? How about the bride?"

Dominic tilted his head. Maybe I'd given him something to think about; maybe I'd ruined his consumptive fantasies.

"Well, what makes you like that? That's crazy. A good-looking woman being queer. I mean, one can understand why Patty is the way she is. I mean, what man would want her? And even if you were one of them queers—which I don't believe—you could get a better specimen than old Patty here. I mean, there are movie stars now and everything that are like, well, funny. That tennis player. Why would a gal like you want Patty?"

"She's kind . . . and smart . . . and really responsible . . . and sincere. But I got to be honest with you, Dominic. I can be candid with you, can't I?"

He nodded.

"It's sex."

"You're crazy." He curled his own lip in disgust.

"About her. I mean, she's so talented, Dominic. I can tell you this? I mean, I can be candid with you, can't I? She's the best I've ever been with. . . ."

"She may have some family talent," Dominic slurred. "But still, you can shut off the lights, but you can't tell me you can forget that damn harelip."

"Oh, I don't forget it. Not for a moment. It's—how can I say this to you, Dominic, so that you'll understand? It's an advantage."

"What kind of advantage could ugliness be? You mean she's not going to run around on you and give you diseases?"

"No, no, Dominic. I can tell you this? Her lip is a wonderful asset. It's like a tongue. Like a second tongue. Simply amazing." I closed my eyes and let my hand wander to my lap.

"Jesus, Mary, and Joseph." Dominic stood up, using the table for leverage. I remembered Patty's comment about the possibility of chairs being thrown. But Dominic just kept repeating "Jesus, Mary, and Joseph" over and over and holding onto the table. Until Didi stood up beside him and said, almost cheerfully, "Time to go, honey."

"It was so nice meeting you." I extended my hand to Didi.

She looked at me, probably trying to decide what she thought. Then she patted me on the arm. "Nice meeting you, dear. And take care, Patty. And apologies for Dominic. You know he thinks the world of you."

"He does?" I interrupted.

"Of course, dear." Didi turned to me and my breasts. "Patty reminds him of her mother. Dominic always had a crush on her. When he was younger. He still grieves over her murder. I'm sure Patty has told you."

I nodded.

"Take care, Didi."

After Dominic and Didi left, other relatives wandered over to our table. Including the new bride and groom. Almost all of the men and more than a few of the women seemed to concentrate on my breasts. Including the new bride and groom.

"So, how is Obnoxious Dominic doing these days?"

Patty is matter of fact. "The same."

One of the things I like about Patty is that she has never tried to discuss—what some others might call process—the incident. We did not even talk about it that evening on the ride back from Staten Island. Instead, as I recall, she talked about bullet-proof glass. I did not mention her mother, although I wanted to ask whether she was actually murdered. I wanted to ask how a nice girl like Patty got involved in bullet-proof glass. I wanted to ask Patty about all her cousins from Staten Island. But I didn't ask anything. When she reached 81st Street, she double-parked the Continental but left the engine running. She handed me an envelope, embossed with her business address, containing the agreed upon second half of the fee.

"Thanks," I said. I had no idea whether or not I would ever see her again.

A month or two later, we went to another wedding. Then a christening. I even escorted her to a funeral. I had not been to church so much since I had lived with Betty, but both the money and the hours were good, so I did not refuse the work. Dominic never ventured near us again, which I supposed was the reason Patty liked to have me as an escort.

This date is different, though. Labor Day Weekend. Not a family function at all, but a lesbian festival. Patty's invitation and our negotiation had been brisk, so I assume she was embarrassed. And she still seems slightly uneasy, shifting her top from shoulder to shoulder as if it is uncomfortable. She is wearing some sort of overblouse, navy blue in a sailor motif, complete with a red bow that dangles on her stomach. The slacks match exactly, and the outfit looks brand new, shiny and synthetic. I glance at her again, worried about the way she is dressed. Sure, maybe we will wind up walking around naked, but first we will have to get through the gates. Despite the festival pamphlet celebrating solidarity and diversity, I would bet that these dykes could be as cruel as any cousin.

"Have you ever been to one of these things before?" I venture.

"No," she admits.

"Me either." I smile. "Well, then I think we should celebrate. Let's get some new clothes! Turn here."

"Oh, Jesus," she complains, but makes the turn.

I worried that the store would not be open this early, but once we are inside, I am still worried. The narrow clothes in the narrow aisles are not meant for her. Then I find a rack of Indian print harem-style pants. A hot pink T-shirt. Outside the dressing room, I advise her to ditch the bra. And the loafers. And the socks; I refrain from commenting on their plaid ruffles. I bring her some thongs.

"You look great."

"Well, thanks. Why don't you pick out something for yourself?"

"I have. How's this?" I hold up a black sleeveless tank top, ripped low-cut. When I try it on, it fits tight in my cutoff jeans. My nipples protrude in the air conditioning.

Patty pays for the clothes after seeing the manager to solve two problems: It is against store policy to allow customers to walk out of the store wearing their newly purchased clothes; it is against store policy to accept checks. I try not to show my surprise that Patty wins both battles. Or my surprise that her car is exactly where we left it; double-parked outside the store.

In our new clothes, we ride through the tunnel, sliding away from Manhattan so easily in the relatively light traffic of Saturday morning. If only I could change the car as easily as our outfits, but it is undoubtedly true that the seats are luxuriously comfortable. Once we are in New Jersey, the sky starts to spread, flattening out into a horizon just above the mountainous piles of rocks and highways. It seems as if this—and only this—is reality. The city a false enclosure. We cross the Delaware River. Follow the directions on the hand-drawn map. Spot the signs on posterboard.

The gate is wooden. A woman holds up her hand to stop Patty's car. Leans into the car window, tapping on a spiral notebook. She looks like she's wearing a uniform, but she is not. She is simply acting like she should be.

Patty's name is in the notebook. Marked paid.

"And your name?"

"Friend," Patty answers before I open my mouth. "I paid for two."

"I can see that." The woman taps again on her notebook. "But I need to have your name."

"Moonflower," I answer.

The woman smiles at me.

"And what's your name?" I asked her, smiling back.

"Donna. Security." She nods curtly, her smile yielding to her officiousness.

"Let's see. Cabin or tent? Okay. Cabin. The Susan B. Anthony Cabin. Just park up the hill there, then unload and follow the signs."

She hands Patty our braided bracelets, admission tickets into an attempt at another world.

We find the Susan B. Anthony cabin. It is larger than I expected, and I realize I expected a private cabin. Despite its pink posterboard, it smells. Bad. I guide Patty toward the bunks farthest from the toilets. We push two of the bunks together. Spread the sleeping bags out. Look at each other.

Look at the schedule on the wall. We're just in time for the ageism workshop and the racism workshop and the poetry reading and the separatist roundtable.

There is also softball, but not until tomorrow.

There is also a dramatic monologue, but not until tonight.

There is swimming in the lake and hiking on the trails.

There is also fucking, in this damp shit-smelling cabin.

We choose the ageism workshop.

Find the Harriet Tubman Cabin. It is crowded, even by city standards. There are voices—the discussion has already started, I guess—and tension as pungent as the smell.

"Weaver loves older women." A young woman says this. At first I think Weaver is someone like Susan B. Anthony or Harriet Tubman; someone I should know about. But it turns out Weaver is the woman who is speaking.

"All older woman?" Another woman challenges. She has on a T-shirt that reads OLDER LESBIANS FOR EQUALITY.

"Oh, yes, Weaver does."

This dangerous moment shimmers in the cabin. I try not to cringe. Patty leans forward. Killer instincts, I note.

"Even in a sexual way?" The OLDER LESBIANS FOR EQUALITY T-shirt is a costume for a someone who enjoys the long labor of setting hand-made traps.

"Oh, especially that. Yes, Weaver loves sexual expression with older women."

Margaret Smyth will never be a trial lawyer, I think, because I cannot tolerate this.

But Moonflower is ingenuous, attentive.

And Melanie is only interested in Patty's responses.

Patty leans forward even more.

"All older woman?" Another woman jumps in.

"Oh, yes. Weaver loves sexual expression with all older women."

"And so you would have sex with Nancy Reagan? Or the Head of the Daughters of the American Confederacy?"

The trap springs. The steel of politics glints. But the sharp edges do not pierce Weaver, who believes in her own innocence.

"Oh, yes. Weaver would. For all older women are loved by Weaver."

The women hiss. The older women and the younger women and the women somewhere between those two categories, all hiss. Except for Patty. Except for Weaver. Except for some woman in the corner who is excused because she is blowing her nose. Except for Moonflower and Melanie, who put their hand on Patty's leg.

"I don't see what's so bad about Nancy Reagan," Patty says, later. We are sitting alone, near the lake.

I murmur.

"I mean, she did the best she could. And besides, isn't that all over now? For Chrissakes, leave the poor woman alone."

"I guess they were just making the point that you can't generalize about older women." I am conciliatory.

"Well, you can't generalize about anybody. So what?"

I don't answer.

"And besides, why wouldn't you have sex with Nancy Reagan? Could you say *you* wouldn't?"

For the right price, sure. But I don't say this. I don't want to think this.

"It's a little hard to imagine." I do say this.

"But would *you*?" Patty is insistent.

"I really don't know. Would you?"

"Of course not," she says loudly, as if I have insulted her.

No more workshops, I vow.

I'm not sure Patty qualifies for the separatist roundtable.

Which leaves the poetry reading.

Or fucking.

By the time we get to the poetry reading, it is over.

We drift with the other women toward the eating hall. Rice and eggless eggs and beans and sprout sandwiches. The organic pizza is long gone. We sit at a long table with some women speaking in sign language. When the other women drift away, we drift with them. Down a long path. Past the Harriet Tubman Cabin and the Susan B. Anthony Cabin and the Sojourner Truth Cabin and the Florence Nightingale Cabin (Medical Emergencies). Past the softball field. I assume we are on our way to the dramatic monologue. The stage looks makeshift, but large.

Music.

Flyers float around announcing the schedule changes. I recognize some of the names of the performers. One I recognize a little too well. I calculate the number of women in the growing crowd. Not as many as I would like, but enough to ensure a bit of anonymity.

A lesbian comedian introduces herself as emcee. The women applaud and whistle and stamp their feet on the grass. She holds up her hand, as if she is modest. "First, of course, before the entertainment, or at least the official paid entertainment . . ." The comedian pauses; taking the cue, the crowd cheers and hoots. The comedian holds up her hand again. "We are going to do a little bit more to help pay for our entertainment." The women cheer some more. "And give you, all you beautiful, beautiful women . . ." The women yell and scream. "Beautiful women. Maybe some of you are lesbians?" The comedian shapes her face into a question. The audience yells out various positive responses, but not in unison. I am beginning to feel like I am back at Betty's church. "No, no." The comedian continues, "You can't be lesbians." She says lesbians like it has a hundred and one syllables. "You can't be. Though you're all beautiful enough to be lesbians, that's for sure. But nah. You can't be. You know how I know?"

The comedian pauses. The crowd waits.

"Because you have your fucking shirts on. Like you're embarrassed to have breasts or something. That's how I know. Lesbians don't wear shirts."

We take off our shirts. The women in front of us and behind us and next to us. Patty discards her hot pink T-shirt. She has large, even breasts that swing sturdily as she struggles out of her T-shirt. Her nipples are small, or perhaps they just seem small against the landscape of her breasts. I realize I have never seen Patty's breasts before as Melanie squeezes the ripped-to-be-low-cut black sleeveless tank top into Moonflower's pocket.

"That's better. Now I see lesbians." One hundred and two syllables. The crowd screams again, applauding itself. "Okay. Now that we've got that settled, let's get down to work. The auction. With some very fine and wonderful things donated by some of our craftswomen—craftslesbians!—at the festival. And if you haven't visited them—at the Alice B. Toklas Hall? Yes, the Toklas Hall, then you need to do that. Or better yet, just buy everything you want right now, so that you can pay higher prices and all the money goes to the festival."

The crowd laughs appreciatively and cheers still more.

Patty is laughing and cheering also. And licking her lips.

She starts bidding on the first item. A ceramic mermaid pin. Donna—Security—is bidding against her.

Thirty dollars for a piece of clay.

Thirty-five.

Patty leans forward. Killer instincts. Fifty dollars.

"Sold." The comedian is picking up the next item. A woman approaches to get Patty's name. I recognize her as a lesbian singer, though she used to be more famous than she is now. Thankfully, she is not the one who is becoming more and more famous since I met her last year.

Twenty dollars for a bolo.

Some potholders.

Forty-five dollars for a little metal statuette. It is not Joan of Arc astride a horse or otherwise. It is some sort of goddess with a very huge stomach. Patty clutches it for a moment and then casts it aside, ready for the next item.

"Let Donna get one." I touch Patty gently on the arm.

She laughs. "Moonbeam, you are such a soft touch." She lifts her arm and puts it around me.

"That's Moon*flower,*" I whisper, kissing her under her ear. Donna

45

gets a handmade teapot for only seventy dollars. Also a crocheted blanket. From what I could see of the blanket, it seemed like something Patty would really like.

The next item is a lapis lazuli necklace. Patty is seriously back in the action. And I find myself silently cheering her on.

When the last item is sold and the comedian is orchestrating her transition to the musical acts, I follow Patty toward the front of the crowd, near the stage. Donna is already there, smiling, standing under the posterboard which proclaims CLAIM AREA but fails to bear the name of any famous lesbian. While I wonder who would be appropriate (The Sappho Bidding Claim Area? The Audre Lorde Bidding Claim Area? Perhaps Vita Sackville-West or one of the other other rich ones like Romaine Brooks), they pat each other on the back, as if they are old friends or at least old rivals.

"You know, I can see why you bid for all those things. If I had a girlfriend as pretty as that . . ." I wander off. Moonflower would not tolerate being talked about as if she is not present, but Melanie tolerates Patty's need to have others comment on her girlfriend's appearance. And maybe I hope that Patty and Donna could become friends, lovers even. Although that would probably mean the end of Patty as a client.

When I return, Patty and Donna are talking about bullet-proof glass. Donna's security interests apparently extend beyond lesbian festivals.

"Did you get her phone number?"

"You're jealous." Patty smiles a very crooked smile. A smile I cannot decipher. So I don't mention any of my own matchmaking fantasies. I do approach Donna on my own and get her phone number. On the pretext I might need her for "security work." And put it in Patty's purse. Among the ceramic mermaid pin and the bolo and the potholders and a little metal goddess statuette and a piece of lapis lazuli entrapped by some wire and a piece of black string.

We are sitting on the grass as the summer sky darkens, listening to the music, swatting at mosquitos with the shirts that we still have not put back on our backs. The comedian announces the next singer. I suggest that we leave and I am surprised when Patty agrees.

On the way back to the Susan B. Anthony Cabin, I reach for Patty's hand. In the dark, it feels uncomfortably like it is me—not Melanie or Moonflower—who reaches for Patty's hand. And also uncomfortably like me who allows Patty to put the lapis lazuli necklace around my neck, the stone heavy between my breasts. I know I need to have a plan for Melanie, if not Moonflower, by the time we get back to the cabin, but the stone knocks against my chest in a lulling rhythm that seems to prevent any analysis. And once inside the cabin, the odor barricades my efforts at concentration. No matter how many times we reshuffle our sleeping bags, we cannot ignore that distinctly latrine smell. I suggest that we leave (maybe find a hotel, come back tomorrow? Or drive back to the city, we can stay at my place?), and I am not surprised when Patty agrees.

The dark parking lot. Patty the car waits in the grass for us to find it as we wander among the rows without a flashlight. For some reason—for no reason—Patty the woman and I (Melanie/Moonflower) are laughing. Holding onto each other for support as our sides start to surrender to the assault of the laughter. Hugging each other when we find Patty the car, subdued but still shockingly citified under the starlight. Falling, with some mix of voluntariness, to the damp ground, a tangle of sleeping bags beneath us, our bare breasts rubbing.

Kissing. Deep and liquid. More deep and more liquid than is appropriate. Too quick to be so crushing. It's better to move slowly. To tease. To focus on the client's anticipation and ultimate (but not too soon, never too soon) satisfaction. To be professional. In control.

"Have you ever seen so many stars?" Patty says this, more declaration than question. Or perhaps it is not Patty. Maybe it is Moonflower, although Moonflower would be used to seeing stars. It cannot be Melanie; all her attention is elsewhere, concentrated on her client. Margaret? No. Margaret is home studying criminal procedure, isn't she?

My cutoffs are around one ankle and Patty's head is between my thighs; her tongue is between everything. It does start to feel like she has two tongues, although one must be her wet finger. My head bangs against the pillow of ground until Patty sits up and shifts the sleeping bags so that they cushion my skull. I struggle against the comfort.

I struggle to control my thoughts. This is the one talent that remains. The one talent I must maintain. My one talent. But Patty's whole mouth is like a storm with my clitoris as its eye.

Mine. Not Moonflower's, not Melanie's. Me. Margaret or whoever the hell I am. Me, who should be Moonflower. Or Melanie. Yes, Melanie is the woman on the ground with Patty. The woman earning her pay. Not me.

No, not me.

But it is me who can feel tears streaming from my cunt like rain. I can taste salt, a tide of saliva against the reef of my teeth.

It's me who can hear Patty's cousin Dominic sneering at her harelip.

And it's me who can feel Dominique's fist in my cunt.

And it's me who can see—who?—that woman, waiting in a hallway at school. A vision with a red bucket bag slung over her shoulder. Her tentative smile. Her. Her. Her.

It's me who is laughing. Turned inside out. Well, almost.

But as close as I am going to get.

Closer than I want. Not as close . . .

I pull Patty's wet face to my shoulder. I start laughing again. Then Patty is laughing.

And I tumble against her, positioning both hands in places Melanie knows will be pleasurable. Patty's body jolts. And then Patty is laughing, almost screaming really.

The next day, Patty is dead.

It's in the Metro section of *The New York Times* on Tuesday. Bottom of the page. I'm sitting in the law school student lounge, having picked up a discarded newspaper, ten minutes to kill before Criminal Procedure begins. CEO of Protective Products, Inc. Found Dead. The article has no details. No suspects divulged.

In class, we all open our textbooks to the appropriate section according to the syllabus. "We will continue our discussion of confessions," the professor announces. I take notes. Or try to. I pray Professor Yarnes does not call on me. She doesn't. I skip my next class; very unlike Margaret Smyth.

I search my apartment's coffin of a closet for bloodied clothes. I am looking for physical evidence to seize. Search and seizure. Next on the syllabus. But if I killed her—no, impossible—there would be some sign. Where are my cutoffs? That black tank shirt?

Killer instincts? Not Patty, but me. Me.

Me?

Not me. Not me. Unless I'm like that case in criminal procedure. The guy with the multiple personalities who confesses that one of his other personalities murdered the victims. Multiple victims, wasn't it? Was the confession knowing and voluntary? I don't remember.

I can't remember.

But don't I remember Patty dropping me off on 81st Street? Late, late on a Saturday night. Early Sunday morning. Of course I remember.

I am letting my imagination run away with me. Like a hypochondriac who experiences the symptoms of every disease he hears about, I am overly susceptible to suggestion. It comes from being alone too much. Next I'll start talking to myself like some elderly spinster.

"Just check the closet," I say out loud, just to test my own reactions, just to make sure I recognize my own voice.

The cutoffs are there. The black tank shirt in the laundry pile. Not a drop of blood anywhere.

That doesn't prove anything, I say, but not out loud.

Maybe I was the last person to see her alive.

I should call the police. Call the police, who am I kidding?

I should calm down.

Make myself something to eat.

My kitchen is small, but neat. The refrigerator is clean, too clean.

I open the door to the freezer compartment, half expecting to see a frozen arm with fingers spread wide in a final plea for mercy. But there is only coffee. Some ice cubes. A bottle of Tanqueray. And a quiche Lorraine from the best deli in the world. I contemplate heating it up, although I really should cut back on cheese.

six

*P*hyllis got my name from an L.A. women's paper. A small discreet classified: *Escort, Travel, New York.* Her voice on my Midtown voice mail service reeks confidence: "In town for a few days."

Phyllis. Her name. Or so she says. And my name? I'm running out of names, *Les Guérillères* notwithstanding. Only the exotic names remain. And I refuse to recycle. Melanie, for example, is now available. Not to mention Moonflower.

I'm not only running out of names, I'm running out of colors. Sea green and mint green are no longer distinguishable. And neither is interesting. I love every color as long as it's black.

I'm running out of time. *Plan for forty:* Dominique's rule. The one she violated, by dying. This will be my last classified. My last round. I'll just make do. I have to. These last two years of law school.

I calibrate my efforts. Or try to. But I risk miscalculation. Like last year. I understood that hibernating during class is not a mistake. There is no need to volunteer to answer any professor's entrapping questions. There is no need to impress professors (or even fellow students) with scintillating responses when called upon. Every professor chants the same chant, or at least puts it on the syllabus: Class participation does not count; the final examination determines the grade for the course. Yet on the final examinations, I held back too much at first; a habit forged by an undemanding undergraduate education. To excel is to attract attention and I did not want Margaret Smyth to attract attention. But she needed to be better than mediocre. So I adjusted that by the second semester. I am now in the respectable top twenty-five percent.

The more serious miscalculation was last summer. It was not just my lackluster first semester grades that prevented me from landing a summer position. I started looking too late; I somehow missed the messages about deadlines. But I also missed any messages attaching importance to a summer job. After all, I had a summer job—the same job I had all year—and was not worried about extra income. I should have figured out that my classmates—with their planned winter vacations to Switzerland, Aspen, and St. Kitts—were also not worried about extra income. The concern was the resumé. A summer associate position with a prestigious law firm enhanced a resumé, improving one's chances of being offered an associate position with that same—or some other—prestigious law firm upon graduation. But prestigious law firm or not, a summer job provided "practical experience," improving one's chances of being offered a permanent job. Any permanent job.

Not even one month into the academic year and the interviews for next summer—those crucial second summer positions—have already begun. And this time, I am in the pool. I even have a call back: I have passed the test of the first interview at the law school and am being called back to the office. Sure, it is the District Attorney's Office and I have no desire to be a prosecutor, but a call back is a call back. And I need the practical experience.

Including the practical experience of interviewing. For that was my real problem last year. Yes, I was dreadfully late, but a few of my classmates who hesitated out of shock or fear eventually got summer jobs. I did not even get a call back. Not a single one. Because I could not pass the initial interviews.

In a room—a small interview room, a closet really—with a man. We sit face to face, a desk between us. He has on a suit, navy blue. He smiles at me. He might as well be from Mars. How many men have I been this close to in my entire life? Less than a handful. I remember a male social worker. I remember a foster father or two, but that was in bed and in the dark and I did not have to look at their smiling faces. What are your hobbies? He asks me this, over and over, this man from Mars in the white shirt and the red striped tie. I thought I was going to be a summer associate, a legal intern, doing research in law books. I feel like I'm being interviewed for a date on a television game show. Hobbies? I don't have any. I study all the time. Hobbies? I imagine the coastline of Australia. Hobbies? I like to travel, but mostly I stay in the city. Hobbies? I date. A lot.

In the interview closet with a woman, it is no better. Only different. Her suit, also navy blue. How many women? More than a hundred. I remember each of them, especially the dead ones. What are your hobbies? She asks me this, only once or twice. What do you want them to be? I ask back, silent, but with an arch to my back against the hard chair, a tilt of my head in the fluorescent light. I concoct hobbies that I think will interest her. But I do not interest her. She regards me coldly, as if I am frivolous. And the one or two times in which she does not regard me coldly, it is even worse. Much worse.

So I went to the interviewing workshop put on by the Placement Office. I watched the placement personnel role-play successful and unsuccessful interviews. I went to the library and borrowed books on interviewing skills. And I decided upon some hobbies for Margaret Smyth. She likes to quilt. And now the District Attorney's Office thinks she might make a suitable second summer intern. I still want to talk to my Criminal Procedure professor about this. I would rather be a research assistant for her. Was supposed to talk to her about it. Had an appointment. Maybe she has chosen someone else.

Meanwhile, I have to get through my third semester courses. Not only Criminal Procedure, but Tax. Federal Income Tax. The professor, unlike Professor Yarnes and like most of the other professors, is male. Some of my classmates think this professor is famous, but I have never heard of him, which I realize does not mean much. There was a waiting list to get into this class, an elective. They did it by lottery. And I got in. Lucky me.

Margaret Smyth, sitting in Tax class. The topic is definitions of income. Again. Still. His left hand juts into the air punctuating another monologue about the market economy. Maybe this is vaguely interesting. But I know it is not what I need to learn. What I need to learn is in the Tax Code, a huge beige book that I carry around but never seem to open. What I need to learn is what will be on the exam: the provisions and manipulations of the Tax Code. Or so the common wisdom goes, passed down and around the students. Though perhaps a theoretical question on the exam: He sometimes makes the student pose it as well as provide the answer.

What is income? I write at the top of a fresh page in my notes.

"While we might believe there are legitimate and illegitimate markets, crediting the existence of the black market, if you will, such distinctions are based on a morality that is absolutely—yes, absolutely—irrelevant to the definitions of income. Income is amoral."

Pause. The professor's left hand scratches a place in the back of his neck.

"Amoral. Yet, this very amorality in the definition of income assists the government in implementing its moral judgments. Does anyone know how this operates?" Hardly a pause. Hardly a glance for raised hands. "Well, think of Al Capone. The government finds criminal liability for all the scoundrels it cannot otherwise entrap through tax evasion. Unpaid taxes on income."

Pause. The professor laughs.

"Income has no morality. Which is not to say the tax structure does not. Rates, deductions . . ."

My pen stalls. Income tax returns. Margaret Smyth has been filing them since she started college and qualified for student loans. Margaret Smyth. Tax payer number 041-50-1847. Born in Australia, but to American parents. Both of them deceased. Margaret Smyth, herself, is also deceased. A family car accident? A triple murder-suicide? The details are undoubtedly sad. Tragic, probably. But Margaret, aged fourteen at the time of her death, has been resurrected. By me. The papers are good. Golden, almost. The name Margaret an omen of good fortune, a delicious coincidence. Not as expensive as I thought she would be. Not as much as I was prepared to pay. The only certificate of death is from Wollongong. New South Wales. Australia.

Tamara doesn't pay taxes. Doesn't need to. Doesn't have a social security number or even a last name. She exists only in Ann-Marie's fantasies. And Melanie is dead. And Olive and Violet and Cassandra and all the rest of the women from *Les Guérillères* are safe. It's Sarah Tudor I worry about.

Though I sometimes have a flash of anxiety for Wendy Redfern and Maria Bennett and Charlene Nadvorney and Crystal Werner. Sleeping women, waiting for me in my tapestry attaché in the back of my closet. Their passports and drivers licenses sandwiched between some cash and a few official-sized black-and-white photographs. I keep the documents current by sending sacrifices—in the form of money orders—to the appropriate governmental agencies. I keep them locked away, hoping I will never have to resort to them, my alternate plan, in case all else fails.

My notes spread to the bottom of the page. I try to transcribe the professor's attempt at a lecture, almost word for word. When I started law school (was it just over a year ago?), I thought I would not have to take notes. I barely took them in college, except in a science class or two. I thought it was important to listen. And to think. It's also handy that I have an excellent memory. Honed in a rather odd way, some might say. Names and colors and sexual styles of women. I must not only remember each of them, but also myself— who I am when I am with them.

And then a few numbers. The telephone numbers of my various voice-mail message services. Contact numbers left by a possible new client: Phyllis. I try not to write anything down. It seems safer. Although, I have annotated my copy of *Les Guérillères* with little scraps and stickie-notes that I tear up and flush down the toilet, probably more heavily than last year's *Cases and Materials on Contracts.* Although not with words such as *rule, issue, reasoning, dicta,* not with words someone else might understand. I hope. Sometimes not with words at all; just a little symbol to jog the memory.

But since law school, my memory is failing. Perhaps, like a computer, I am running out of capacity on my hard drive. Section 1061 of the Tax Code defining income and Tamara's required motion on Ann-Marie's clitoris compete for space. Or perhaps, like a mere mortal, I am simply getting old.

I am still good with names. I can remember the name of every case we study. *Jones v. Smith. Palsgraff v. Long Island Railroad. DeBunkke-nenkunk v. Akron-Oneida Refrigerator Systems, Inc.* Even the odd names; especially the odd names.

Though names are only names.

And names are not the only labels.

Take the Musician. Her name makes many women scream and swoon. Long a dyke icon, she is beginning to make it in the mainstream. Long recognized in any lesbian bar, she is starting to be recognized in the grocery store. She sees me privately. She always telephones unexpectedly. I charge her exorbitantly. I turn her down, more than occasionally. I greet her at the door, casually. I suffer her seduction, almost noncommittally, interrupting her to go to the kitchen and get a glass of water. This always excites her. "Olive. Olive. Should I take off my jeans?" Her whisper is hoarse. I tell her to suit herself, if I say anything at all. This is the way she wants to be loved. As if she does not matter.

Or the Professor. Not a law professor, but drama or literary criticism of some sort at an expensive university. She tells me her name is Teodesia and takes me to dinner and tells me to tell people that I am a prostitute. But there is no one to tell. She tells me she likes to be fucked in the ass and takes me to a hotel and tells me to watch television while she masturbates on the bed, screaming out my name, "Violet, Violet." She makes it sounds disturbingly like "violence." She invites me to a talk she is giving at an important conference at the Hilton and I sit in the back of the room and she uses huge words and complicated syntax to talk about her love affair with a sex worker and how it illuminated the previous scholarly interpretations of certain nineteenth-century texts. She does not pay me for showing up, and although she winks at me when she is leaving, she has not called since.

56

And the Writer. She always suggests we meet in front of a book-store and she always requests that I go inside and see if *she* is in there and if *her* spine is in or if *she* is face-out and whether *she* is on a staff favorites table or some other prominent position. And although I know perfectly well what she means, I always ask, "You mean your *book?*" and she nods. I shake my ass as I walk into the bookstore. I always half expect to see her body shriveled into book size on some shelf, but I dutifully look for her book. And then we rendezvous and I tell her the news. I always lie. If the book is there, I tell her it is not. If the book is nowhere to be found, I tell her it is displayed promi-nently. If it is spine out, I tell her it is face-out, and vice versa. Silly lies. Not meant to manipulate, but only to spite. Did I expect her to give me a copy of the book? Did I expect to be listed in the ac-knowledgments: "Thanks also to Cassandra, my faithful whore"? But I bought the book and read the sex scenes, hoping for ideas about her or maybe just ideas. I found it rather brutal. Lots of hard fuck-ing, mostly lesbian, once with a beer bottle that breaks. Clichéd, but rather well done, I supposed.

The Minister's Wife. Ann-Marie. Thursdays.

Patty. I could think of her as Protective Products, CEO, but I never did. I never really had a category for her. But now I do. The category of those who need to be forgotten. I considered going to her funeral, a memorial service at a Catholic church. I could have pushed up my breasts and poked them at Dominic. Or I could have worn some drab disguise and sat in the back. But I didn't want to see any coffin or flowers, didn't want to look at the relatives who were probably plotting how to carve up her company as the hymns were being sung. No, it is best just to try to forget.

And Jeanine. To label Jeanine would require too many hyphens. Imposter lacks both precision and tact. And I happen to like her, not only because she is likeable, but because she is a reliable client. Di-rector of a West Coast gay and lesbian rights organization of some kind. Her trips to New York are scheduled well in advance and usu-ally include a fund-raiser with excellent food, a few boring speeches, and lots of intelligent conversation, which Ursula, always wearing yellow, enjoys and enlivens. Jeanine is considerate in other ways as well, sending me little notes and holiday presents as if she actually believes her story that I am her East Coast lover, the one who cannot leave New York due to a combination of my business in Manhattan and my ill mother in Brooklyn. When her acquaintances sigh at this sad tale, she grabs my hand and says something about absence really making the heart grow fonder and sends a smile which convinces even me with its salacious quality—as if we still have great sex while everyone else is battling bed death—and then Jeanine will be the object of envy. Or sometimes, she grabs my hand and says something about being three thousand miles apart allows her to give all of her efforts to the organization—as if everyone does not know that Jeanine works like a loveless dog—and then Jeanine will be the object of pity. And if any one of these acquaintances, or even a few, see me somewhere in this city, out to dinner with another woman, they will only envy and pity Jeanine more. And have less reason to doubt the persistent rumors that Jeanine is straight.

What worries Jeanine most is the possibility that someone in her wide bicoastal circle of acquaintances will become my client and thus deduce her own relationship with me. But what would that mean? I ask Jeanine. Would it mean that the rumors of heterosexuality are true and thus she is somehow not qualified to head a lesbian and gay organization? Or would it mean that there should be new rumors, of her desperate attraction to a prostitute, or her unorthodox sexual proclivities? And who could this new client tell, I ask Jeanine, without implicating herself? Jeanine thinks about this, but is only partially consoled. Gossip has a strange way of leaking across the continent.

Which is what worries me about Jeanine. I do not discuss my anxieties with her, of course, but the plethora of attorneys I meet at her side is disturbing. I catalog their names and their locations. I solidify my plan to burrow in the interior of the country: St. Louis or Louisville, Topeka or Tulsa, Lincoln or Little Rock, Charleston or Charleston. I have fantasies about cities the way other women have fantasies about lovers. A city small enough to be removed from the orbit of New York and small enough to be warily impressed by a recent law graduate from New York. A city large enough to have jobs and a measure of anonymity and more than a handful of lesbians. A city in which, even if I run into one of Jeanine's acquaintances, I can fend them off with something vague about law school and kill off the mother in Brooklyn. Or pretend I do not recognize the acquaintance. Ursula? You must be mistaken. My name is Margaret Smyth.

I'm hoping that Phyllis, from the same newspaper as Jeanine, will be as good a client. A steady client. What label will Phyllis have? Occupations are often easiest, but I suppose that's because women without occupations cannot afford to be my clients. Or maybe my clients lie, inventing themselves for me—or for Tamara and Melanie and Ursula—as I must invent someone colorful for them.

I will meet her at the city's best Japanese restaurant; the best according to all the sources that mattered, accepting only American Express and cash. I will be Cynthia and have red hair. I will be careful, as always.

I am wearing Margaret's black leather jacket. Lambskin, soft against my shoulder as I turn my head to look for her. I could feel tough. I could feel sexy. I could feel anything at all because the only accurate feeling a black leather jacket provokes is that it is not L.A. Still, summer in Manhattan can linger until Halloween and a rivulet of sweat runs down my back.

I am wearing black jeans and a simple black shirt. I am wearing Margaret Smyth's clothes. Because in Margaret Smyth's closet, I could not find any color for Cynthia. I am getting restless. I am getting careless.

The horizon of the river opens up, like the wide mouth of a funnel, beyond the narrow tube of 13th Street. But I can't see it. The sun, some irradiated orange, obscures everything with its melodramatic descent. The same sun as Uptown, but Downtown is always more passionate. The same river I crossed with Patty. Patty. Bend the mind in another direction. The same river I will cross when I leave.

I am waiting for the city to be swollen with darkness. I am waiting for Phyllis. I am Cynthia. Cynthia.

I should have chosen orange for Cynthia.

"Violet."

I turn toward the voice. The city shrinks. Her hair has a tint of purple. My red hair did not protect me from Teodesia's gaze.

I have less than a second to contemplate my options. I acquiesce. Hoping that if Phyllis shows up she is the kind of client who will be excited by another woman instead of threatened.

"How are you?" I do not extend my hand.

"Oh, just great. I published the paper you heard me present and it's really making waves. And I'm hard at work revising my book. The one analyzing soap operas as postmodern feminist texts. It's quite fascinating. I'm sure it will make a splash."

"Good luck."

"You look well, as usual. Though I'm not sure the hair does anything for you. It's a very nice jacket, though. You look quite the butch. Except for the hair, of course."

I definitely should not have worn black tonight.

I can smell Teodesia's harsh perfume as she kisses me good-bye. "I'll call you," she promises. I watch her purple-tinted hair waft down the street. I close my eyes and wish I could open them in Tulsa. Topeka.

"Cynthia?" A woman approaches. She is short and rounded with a loosely wrinkled face.

"You must be Phyllis."

We shake hands.

Over sushi, she tells me she is a filmmaker. Ah, The Filmmaker. But she does not seem to want to talk about her films, despite my prompting. Instead, she wants to talk about me.

"Aren't you numb?" she asks.

"What?" I look into her eyes. They are a soft shade of brown.

"I mean, I suppose it must be numbing. Being a sex worker. I think you are very brave. I mean, one summer I was a waitress, and even that was numbing. I mean, a guy grabbed my ass, can you believe that? It was so degrading. Numbing really."

"I've never been a waitress."

"How long have you been a sex worker?" Phyllis is direct.

I deflect. "What makes you think I'm a sex worker?"

"Oh, I don't." Phyllis yields, but only temporarily. "What did you think of that sex survey?"

"Which one?"

"You know. That lesbians don't have much sex. That the median number of sexual partners for a woman during her lifetime is two."

"Interesting," I say.

"You must have some thoughts."

"Do you?" I ask.

"Well, I know that the median number of sexual partners for men—five!—simply can't be true. Given the number of prostitutes in this country, it simply can't be true. It's statistically impossible."

"Perhaps no one counts a prostitute as a sexual partner."

"But that would be inaccurate." She points at me with her chopstick.

I eat tempura, longing for a cup of coffee. I ask her about her films, her self, L.A. She keeps talking about sex, about surveys, about prostitutes.

I insist we split the check. Accurately.

"Where to next?" she asks eagerly.

I have already wasted enough time. I should be reading Tax or Criminal Procedure. But she tells me—twice—that she has never been to New York and she has always wanted to see the Stonewall Inn, shrine to lesbian and gay rights.

So, although it is not really on the way to my subway, I agree to guide her there. And besides, she seems so naive and I feel so responsible.

I touch her elbow with my hand on the crowded streets.

But Phyllis does not seem to need my navigation. Something about her stride is confident. Not just dyke confident. But knowledgeably confident. Comfortably confident. She does not flinch when a young man jostles her.

Of course, L.A. is not so different. Is it?

I hesitate at a corner, checking a zipper on my jacket. Phyllis plunges toward Stonewall Inn, turning left. Accurately.

At our destination, Phyllis does not seem disappointed. Shouldn't she have expected something a little more noble, if not spectacular? I suggest a certain lesbian bar. Ask her if she has heard of it. "I think so," she says with a measured degree of doubt. I try to let her set the pace. She seems to, then pauses at a corner. She touches my arm. "Nice jacket." She smiles. She leaves the curb before the light changes, just like a New Yorker. She smiles at the bouncer, just like a dyke. I pay my own cover. I tell her what I would like to drink and send her toward the bar. I slide into a crowd of women in black leather jackets. Finally grateful for my own jacket, now camouflage. And escape, through the wide front door.

"Smells like rotten fish," Betty used to say. Probably still says it. If she is not dead. Strange how some phrase of some better-forgotten foster parent still floats in my head. Still. Accurate.

And necessary. For survival.

The selection of clients is not simple. It requires the sharpening of instinct. I have rejected women who seemed perfectly acceptable; that was probably their fault, being perfectly acceptable.

Still, sometimes there are reasons.

She said she had never been to New York but knew her way around the Village.

But all my clients lie. Maybe she simply wanted to pretend she was a filmmaker from L.A. and is really a New York secretary.

She wanted to talk about prostitutes and sex.

But all my clients have sexual idiosyncrasies. Either not wanting it or wanting to seem like they have it or wanting it to be with a woman or wanting it to be—or not be—a certain way.

Back in my apartment, I decide I am becoming paranoid. Phyllis could be a fine client, once we worked past her anxieties.

On the way to Tax class, I decide she really is a filmmaker—from New York—trying to do a film about sex workers, a trendy topic these days.

In the District Attorney's Office, I decide she is dangerous. I am wearing a blue suit (pinstriped and modest skirt length) and a white blouse. She is wearing some sort of dark jacket over dark pants. I recognize her walk as she strides down the hallway, like she knows where she is going.

I am sitting in the cage of a glass cubicle with the man who is interviewing me for an internship. She turns toward us. Camouflage can trap the animal who wears it. But only if it panics. I must refuse to freeze in the headlight of her eyes. I smooth my brown hair back from my face, tucking a stray strand back into the knot at the base of my skull. I watch her turn away from us, walk back down the hallway. I try to notice everything about her. Does she have a briefcase? A file folder? A badge? Does anyone talk to her?

I look at the interviewer looking at my resumé. My name is Margaret Smyth. My hobby is quilting.

part three

BJ

seven

Coffee and just a few saltines—the no-salt type—are carefully poised on the painted blue chair. It would be dangerous to put the crackers on the table. Not just because they would be within easy reach, and I would eat them without realizing I ate them and still be hungry, but because I could get unsalted crumbs in the computer. Then I'd never get it fixed, never get my assignment finished. The new publicity person for the show says she thinks there should be more of a "family feeling" on the set, though some of us think she just wants to pawn off her work. So when she learns that *Soap Opera Universe* is doing a special anniversary issue on twenty-year characters, she doesn't even bother to look in the files, but just calls me and tells me she has a "little assignment" for me. Just one hundred words on myself. Who I "really am."

Like I know. Like I know who it really is who looks out the window from this cliff-perched house in Grandview, looking for a horizon but seeing Westchester. Looking for an answer in my red bucket bag; hadn't I made some notes this morning? But except for a stray yellow appetite suppressant, I find nothing worthwhile. I should have thought more about this, instead of watching that woman all morning and waiting for a law professor who stood me up.

I call out to Malcolm. I must sound irritated, because he comes running. When I ask him some questions about the computer while

I'm trying to get it to work, he just stands there motionless, as if he's been practicing to be a mannequin for all of his eleven years. Like I'm going to yell at him. Like he's done something wrong. But it turns out only to be a problem with the surge protector. Something had turned it off, some flood of electricity I suppose. So I explain that to him and he smiles. And I explain how to fix it, what to check for next time. I want him to know these things, these little things that make it so much easier to get along in the modern world. I know I'm the only one around who is able to teach him that.

Which is why, I suppose, I purchased the computer for him in the first place. It seems that's what parents do. Try to buy things to make their kid's life easier. Try to buy a life that might be easier. Like my mom and all those years of dancing lessons. My mom thought she could purchase me the glamorous life of a Rockette at Radio City Music Hall.

But I didn't grow up to be a dancer. Still, those lessons weren't useless. They taught me something. Not just plié and tour-jeté. Not just shuffle-ball-change. Years of ballet and then toe, years of tap dancing. But no acrobatics at Bambi's Dancing Studio. Though it was offered and I wanted to take it. My mom, Evelyn, said there wasn't enough money. I was already taking three lessons a week and we were already stretching things into four nights a week of pierogis, she said. So I suggested changing one of the lessons into acrobatics. It was even cheaper, according to the fee schedule that hung over the front desk where Bambi sat when she wasn't teaching classes. But Mom still said no.

Later I figured it out. Or maybe Mimi told me. Mimi lived upstairs from us and was—and still is—my mom's best friend. Like a second mom to me, really. They rotated shifts with me just like they did at the mill. Mimi is the kind of woman who would just say it out loud, even to an eleven-year-old kid. Just say, "Your mom doesn't want Barney's slimy hands all over you." Barney was Bambi's husband, the acrobatics instructor, and—at least in the judgment of Evelyn and Mimi—he touched his students too long and too frequently as they did their trampoline tumbles and somersaults. Later on, when I was older and watched Barney as I waited to instruct my own dance class—Dance for Tots—I agreed with Mom and Mimi and was glad I'd never taken Barney. I did learn to do some cartwheels, though, after a few disastrous attempts in our apartment. After I broke my mom's favorite candy dish, a little blue milk-glass boot, Mimi took me to a park with shorts on under my skirt and coached me on the finer points of keeping my knees straight and toes pointed to the sky.

But dancing, even without the acrobatics, made me brave. It gave me some sort of discipline. And some sort of confidence in myself. And, of course, it helped me resist the pudginess that was always there, lying in wait for me all through adolescence. Lying in wait for me even now. Sometimes I think I should take some classes again. But it's difficult to find adult classes that aren't more serious than I want to be. Competitive, almost. So I flit in and out of the local aerobic class at the Y. It's hard not to point my toes.

Though the classes helped me, I really didn't consider dance or even acrobatic lessons for Malcolm. I thought about karate, but he wasn't interested in that. He jumped at the chance for a computer, though. I used the excuse—to myself, more than anybody—that his handwriting was awful. His teacher complained so much it got to where Malcolm would not do his homework, except for math. "I can't write," he'd say. "Of course you can," I'd encourage. And after sitting at the table for a half hour he'd have some awful looking scrawl across the top few lines of the paper. No spaces, so that I couldn't tell where one word ended and another began. So, it was hard to get the point, but I told him he was improving and made him read it out loud. It was usually a story about elves or dogs. Or elves and dogs together, living in a little stream, chasing each other but not in a mean way.

If Lenore walked by and she was in one of her bad moods, she'd say the story was "juvenile."

I'd long since stopped reminding Lenore of Malcolm's age.

She'd stand in a doorway, usually, leaning against it with her arms crossed, sometimes holding a drink, and she'd shake her head. She'd look sort of beautiful but also sort of ugly, especially if she had on her scruffy slippers. Like she was supposed to be playing the part of a demented housewife. Then she'd look over Malcolm's shoulder at his paper and snort: "Chicken scratch."

"Pretty smart chicken," I'd joke.

And no one would laugh, except for me.

His teacher would spend the entire teacher-parent conference talking about Malcolm's handwriting. "How is he in math?" I'd ask, knowing he was doing work two grades above his own.

"Fine, that's no problem." She'd smile. "Except when I can't read the numbers." She'd smile more. "You know, for a child his age, he just doesn't seem to have developed the fine motor skills necessary. Something must be done about his handwriting."

So I bought the computer. Expensive; more money than I thought possible. A typewriter would have been cheaper, but this is more modern and has all these neat things one can "access." Like games. Malcolm plays some intricate programs, rescuing gold coins from dragons and being lost in the ancient tombs of Atlantis. But it is better than lots of other things, I suppose. Like television. And I only allow the computer programs that are labeled EDUCATIONAL ENTERTAINMENT.

Now he does all his writing homework in a word processing program. Long stories, mostly still about elves and dogs, though some cats and kangaroos have been appearing lately. And he's doing a research paper: The Animals of Australia. We go to the library on Saturdays. He started out with a card catalog, which I remember using in junior high school, but mostly it's all on computer now. So the librarian helped me while I tried to help him.

I wish it were so easy to research my own life. Go to a card catalog—or computer—and find some entries about me. All neat, with a beginning, middle, and end. I wonder if I'd read the end. I would; I'm sure of it. I want to know whether I'm still playing Mavis Paige on *In the Name of Love* when I'm eighty. I want to know what Malcolm grows up to be. I want to know if Lenore ever recovers.

Though, of course, the article or the book or even the unauthorized biography wouldn't tell me what I want to know about Lenore.

Couldn't tell me if she gets better, because it would have no way of knowing how bad she is. No one knows. Not even my mom or Mimi. Though both of them know about Lenore's little breakdown. That's what we call it: Lenore's little breakdown. Like she was a car that had run out of brake fluid or something. Like it had all drained out when she gave birth to Malcolm. So that she careened around after that, unable to stop, even when she was close to killing him. So close. I still shudder to think about what would have happened if I hadn't come home from work at exactly that moment on that day.

But it wasn't just that day. It was the next and the next. Shaking the baby. Screaming at him. Throwing him down so hard on the bed. Holding a cigarette close to his face when he cried, so that he cried more. It got so that I couldn't leave them alone together. I called in sick, but I was petrified of being replaced. It was a time when the story line could have gone either way. I was working hard—working double—playing both Mavis and the evil twin, Renée. Mavis is a good girl, the essential wallflower of daytime drama, so she has to be made interesting now and then. Usually, I'm doing battle with one of the bad girls over some male love interest, or sometimes over some other sort of property such as developing the land underneath the old age home for a gambling casino. But when Malcolm was born, I ricocheted between Mavis and Renée, good girl and bad, stealing my own male love interest away from myself.

I could barely handle my job, let alone the evil twin who had come home from the hospital in place of Lenore. So I called my mom. And Mimi.

It was Mimi who came. Came and stayed with us. Stayed with Lenore and Malcolm. Until it was difficult for either Mimi or me—or both of us together—to subdue Lenore when she started. Afraid Lenore was going to succeed in killing Malcolm, or herself, or both.

So, I finally did it. Finally took her to a pricey psychiatrist in Manhattan, not far from the studio. Dr. Sidney Henry. Who sedated her. And then institutionalized her. Voluntary, at least officially. A nice private place, of course.

*   *   *

Lenore's father blamed lesbianism. "What can one expect when a lesbian attempts to have a child?" He said that artificial insemination was "just that—artificial." He told us he wondered how any daughter of his could insert sperm from "some medical student jerking off to dirty pictures." I didn't argue. He was a surgeon, after all, which meant he would have been a medical student once, and so must know all about the procedures.

Mimi blamed Lenore's father. Not just because he wasn't supportive of Lenore, not even making the trek from Scarsdale to visit his daughter either at home or in the hospital. But because he allowed Lenore to be named Lenore. Just like her older sister. And her younger. And his three wives. All Lenores. "Like it's a common name." Mimi scowled. "I mean, except for that stupid bird poem that I had to learn in school, who ever heard of it?" It didn't matter to Mimi that each Lenore had a different middle initial. Lenore's middle initial was E, for Elizabeth, which meant her father, her mother, and the mothers of her half sisters, and her half sisters all called her E. She called them Dad, Mom, B, R, P, and A.

Dr. Sidney Henry did not blame anyone. He told me he was not "in the business of allocating blame."
    Dr. Sidney Henry diagnosed. He said that was his profession.
    His diagnosis was postpartum depression.
    Mimi agreed. "I could have told you that."
    Lenore's father agreed. "Lesbians should not be giving birth."

Renée was diagnosed as schizophrenic. Not really diagnosed, but that's what Bob, the show's resident wiseman and medical doctor, pronounced in a segment featuring dinner with his wife. Soon after that, Renée set a car on fire, trying to murder Mavis. The flames started on Friday, but by Tuesday it was evident that Renée was trapped instead of Mavis. Though Mavis tried to rescue Renée, getting badly burned. I was relieved to get the script with the scene of

Mavis in the hospital, looking at the flowers brought by the male love interest. Though he eventually turned out to be rather evil, not exactly an evil twin but a conniver who only ever wanted Mavis/Renée to make another character—Patricia, I think—jealous.

Before I got out of the hospital, Lenore came home. But she was never the same. Or maybe she was the same, only more so. Though the same as what? I often wondered. Because I couldn't remember her anymore; couldn't remember the her she used to be before Malcolm was born. The her who I loved. And the her who loved me. The her who had a beautiful laugh, long and low, without a trace of cruelty or cynicism.

It is that Lenore who I want to be in the biography. Not just the hundred words I need to write for *Soap Opera Universe*. But the real biography. Real life. Life without story lines or evil twins or cliff-hanging episodes. Life without explosions and melodrama and mis-apprehensions that could change everything in a moment. But I don't think life like that exists anymore. At least not for me.

Did it ever? I wonder. It did. I'm sure of it. Life was once a progression. Orderly and secure. Sure, it had its twists and turns. Its little visitations from fate. Its bonuses and disappointments.

Like my career. I came to New York to model.

From Philadelphia. Leaving Mom and Mimi in their twinned apartments in the Roxborough duplex. The small rooms crowded with glass figurines and smelling of pierogi and kielbasa and the television tuned to the "stories," as they always called soap operas.

Leaving the mall where I worked. One of the first malls in Philadelphia—the world, probably—and I worked there. In a small boutique named No Name, with black walls and black lights, selling short dresses and long ones that easily slipped over my body now that I had discovered Dr. Randy. Ten dollars for a supply of black beauties and a scrip for some less intense diet pill to fill in the gaps and a mimeographed monthly menu which included boiled salmon but no pierogis. While my classmates were drinking alcohol and getting stoned and considering algebra, I was popping amphetamines and working forty hours a week in a boutique. I loved the feeling of freedom, of having money and spending it. I was determined to stay out of the mills, the factories. I wanted to enter restaurants only as a customer. And if the pay at the mall was even less than at the mills, the glamour and employee discounts compensated.

The black beauties made it difficult to mannequin, though. Besides selling clothes, I posed as a model for No Name. Standing as still as death in the black windowless window, I pretended to be made of plaster. People touched me to see if I was real. Once a child pinched my thigh and I did not scream or even flinch, though the red mark lingered there.

As a mannequin, I could watch the people who watched me. And watch the ones who didn't, who just walked by. Mostly I watched the girls from the other stores, coveting their clothes and their roles as if I were an understudy. But also coveting them, in some way I couldn't seem to figure out. I especially loved to watch Penelope, an extravagant nineteen-year-old with a boyfriend in jail for possession. Penelope always wore white stockings and black mini-dresses. I thought of her legs when I shaved my own. Smoothing my own hands down my own calves, pretending I was Penelope and my calves were Penelope's calves. But I would fall back into myself, though the calves remained Penelope's. My hands, Penelope's legs. My hands, higher on Penelope's legs. Unsure whether it was my thighs or Penelope's thighs that squeezed so tightly together.

I had talked with her a few times, going to her store—a bigger boutique named Canadians—to borrow quarters, or seeing her in the dark parking lot as I waited for Mimi to come pick me up. One night, after talking with Penelope near the fountains on our respective breaks, I telephoned Mimi. "You don't need to pick me up; I've got a ride." It was a risk, sure, though I figured I could always call Mimi later if it didn't work out as I hoped.

It was more than I hoped. Penelope rode me home on the back of her still-in-jail boyfriend's motorcycle. I held her waist tight and squeezed my thighs even more tightly against the hot machine. She pulled up in front of a dark club, and all at once I knew it was the kind of place that I wanted to know. I wasn't even carded when

I walked in, safe under Penelope's casually possessive hand on my arm.

I telephoned Mim and told her I was sleeping over at a friend's house.

I could always call her later if it didn't work out as I hoped.

It wasn't as much as I hoped. But it was enough.

I wore the same clothes to No Name the next day. And the next.

During those nights with Penelope I touched her thighs, which did not feel anything like my own. Penelope's thighs were dry, although she was always rubbing cream on them. And Penelope's crotch was dry, although I was always rubbing my spit on it. She blamed it on the drugs. I blamed myself.

My mom called me at the store—which she never did—to say she was worried. So I showed up at home now and then.

"What about graduating high school?" She bit her lip and gave me a plate of potato pierogis with onions.

"I'm not sure I can do it." I told her. I didn't eat the pierogis.

"Well, you need a plan. Something to do with your life." My mom, who I only ever called Evelyn these days, was screaming.

"Let her go," Mimi advised. "She'll be all right." Talking as if I wasn't there, wasn't really real.

"I want you to have a plan," Evelyn said. "A plan, you understand? A goddamn plan." She was screaming now and she hardly ever screamed. "Without a plan, you wind up a whore, you understand that? A damn prostitute. That's what happens when you don't have a plan."

"Let her go," Mimi said again. This time, she was a little more serious. Evelyn was holding me by my hair.

"Just promise me you'll get a plan." Evelyn had let go by now. She was crying.

I nodded, escaping from the yellow brick duplex where the twin apartments straddled each other. I didn't need plans, I thought. I had the diet doctor and I had Penelope. And both of them had plans for me.

Penelope's first plan was that I try out for the teen board of the department store, which pissed me off. Didn't she know I was too hip for any teen board in any fuddy-duddy department store? Or at least I tried to be. And I knew that the store consultants would judge my school grades and my neighborhood too low. The store wanted scrubbed cheerleaders from a suburb, not hungry girls from Roxborough.

"Would *you* try out for the teen board?" I asked her sarcastically.

"No," she admitted.

"Then why do you think I should?" Daring her to name a difference between us.

"Because you look like you could be on the teen board."

"I look like some cheerleader?"

"You could."

"Thanks a lot." I pushed my lips into a pout.

"It's a compliment."

"Right."

"Don't you know you're gorgeous?"

"Right."

"And you need a chance to get out of this place."

"By getting on the teen board?"

She laughed. Her teeth were small and even. They matched the mark that glowed on my shoulder. "You're probably right about that. Those girls become debutantes and join the garden club. We need a different plan."

I savored the word "we." I even liked the sound of "plan"; perhaps there would be something I could tell Evelyn. "Any ideas?"

"Not really," she answered, looking at her watch. "Hey, my break is over." She took her white legs back to Canadians.

Though it wasn't long afterward that she did have an idea. Photographs. Some photographer she knew who was trying to get his own portfolio together was looking for "beautiful girls" to photograph. And we had an appointment. Or I did.

"Come with me," I begged.

"Oh, he's perfectly safe. A faggot. But bring some makeup. And a few changes of clothes."

The camera was mesmerizing. At first, I couldn't watch it watching me, it was too quick and I was too self-conscious. But then it became just like a person, some critical onlooker at the mall, trying to determine whether or not I was really real.

"What was your name?" he asked after it was over and I had changed clothes more times than I could count. He tried to feign a European accent, but he sounded like South Philly.

"BJ."

"That's it? BJ?"

"Yeah."

"Perfect," he proclaimed, racheting up the intensity of his adopted accent. But when he gave the promised prints to Penelope, his enthusiasm was gone. He said that "BJ's essential tomboy goodness" was not "present in the print."

But I liked the photos.

And more important, so did Penelope.

So, she showed them around. She seemed to know a lot of people. Artsy people. Photographers and dancers. Musicians. Professional types. People with drugs. I still went to the diet doctor's office, but I also saw Dr. Randy in the club now. "You look great," he'd tell me. "Thanks," I'd say. And he'd smile, as if he knew my gratitude was not just for the compliment.

"Have you thought about being a dancer?" Dr. Randy asked. He was dancing next to me.

"I am." I laughed.

"No, I mean professionally."

"Like a Rockette?" I laughed. I imagined Evelyn's pride, despite myself.

"No. Something more lucrative." It turned out Dr. Randy owned an interest in some of the other clubs, the ones with "dancers." I imagined myself with white boots in a little cage, watching the people watch me.

"For men, you mean?"

"Mostly," he said.

"No chance." I tried to say this airily, but the possibility scared me.

"Suit yourself," he said.

Which is exactly what Penelope said when I told her I was leaving for New York. I tried to say it in a way that meant that I was leaving her, although the effect was diminished by the fact that she had already left me. Left me for her boyfriend, back from prison.

Or so she said.

And said it again even when I saw her in the club—our club—with someone else. In a brown leather jacket and tight jeans. Probably twenty-two at least. A woman; definitely not a girl. Certainly not any ex-boyfriend, from prison or elsewhere.

When I was a famous model, Penelope would be sorry. And the brown leather jacket woman would swoon with jealousy every time she saw me on a cover of *Vogue,* or maybe even *Cosmo* if I could manage some bigger breasts without getting the rest of me fattened.

But it didn't work out that way. The major agencies didn't want me. I was too this or too that. Not blond enough or tall enough. Did you know your teeth are uneven? Can't you do something to remedy those eyebrows? You're not serious about bathing suit work with those hipbones? Has your nose been broken or something?

A few compliments: dancers' legs, nice posture, a good walk.

The most hopeful predictions: perhaps some catalog work, a few runways.

A minor agency took me on. But then I had to run around town with a photo album filled with photographs of no one but myself, showing up at strange doors to wait for photographers to deign to glance at my legs. The agency called this a look-see, but I noticed the photographers usually wanted to add touch to the appointment. I longed for my Philadelphia faggot photographer. Hell, I longed for Philadelphia.

Mostly I pretended I was still in the window of No Name.

At one look-see, a woman looked and looked. She wasn't the photographer, but she wasn't another model either. She wore a men's suit, sort of dove-colored with fine white stripes.

"Have you thought of acting?"

I hadn't really, so I moved my head in a gesture I hoped was non-committal. Acting: It was supposed to be the dream of every model, but I wasn't even a model yet. And Hollywood seemed very far away, even farther than New York.

"Can you read?"

I nodded again.

She fished for something in a her briefcase. "Read this."

I did.

She nodded.

"Again," she commanded.

I did.

She nodded again.

"Tomorrow. Ten o'clock."

"I've got another appointment."

"Oh?"

"Bloomingdale's." I was telling the truth. What I wasn't saying was that it was for a sales position.

"Forget about your other appointments. Be there." She wrote an address on a piece of paper she tore from somewhere in the depths of her briefcase.

"Ask for Max," she said.

And I was there the next day at ten. When I asked for Max, she stood up and smiled and shook my hand as if we were both businesswomen at some important event. She had on a white shirt, navy blue pants with wide cuffs, and a men's tie. Her eyes were lined with something more smoky than the kohl Penelope had taught me to use—top and bottom—on my eyelids.

But she couldn't convince the other people in the small room that I was perfect for the part of the runaway.

"Too wholesome." The man who seemed to be in charge pronounced.

"Leave your information," she told me.

She smiled, but didn't shake my hand.

The next day, she left me a message to come back to the studio.

But not before I got an agent. She gave me the number of one. She even called Mimi and said she'd look out for me.

And so I became Mavis Paige. Not a runaway, but a good girl. Someone's long-lost daughter.

And so I became Jill Willis. The agent thought BJ was "inappropriate" and Willensky "too difficult."

And so I was introduced to a new world by Max. Most of the prop girls were gay. So was Max, though she preferred the term "lesbian" during the day and "dyke" at night in the bars. I saw her a lot during those first years. Even danced with her once or twice. Fast songs, not even touching. I watched her dance once with Penelope, who came up from Philadelphia and visited me a few times. "Nice girl," Max had said about Penelope, but for some reason I thought Max was being less than sincere. It wasn't working out with Penelope anyway, the sex was as dry as ever. Only now it seemed worse because I had spent the night with a prop girl and then another and then another.

It was actually a prop girl who introduced me to Lenore. They were dating and I had dated the prop girl and we just started talking in the bar one night. I liked Lenore right off; she had a great laugh. And she didn't seem to recognize me as a character on a soap opera, which I considered a plus. I tried never to date anyone who wanted to date Mavis Paige, especially after I had been enjoying the incredibly wet thighs of one of the prop girls from another show until she had called me Mavis during what should have been an intimate moment.

On my first date with Lenore—the night we met at the bar—she slipped away from her girlfriend and met me in the bathroom and we kissed in one of the stalls. On our second date—the next night at the bar—she told me she had broken up with the prop girl and we flirted and held hands and bought each other drinks and exchanged phone numbers. On our third date—the next Friday—we went to dinner and back to the apartment she shared with two roommates. I could hear the roommates arguing about the dirty kitchen as I dove into the ocean between Lenore's legs, the waterbed sloshing around my head. On our seventh date—two weeks later—she moved in with me, supposedly to get away from her roommates.

Then we moved out of the city because we had decided to have a child. Or Lenore did. She always said that not being able to have a kid was the only thing she regretted about being a lesbian. So, when some women she knew went to a sperm donor clinic and got pregnant, Lenore was so excited she could hardly stand it. Her laugh was lower and more lusty than ever. I wanted whatever would make her happy.

Maybe I still do.

Though now, all I need to do is reduce my life to a few sentences:

> *Beverley Jane Willensky grew up in the Roxborough section of Philadelphia, raised by her mother, Evelyn Willensky, a garment factory worker, and her mother's best friend, Mimi Hindell. She spent many years taking dancing lessons. She started working in boutiques as a teenager and was encouraged to model by her best friend. She came to New York to pursue a modeling career, but was unsuccessful. Based upon a chance meeting, she read for a role of a teenage runaway on* In the Name of Love *but afterwards got the role of Mavis Paige, a role which she has had for almost twenty years.*

Of course, I won't give Penelope the satisfaction of letting her know I remember her name. And maybe I should mention Max, although she hasn't returned any of my calls in fifteen years. But I'd like to have both Evelyn and Mimi mentioned by name. They keep all these clippings. Watch me everyday, easier now that they are both practically retired. And if they aren't home, they tape the show on the VCR I bought my mom, Evelyn. Though Mimi is the one who works it, never Evelyn.

But what about Lenore? I want to include her, of course. I'll need to describe her, give her an occupation in the world. A photographer?

The darkroom downstairs unused since it had been light-proofed and equipped. A weaver? The closet full of rags for the rugs she started to weave. An interior decorator? The habit of rearranging the furniture, not just within a room, but from room to room. Poor Malcolm, his bedroom is never in the same place more than three days in a row.

Lenore, an artist without an art.

Yes, an artist.

She shares her life with her partner, an artist.

Yes. But how to say that this partner is a woman? That Beverley Jane Willensky is a lesbian, who lives with another woman? What I've been trying to say for the past twenty years. Or maybe only ten, but didn't hide it before then. Maybe I did get a little nervous now and then, but not much. After all, it seemed like half the people who were around me were gay. I mean, most of the writers of the steamy heterosexual story lines are screaming faggots. Drama queens, surely. And a few directors, certainly, though I am never quite sure which ones. I always think I know, but then I'm not sure.

And dykes? I mean, the entertainment industry bubbles with them. And soap operas are no exception. My angel, Max, in the dove-colored suit isn't the only example. But none of the others are like Max. Sometimes I still miss her. She's still in casting, but not in New York. Moved to L.A. with one of the West Coast soaps.

I just wish the story lines would catch up with reality. That's my last ambition. To have Mavis Paige come out as a lesbian. She has all the potential, of course. It would explain all those unsuccessful affairs with men. And her goody-goody independence. She's a role model, really. One of the first female characters to have a career that wasn't based upon inherited power. And who was not a nurse. A few female surgeons before her, but she was definitely the first attorney. And still one; didn't give up her career for some husband. Even though it's not a powerful career. Even though she's the do-good foil, defending the downtrodden, spoiling the plans of the real characters who are greedy and interesting. She should be the first dyke on daytime drama. The first dyke character, I should say. Not that there haven't been a few titillating possibilities. Once a character almost—

yes, almost—revealed herself as a lesbian. But it turned out she was merely confused. And now there are a few gay men. So, I think the time is ripe for a dyke on daytime drama. And I want to be her; to have Mavis Paige be her.

But failing that, at least the actor who plays Mavis Paige should come out. I should just call *Soap Opera Universe* and *Soap Opera World* and *Soap Opera Encyclopedia*. I've implied it in interviews with *Soap Opera Universe* and *Soap Opera World* and answering the questionnaire from *Soap Opera Encyclopedia*.

But it's always edited out.

Probably from our show's publicity department, before it even reaches the damn magazines.

I've even tried a gay and lesbian magazine. Telephoned and left my name and number. Thought I could give an interview. It might be an exclusive: Soap Opera Lesbian. I don't really flatter myself, don't think it's newsworthy or anything. But thought that the heterosexuality of the soap opera might be a good hook. The interviewer could ask me: So, what's it like to kiss all those men when you're a lesbian? I thought it was probably remotely interesting. Or at least as interesting as some of the other people I see profiled, a bunch of movie stars who don't seem to have acted in any movies. But the magazine never returned my call.

They act like they don't know who I am. And I guess they don't. It's the difference between Hollywood and New York, I suppose. The difference between night and day.

Maybe I shouldn't have left them my real name: BJ Willensky. I could have left a message from Jill Willis. Or Mavis Paige. Maybe then I would have been important enough to have gotten a return call.

But now I have another chance. Perhaps describe the partner as a female artist? Or is it enough to use her name, the gendered "Lenore"?

She shares her life with her partner, Lenore, an artist.

She shares her life with her partner, a female artist.

She shares her life with her female partner, an artist. Shares her life? Isn't that a little sentimental?

Her partner is a lesbian artist. Lesbian? Too explicit. No need to set off the new publicity woman's alarm.

Her partner, Lenore, is a renowned woman artist. Omit renowned. No need to compound the lie beyond belief.

Her partner, Lenore, is a woman artist. Both Lenore and woman? Yes. No room for confusion.

No. The confusion is partner. We could be business partners. In a woman's art gallery.

She shares her life with her partner, Lenore, a woman artist. Partner is still just too ambiguous. I might as well risk lover. A little too explicit, but certainly a compromise from lesbian. And not true; not true for a long time it seems. But hell, I abandoned truth several drafts ago.

She shares her life with her lover, Lenore, a woman artist. It will have to do. I can't fuss over Lenore forever.

> *Beverley Jane Willensky grew up in the Roxborough section of Philadelphia, raised by her mother, Evelyn Willensky, a garment factory worker, and her mother's best friend, Mimi Hindell. She spent many years taking dancing lessons. She started working in boutiques as a teenager and was encouraged to model by her friend. She came to New York to pursue a modeling career, but was unsuccessful. Based upon a chance meeting, she read for a role of a teenage runaway on* In the Name of Love *but afterwards got the role of Mavis Paige, a role which she has had for almost twenty years.*
>
> *She shares her private life with her lover, Lenore, a woman artist, and their twelve-year-old child. She enjoys women's music. She supports the Humane Society.*

Just thought I'd add the Humane Society for good measure.

When the next issue of *Soap Opera Universe* appears, my photo is on the cover. Along with twelve other photos, all about an inch square, surrounding the magazine's design for its two decade award. As if simply surviving on a show for this long merits an award, which I guess it does. Still, a cover is a cover. The publicity department will love it. And inside, in the Private Profiles section, the same photo, only slightly larger. Over my biographical statement:

> *Jill Willis grew up in a suburb of Philadelphia. After a successful New York modeling career, she captured the coveted role of Mavis Paige on* In the Name of Love. *She loves the excitement of New York, but also gardening and raising miniature horses at the Connecticut farm where she lives with her husband, a lawyer, and their son.*

Only the horses are a surprise.

eight

*T*oday is watermelon day. An entire watermelon, except for the thick green of the rind. Eat nothing else, except for drinking some water, as if that were necessary to thin the sticky pink of the flesh, to digest the crunchy black of the seeds. Water, water. That bloated, floating feeling. Which is exactly what this diet is supposed to cure.

Along with the cleansing of toxins: pesticides and chemicals and sugar and salt, which will be absorbed by the water and then eliminated from my body in the usual manner. Frequently eliminated.

Unfortunately, I'm on the New Jersey Turnpike.

I have to pee so bad, I think I can't stand it for another mile, but I also can't stand to pull over in a service area. I think Molly Pitcher is next. All the service areas on the New Jersey Turnpike have names: Walt Whitman, Clara Barton, Joyce Kilmer, Woodrow Wilson. I guess that to become famous in New Jersey means to have a rest area named after you.

Although no matter how famous you are, the service area will be dirty and dangerous. As much as I hate to go into the grubby bathrooms, I hate to leave Malcolm alone in the windows-rolled-up-and-door-locked car. Sure, he's probably old enough—meaning that he's too old to come into the ladies' room with me any longer—but I have my doubts whether anyone is ever old enough to be alone in a rest area on the New Jersey Turnpike. Perhaps for some magic moment, possessed of one's full powers, but then that moment passes and one is too old to be alone in the service area off the turnpike. Unless one is a woman, in which case there is never any magic moment at all.

We slow, and then halt. Tune to the special AM radio station: the New Jersey Turnpike. There's a thirteen-mile backup.

"It's a good thing Lenore left earlier," I tell Malcolm. "This traffic is really something. And you know how she hates traffic."

"Why is there such a jam?"

"Well, it *is* Labor Day weekend. But why right here? I'm not sure. Look at the map. Everybody getting off at the Clara Barton rest area? A couple of highways converging? No, probably the toll bridge. At the end of the turnpike. Over the bridge and then we're almost there. Though it's always farther than we think. But when we get there, maybe Lenore will have some crab cakes ready for us."

"I'd rather have ravioli."

I have to smile. Those little pieces of wrapped dough, pierogis in a different language. The thought of Malcolm enjoying his dinner always brings me a reflexive grin. I want to feed him, need to feed him. To have beautiful meals overflowing with comforting food. Dinners so brightly memorable that all Malcolm's other dinners will fade into the shadows of his memory. The dinners attempted by Lenore: elaborate affairs which collapsed from the weight of their own complications and multiple cookbooks, the sauces burnt at the bottom of the pot and the whole house smelling like scalded milk, Lenore sitting on a stool at the kitchen counter, crying.

I start to worry about the possibility of crab cakes.

"This traffic." Malcolm sighs. Sometimes he seems so adult, I forget he's not even adolescent yet. He's actually a really good companion. Sometimes I think he and I talk more than Lenore and I do. Especially on these long drives. He takes my mind off how badly I need to get to a bathroom, how far away our destination remains.

At first, I think the smell is my sweat. Full of the poisonous salts the watermelon is cleansing from my bloated body. Sucked through my pores, since it can't get out otherwise. But it isn't me; it's Route

13. We are finally past the turnpike and the bridge and into the marshes. The smell is the ocean. I wish I could just pull over and leap from the car and spread my skin on the ground, on the highway meridian so thoughtfully blooming with the last of the summer's wildflowers, and inhale the entire world.

"Dead fish," Malcolm proclaims.

"No. That's the ocean."

"Yeah, I know. You act like we've never been here before."

"Not often enough, if you ask me." I am serious.

"And what's the ocean full of?" Malcolm refuses to mimic my seriousness. "It's full of fish." Malcolm laughs, with rhythms that are neither unkind nor sarcastic.

"At least they're not dead," I retort.

"Only some of them. Pollution, you know." Only now he is serious, suddenly, but it doesn't last long. "And some are being eaten by other fish, sharks and stuff, their heads are sort of torn off and dangling, blood streaming behind them, smelling really terrible."

I reward him with an outraged "How disgusting" and he laughs again.

The smell softens as we reach the coast. Or perhaps we simply become used to it.

Or more attentive to other sensations: the darkening late summer sky, the wind hushing through the pines, the dampness settling on our arms.

It isn't only the sky that is dark when we finally arrive. It's the house. I try to angle the car so that I can shine the headlights on the door, but it's still a prolonged fumble to get the key in the lock. Urine starts to trickle, despite my crossed legs. I can hear the phone ringing inside the house, can feel a stream down my legs. I want to laugh and cry and curse. Which is what I'd do if I was alone. Or I'd go behind the house and squat. But Malcolm's presence makes me act calm. It always does; I figure one crazy mother is enough. When I eventually persuade the door to open, I run through the house into the bathroom. It seems like I pee forever; I'd swear I lose two pounds.

The phone starts ringing again, or maybe it is still ringing. It is olive green and rotary. The first time Malcolm saw it, he barely knew what it was and didn't know how to use it. He still finds it amusing to dial, shaking his head when he dials the number of the beach radio station to request his current favorite song or when he calls one of his local friends. But he never answers the phone, so he doesn't now.

Of course, it's Lenore.

Lenore's voice, sounding deeper than usual, as if she is feigning a cough.

Lenore's voice, saying she got a late start.

Lenore's voice, promising "tomorrow."

I act patient.

I act understanding.

I am very good at acting patient, acting understanding.

Even when I am acting like BJ instead of Mavis Paige.

"Let's go to the boardwalk and get some pizza."

If Malcolm is disappointed by Lenore's lateness, the pizza will compensate. I am always compensating.

But it's a hell of a lot easier than driving back to the highway for milk and bread and ravioli.

And while we're at it, we might as well act like vacationers determined to enjoy the last weekend of summer. Since neither of us likes saltwater taffy, we waste our money on games of chance. I win three stuffed penguins, the giant size. I'm pretty good at aiming the water gun, sometimes even getting that stream of water right between the clown's eyes.

Even if we think we should stay home and wait for the rotary phone to ring on such a perfect day, we won't. Malcolm and I are both stubborn that way. A piece of my stubbornness makes me want to postpone driving back out to the highway for groceries: bread and milk and ravioli and maybe some crab hunks for crab cakes. Let Lenore do it, I think. But my good-girl part wins—as it always seems to— and Malcolm does not grumble when I ask/tell him to come along to the grocery store.

Though he does grumble when I pull into the parking lot of Ocean Outlets, tempted by the signs proclaiming end of summer sales. The groceries are already tucked in the trunk, so I prompt him to hurry, as if he needs to be reminded. At the Bugle Boy Outlet, he agrees to allow me to buy him a new bathing suit. Between the green and the blue, he chooses yellow. I pay cash, pleased with a bargain made even better by the lack of sales tax.

"Let's just duck in here a minute." I point toward the Eddie Bauer Outlet store.

"Oh, no," Malcolm groans. "What about the milk?"

"It will be fine for a minute. I just want to check out the bathing suits for me."

"You have that bright pink one. That's nice."

"Yes, it is nice, isn't it?" I laugh. "I got it here last year, at the end of the summer sale."

Malcolm groans again, but this time it is a groan of defeat.

The soothing space of the store absorbs his continuing groans. This store, just like all the others at Ocean Outlets, is not like the any of the factory outlets that my mom and Mimi took me to in Philadelphia. Those "stores," usually only open on Saturday mornings, were really just a roped-off section of the cement-floored factory and sold irregulars. The sewing machines and cutting tables beyond the ropes were not placed there for effect.

"Hey, look at this." Malcolm, who has wandered off, returns to tug at me. He leads me to a circular rack so full that he can barely move the hangers.

"Coats?"

"Aren't they great? So fluffy and probably real warm."

"Well, you do need a new winter coat. But these are adult sizes."

I look at the price. Even on sale, discounted from the original retail price and marked down from the original outlet price, it is too expensive.

"I don't know." I shake my head. I can't help being frugal. Not just because of a childhood spent looking for bargains, but my worries about the future. Sure, I'm making lots of money now, but these thirteen-week contracts are just that—thirteen week contracts. Saving money is the closest thing I have to a religion.

I pull a blue jacket from the rack, assessing it. I look carefully at the stitching; I didn't grow up around millworkers for nothing. "Look for the smallest size," I tell Malcolm, who happily complies.

The men's "Xtra Small" does fit. With a little room.

Malcolm is twisting and turning in the jacket, so that the sleek lining slides over his bare elbows and knees. I tug at the sleeves.

"Look at all these great pockets." Malcolm is zipping and unzipping them. The inside ones and the outside ones and even the one inside the other one.

I look at the price again.

I look at Malcolm again, preening in the parka.

I start to smile.

Maybe because Malcolm, who doesn't ordinarily notice—never mind covet—clothes is so excited. Maybe because it has solid stitching and seems as if it will last at least two winters. Maybe because Lenore is crazy and not here and last night's pizza wasn't enough to make even a dent in all this ugliness. Maybe because there will be no sales tax and anyway I am an employed actor who probably makes ten times what Mimi made when she bought me that white fake-fur jacket one winter.

Whatever the rationalization, I tell Malcolm we can buy it.

"Fantastic," he nearly shouts, taking off the parka. "But can we get the red one?"

The red is Santa-bright. "I guess, if there's one in your size." There is. I fumble for my charge card, hoping the milk is not spoiling in the trunk.

It is still early in this long summer day, I say to myself and maybe out loud, when the groceries are put away and the parka is safe in its huge plastic bag in Malcolm's room, which—unlike at the house in Grandview—is almost always in the same place here. Lenore isn't here often enough to start rearranging the furniture from one room to another.

Malcolm starts off to find his friends, wearing his new yellow bathing suit from Bugle Boy Factory Outlet and carrying his basketball (Herman's Outlet) and riding his bike (Sears) and acting like he hasn't a care in the world. And I'm off alone, putting on last year's hot pink promised-pounds-thinner bathing suit from the Eddie Bauer Outlet and carrying a sand chair (Cost-Cutters) and acting like I'm not acting.

I set up the chair far back from the tide. I have no intention of sitting, at least not now. I want to walk the beach. Like I always do. Like I always have.

As a child I walked this same coast, an inlet and some toll booths farther north. For those precious two weeks every summer, my mom and Mimi saved for vacation, renting a small place at the Jersey shore. I hoarded my quarters all year, worrying that this would be the year we couldn't go. But we always managed. Or at least my mom and Mimi did.

Until my seventeenth summer. When I was no longer with them. When I was no longer simply BJ, or if I was misbehaving, Beverley Jane.

When I became Mavis Paige and Jill Willis. Neither of them was a beach-walker. Both of them were too busy. Mavis was always falling in and out of love with suave and unscrupulous men, even while she performed good deeds as a goody-two-shoes lawyer. Jill was always worried about her career, trying to understand those thirteen-week contracts and waiting to learn that she would not be getting one for the next thirteen weeks and she'd be back to being BJ applying for work as a clerk for Bloomingdale's.

Both Mavis and Jill had perfect childhoods. They summered in a huge house on the corner of Ocean Avenue. It had the reddest geraniums in its window boxes and the windows were always being washed. Because it was white, Mimi and I always called it the White House, and for years I assumed it was where the President——the one after JFK and LBJ, the one Mimi called a scoundrel—lived. But even after I got some perspective, and Nixon came and went, I loved that house. I swore to Mimi I was going to grow up and buy it for her and my mom and me, and all she said was "hmmm."

The place we rented wasn't white and didn't have any geraniums or any window boxes for them. It hardly had any windows. It seemed like a basement, really, except those houses didn't have basements. And once or twice we had to share it with some other women from the mill, but even when it was crowded in the house, I didn't mind. I was walking the beach.

The place I bought isn't white and it isn't in New Jersey. I guess I could have window boxes with geraniums and I guess I should wash the windows. It is never crowded.

And I didn't buy it for my mom and Mimi. Although I thought I did. Thought they could retire here. Thought they could stay here in the summer and I could come down when I had a chance. I didn't notice that after my seventeenth summer they never went to the shore anymore. I didn't pay attention when Mimi told me the sand made her itch and my mom said the sun gave her rashes. I didn't seem to remember that they wouldn't let me buy them better places—in Philly, for god's sake, even in Roxborough. I just told myself I was buying it for them.

Like I told myself I was buying it for Lenore. A place she could relax. The sound of the ocean could sift through the windows and soothe her. A place with a minimum of furniture, so she wouldn't feel obsessed with rearranging it. And a place in a queer-friendly town, so she wouldn't feel exposed.

"This will be great," I told her, when we were looking at houses and I eavesdropped on a man-woman pair walking in front of us near a restaurant flying the rainbow flag: "They have become quite the habitués of this place. You'll see them holding hands quite openly." He had such an instructional voice and her sweater was so sweetly embroidered with blue flowers, that I assumed that everything was as friendly as friendly could be.

"Isn't that great?" I asked Lenore.

"Do you know what habitués are?" I was not sure whether the challenge in her tone was stress or simply sarcasm.

"Actually, I do." And I did. I learn a lot at my work. Especially words. Any strange word in the script and I'm the one who gets asked whether or not I know what it means. "Hey, BJ," the director-of-the-day, or maybe the actor whose line it was, would yell out for me. I'd always be called BJ then, never Mavis Paige or Jill Willis. It was BJ who was the tester. BJ, with her high school equivalency diploma, who would say whether or not she knew what a certain word meant, and then someone would say, "Well, if BJ knows . . ." The sentence never finished, but the implication was obvious. If I know, then the dumb people who watch our show would know. We all believe it is important not to alienate our audience. We don't quite believe the surveys that regularly report the daytime drama audience as mostly college-educated. But it seems true that the worse the economy, the better educated our audience: People who are unemployed drift from job hunting to game shows and finally to the soaps. We can tell from the letters we get. Not just that the letters tell us about former jobs as stockbrokers and philosophy professors, but the words the letters use. Words like habitués.

"Oh," Lenore sounded defeated. Like she wanted me to be less intelligent. It meant that her college degree—the one Daddy bought for all his Lenore daughters—meant something. So she tried a different tack: "It doesn't have a very flattering ambience," pronouncing ambience as if it wasn't a word in English. Like she wanted me to believe something more sinister, more French and sophisticated.

I should have known then that Lenore really would not like it here.

At least Malcolm does. Because, of course, I told myself I was buying it for him. For his college education. An insurance policy should I lose my talent for beautiful crying. A hedge against the death of Mavis Paige in a fiery plane crash or from an incurable disease. Security should my contract not be renewed.

But the investment potential is not what Malcolm appreciates. Like any kid, he's interested in fun, in freedom. The community pool and basketball courts and the ocean so raw and surfable. The kids his age and older just hanging around. Habitués. Until they are old enough to work in the pizza parlors, or as life guards, or guardians of the bumper cars.

Which is not that different from why I love it here, I suppose. But I never told myself I was buying this place for me. To try to recapture those annual two weeks of gloriousness.

To walk on the beach.

To be bordered by the horizon. So far away it seems knowable. Not hidden by the city's buildings or the headlands jutting into the Hudson or even the suburban ranches of Westchester, with the jewel of Scarsdale glimmering but invisible in the distance. The unavailability of camouflage here means safety: There is no available protection because there is no necessity for protection.

To walk on the beach.

To walk north. Not toward my childhood, but toward the state park. Just two jetties and I'll be on the "women's beach." I love that euphemism because it doesn't really seem like one. It seems accurate. Natural. Protective.

Miraculous.

I would have simply have died—at fourteen, fifteen, sixteen—to have been walking the beach and find what I can find now. Even before Penelope and her white stockings, I had fantasies of a beach full of mermaids, or, more frequently, a single mermaid with hair flat and wet against her breasts and with shimmering green eyes that matched her discrete scales. But those fantasies seemed more realistic than the possibility of this. Women in pairs or groups, playing catch or Frisbee or volleyball. Women bobbing in the waves or horizontal on the same kind of styrofoam surfboard that Malcolm has or splashing each other. Women sunning themselves on straw mats or faded quilts or beach chairs or spread on the sand as the waves deposit little ponds of sand on their glowing thighs. Young ones with their lithe bodies tucked so neatly into their little bathing suits. And lots of not so young ones, not so lithe ones, not so neatly tucked ones. Older ones, singly or in pairs or groups, acting as if this women's beach was an ordinary place instead of a miracle.

I lapse into my best dyke walk. In my hot pink bathing suit, the slimming material gripping my flesh too tightly by now, what clue is there that I belong? That I am not some suburban housewife who watches soap operas, on vacation with her family, who just likes to walk on the beach and walked a little too far and found herself on this beach, and after a while, noticed the absence of men and remembered what her husband said: Habitués.

Without Lenore, what credential do I have? Lenore to hold my hand, although she is uncomfortable doing that in public now, even on a dyke beach. Lenore, who does not like to walk on the beach, who maybe doesn't like the beach at all, because if she did, wouldn't she be here with me already, instead of driving down today, probably on the New Jersey Turnpike at this very moment?

Of course, I must have had some credentials before Lenore. I remember stroking Penelope's dry thighs, dancing with Max, picking up prop girls, kissing women in a bathroom stall. But that was twenty years ago.

I reach the next jetty too quickly. I'm walking fast or the coastline is shrinking. On the other side of the rocks, the men control the sand. Singly or in pairs or groups. My squint reveals a little less athletic activity (the volleyball net is taut and lonely), but the same degree of swimming and sunning. I could walk there. I would be safe, feel safe. But that is the safety of knowing I would not be attacked, that these men's dangers are not interested in me. It is a comforting safety, but it is different from the safety of belonging.

So I stay on the south side of this jetty. On my side. With my kind. Where I belong. Or try to.

Sitting on a smooth huge stone. Near the white sign painted with cracked red lettering: DANGER STAY CLEAR. Which could mean the rocks, but I always think the dykes. Because all this safety and belonging is dangerous.

When a woman looks at me a moment too long, I smile. As if to disarm. I assume she thinks I am some former lover's former lover. Or someone she tried to pick up one night, ten years ago, or maybe even did pick up one night, ten years ago. Or someone who simply looks like someone else. For wasn't it true that just like cats, there were only really thirteen or so dykes in the world? They just reappeared and reappeared. The Jock. The Intellectual. The Bar Dyke. The Goddess Worshipper. It was at a party, I remember, and we had laughed as we tried to name the thirteen dykes. The prototypes, someone had said. "Stereotypes," some other dyke had complained, but she laughed and joined in the game. Had that been Lenore? No, Lenore was not there. Wasn't she back in the hospital then? Or was she? I don't remember.

I don't remember ever going out again after Malcolm was born. But I must have. Some party for the cast and crew of *In the Name of Love*. A few prop girls would have been there. We would have told jokes and laughed. Probably lesbian jokes. Probably a joke about there being only thirteen dykes. I can't remember the details. I can only remember that none of the thirteen dyke types was undergoing psychiatric treatment.

"Excuse me." She's standing on the flat rock next to me. My face is level with a swirl of dark hairs curling around the crotch of her white bathing suit. "Aren't you . . . ?"

"Hello," I say.

"Oh, you sound just like her."

It would be useless to ask "who?" I'm trapped, here on the jetty. I could scramble off, but that would be clumsy. And I don't really mind. She's pretty cute, actually. Part Jock. Part Intellectual. With that olive skin that tans so well. And those wisps of hair. I stand up so suddenly I'm almost dizzy.

"And you are?" Mavis Paige says this in her lawyer voice. A little formal, but revealing her sweet nature.

"Alexandra. Oh. I'm just so glad to see you here. I mean, we all admire Mavis. She has such an independent-woman presence, if you know what I mean." I could swear she winks.

I do? I do, really? Like a dyke? Some kind of dyke presence comes through Mavis?

But I say, "Well, I try."

"Though I have to admit I was disappointed to read about your husband."

"That's just publicity."

"Really? Oh, you mean like Rock Hudson? I just read this book about Rock Hudson and Hollywood and how he had to seem straight as an arrow."

I nod. If she wants to compare me to Rock and think glamour instead of grit, that's fine with me.

"Just wait right here. I've got to get my lover. She'll be so excited."

Lover. Such an intrusive word. But that's only an obstacle for BJ, not for Mavis Paige. Sure, Mavis acts like it's a problem, with all her sweetness and sincerity, but she's been involved in more than a few triangles in her time. She usually loses, though. Of course, that was before. When she comes out as a lesbian on *In the Name of Love,* everything is going to be different.

It will begin with a dream sequence. All soft and blurry, so that the viewers have to resist the impulse to get up and try to clean their television screens. I'll be standing in a doorway. No, I'll be on the beach. *Surf pounding in background* the script will instruct. I'll have on a hot pink bathing suit. Bikini. I'll be sitting on a jetty. Sort of sexy and lost. And then she'll walk up to me. My lips will be level with her crotch. A few hairs will be visible—just to me, not to the audience—at the line of her leg. The camera will take my point of view and scan up her stomach, past her breasts, revealing her face.

But it's obscured in the mist. Even to me.

Alexandra? No. Not her, trotting after her lover.

Lenore? I can't even pretend it's her.

Some other character? Grace? Bethany? No. The sponsors will never go for that.

A mermaid? No. I'm too grown-up.

I stand up. The focus is no longer soft and blurry; it's sharp; it's hard.

It's her. That woman who keeps entering my thoughts, as if I had no control of my own mind.

I whisper her name, although I don't know it.

Instead of sneaking looks at each other in some dim hallway, we're staring—glaring, almost—eye to eye in the brightest sunlight. The bluest band from the horizon approaches and then circles us, so that we are a cameo. We'll be appearing with the other cameos in future advertisements.

"Hey." Alexandra seems shorter. Perhaps only because the woman I assume must be her lover is quite tall.

"I love the show," the tall woman says. All Jock. I find out her name, the fact that they are both nurses, and they have always thought Mavis should be a lesbian.

"It must be hard with all that publicity," Alexandra sympathizes.

"Is it all false?" her lover asks.

"Just about," I admit.

"Even the part about the horses?"

I look past them, toward the horizon.

"You mean, you don't have miniature horses?" Alexandra sounds so petulant.

"Oh no. That part is true." My lie is as easy as a line from a script. *Episode #999999.*

"I knew it. I just knew it." Alexandra takes her lover's hand.

And then they are gone.

Before I think to tell them to write the show and say they want Mavis to come out as a lesbian.

Before I could persuade Alexandra to leave her tall lover and come home with me. Home to the beach house I bought for my mom and Mimi, for Lenore, and for Malcolm. He's probably still with his friends, but could be there waiting. And Lenore. Yes, surely Lenore will be there by now. Because if she isn't there soon, it probably won't be worth driving down.

I make crab cakes, in case anyone shows up.

I dial the rotary telephone; no answer. She must be on her way.

I dial again. I dial until my finger is sore and I believe push button phones are the greatest invention since sliced bread.

Malcolm's face is red with heat and happiness when he returns. We play a four-hour game of Monopoly. The time it should have taken her to drive.

The last lights streak the sky with a deep almost-red pink.

Malcolm is trying to convince me to take him and two of his friends to the boardwalk when the phone rings.

We look at each other. He has a weak smile.

It's Lenore, of course. Of course, she's not able to make it. "Something came up."

"What?" I ask my lover, but she doesn't answer. Says something about the car and the yard and the traffic and the sofa. Doesn't say she wants to speak to Malcolm, even when I ask.

"What's wrong?" I ask my lover, again and again.

Until she is sobbing.

Until I stop asking.

And she is suddenly coherent, calm. Says everything is fine. She's just tired. And then there's the "situation with the sofa."

"Oh."

"Love you," she says. And hangs up as if I'm crazy to think anything could be wrong.

I should be used to this. I should never have agreed to her plan that she leave earlier to avoid the traffic and Malcolm and I would follow. I should pack Malcolm and our stuff back in the car and drive back home to see if she's fine.

I should, I should.

"Oh, fuck," I say. This is not a line from any script.

"Yeah," Malcolm replies.

We stand there, looking at the olive green rotary phone. As if we expect it to ring again.

"Let's go to the boardwalk," Malcolm finally suggests.

I win five stuffed penguins. Hit that clown between the eyes every time.

nine

Hearts of California Romaine Tossed with Passion Fruit Vinaigrette, Sun Dried Cherries, and Golden Raisins (hold the Bleu Cheese, please).

Grilled Tournados of Jumbo Shrimp with Green and Yellow Curry Sauces, Thai Coconut Ratatouille, and Cilantro Pesto.

Roasted Rack of New Zealand Lamb with Red Onion Marmelade, Garlic Mashed Potatoes, Braised Swiss Chard, and Marinated Artichokes.

We are at a Midtown Manhattan restaurant. Lenore's suggestion. But convenient, near the studio for *In the Name Of Love*.

It is lunch. Although the prices are like dinner prices elsewhere. Today's blocking is done, but I need to be back by 1:15 P.M. to get dressed. David is going to propose to me this afternoon. I'm not sure yet whether or not I will accept, because I'm still in love with Brad, who is off with Bethany in the Bahamas.

I'll eat a salad. I don't generally like to eat lunch, except for a snack-size bag of potato chips and a diet Coke, or maybe a Snickers candy bar, but Lenore insisted that we meet for lunch. She sounded so happy, so enthusiastic, that I agreed without hesitating. If I thought about it at all, I only thought to be pleased that she offered to telephone the restaurant and make the reservation. And maybe, just maybe, I allowed myself to think that things might be getting better.

The maître d' leads me to the table where Lenore is waiting. Her hair is in some sort of twist on the top of her head. She is not alone.

The man seated next to Lenore stands up but does not extend his hand. I notice several things: his height (tall), his hair (blond), and his watch (Swiss Army red). He leans across the table and presses one lip—his bottom, I think—on my cheek. "I feel like I know you already," he says. It sounds like he's imitating a generic European accent; he sounds like a photographer I once knew in Philadelphia.

I know I should know who it is, but I don't.

Just like I didn't know who it was when Lenore announced: "I finally found him." I had just driven back from the beach, coming back earlier than I'd planned because Lenore had not driven down as she promised. I had decided not to be angry. After all, it never did any good. So, I was unpacking the car and listening to Lenore talk while Malcolm was looking for his bedroom. It could be almost anywhere, with the possible exceptions of the kitchen, the bathroom, and the room in which it was before we left, a room marked as a study on the house plans. But his bedroom was still in the study, which I could tell troubled him. He considered Lenore's constant rearranging of the rooms predictable.

"It's really him." Lenore is almost shouting now. Dancing around me while I carried in the laundry basket, hoping the washer and dryer were still in the basement.

If Lenore were not Lenore, I would know what finally found "him" could bring my lover such joy. Or I could at least take a good guess. But Lenore could be talking about her tenth grade math teacher, an upholsterer for the sofa, a tai chi instructor, or Malcolm's sperm donor. All of whom Lenore has talked about finding over the past few years, with equal intensity. She frequently places advertisements in the classified sections of certain newspapers. She even hired a private investigator for the tenth grade math teacher, but because Lenore would not tell the investigator the name of the high school she attended ("What does he need to know that for?" she had screamed), the search did not get very far.

So I just waited for Lenore's story to develop. I'm in the doorway of what I figure out must be my own bedroom when Lenore shouts, "I can't believe I found him: Dagoberto." It's not unusual that I have my own bedroom instead of sharing one with Lenore, but it isn't usual either. So maybe that's why the name doesn't sink in.

"Dagoberto Luz, isn't that a beautiful name?"

"I guess," I say. I was looking at the double bed, feeling sort of sad. I really hate to sleep alone.

"Oh, you're going to love him as much as I do. We're going to be a real family now." Lenore was hugging me. I almost hoped she would kiss my neck and I would pull her down on the double bed and she would melt in my arms. I almost hoped for a miracle more amazing than any mermaid.

Which is what I'm hoping for now, in the restaurant, with the tall blond man wearing a Swiss Army watch. A miracle that will turn this man into a mermaid. Right here in Midtown Manhattan. Or at least a dyke.

The man who ordered rack of lamb.

Not the most expensive item on the menu; the second-most expensive.

"Get anything you want, Dagoberto," Lenore had said to him. "My treat," she announced.

Which meant my treat. Lenore hasn't worked in twelve years, not since she was pregnant with Malcolm. Not that I really have a problem with that. Not that I really expect her to work. Given her mental health. Or lack of it.

Which can lead to money problems.

Not just the psychiatric bills.

Like the seven thousand, three hundred dollars' worth of embroidery supplies she ordered. Standing hoops in four different sizes, and scissors shaped like little birds, and scroll frames ordered extra large, and crewel, chenille, and tapestry needles in packets of one hundred, and bolts of embroidery fabrics in various weaves, and floss in original hand-dyed colors, and pearl cotton in the highest sheen, and skeins of Persian yarn, mostly pink and red, and metallic threads for "special effects."

She doesn't even know how to embroider.

It was right after the embroidery fiasco that I knew I had to keep everything separate. Her psychiatrist, Dr. Sidney Henry, actually advised me to do this, pointing out that it would be bad for Lenore to "indulge in consumer frenzies."

So, everything is in my name, alone. The house perched on the palisades, looking as if it would surely tumble into the Hudson during any East Coast earthquake. The house safely set back from the ocean, but not so far that I can't hear the ocean's soothing pulse all night. The bank accounts, including the one in the Bahamas. The money markets. The certificates of deposit. I hired an investment counselor—I knew I should be smart about the money I was making—and he advised: "Diversify." But stocks and bonds make me nervous. I am afraid of risk; always afraid—even after twenty years—that Mavis Paige will be written out of the script and Jill Willis will never get another lucrative thirteen-week contract again.

Besides, I trust the nice women at the local bank in Grandview, the one who set up the Bahamian deal. "Just in case," she said. I didn't ask her in case of what.

It's not like I want to deprive or control Lenore. I gave her one Visa card after the embroidery binge, with a five-hundred-dollar limit. I have to keep calling the company to maintain the limit because they keep trying to raise it based upon her excellent credit history. Every month she charges five hundred dollars and every month I pay it. I try to remember to compliment her on the new lamp she bought, or the new bathrobe, or the new umbrella embroidered with real gold thread.

"I've seen your show. You're quite competent." Dagoberto's accent is brisk with its *T*s.

"Oh. And what do you do?" Mavis' accent is clipped with its vowels. Jill Willis is raging: *Competent?*

"I'm unemployed at the moment."

Ah, a former stockbroker or philosophy professor who is now addicted to daytime drama.

"Dagoberto was a medical student," Lenore says, touching his arm.

He nods.

I assume he flunked out.

Or was kicked out for cheating.

I can tell he is unscrupulous. It's the blond hair. And maybe that tiny scar on his chin. I haven't been on daytime drama for almost twenty years without learning a few things.

"Which is how I knew it was really him." Lenore sighs. "Through the medical files. He got all the medical records to prove it to himself before he even answered the ad."

And then even me, goody-two-shoes Mavis/Jill/BJ, gets it.

Though I have my doubts.

Weren't there papers that Lenore signed that said the medical records would always be confidential?

And by the time I have to go, arranging to pay the bill with the maître d', leaving them at the table together talking and laughing, I think all my doubts are confirmed. I think this not just because they ignore me—as if I am not really a real person—but because neither one of them mentions Malcolm during the entire lunch.

"I want a divorce."

It is not the voice of David, or even my own, which rings with such conviction. David and I have only been married for a few episodes. I wore a beige lace dress and although beige is not my best color, all the guests said I looked beautiful. Although Bethany did say I looked "a bit haggard." Not to my face, but to Brad, who I still love and who is beginning to tire of Bethany.

It is the voice of Lenore.

I do not point out that we are not married.

I do not point out anything. I just wait. To see whether she is serious. To see whether she is clearheaded.

She has never sounded so rational. At least not since Malcolm was born.

"You have to admit our relationship leaves a lot to be desired." She is smiling. She is dressed in matching clothes (a green silk shirt of mine and pants I had bought her last year, black with a delicate green paisley print) and her hair is combed.

I smile back, like a reflex. I can't seem to remember my lines.

"We haven't had real sex in years," Lenore says.

I try to maintain my smile. Wondering if Lenore isn't being just a bit too blunt; this should be marked for an edit. Or perhaps I should resort to tears; I should rely upon my talent. I have a beautiful cry. I can make the tears flow without my eyes swelling or my nose reddening. It isn't as common a feat as many people might think.

"We both deserve more." Lenore sounds eerily rational.

"I guess," I admit.

"Like my parents. I mean, they still shower together after fifteen years of marriage."

"Your parents are divorced," I say.

"I know. I mean my father and R."

"R is his third wife. His third wife named Lenore."

"Sometimes you have to try a few times before you find true love."

"With three women that have the same name? And name your daughters . . ."

"BJ, don't get upset."

"I'm not," I lie.

"It's really not your fault, you know." Her hand covers mine. "I guess you couldn't help it, with Evelyn and Mimi being the way they are."

I take my hand from under her fingers.

"But you know, just because your mother is a dyke, you shouldn't have pulled me into it." Her hand covers mine again.

"What the fuck are you saying Lenore?" She must be slipping back into being crazy again. Or she is trying to get even for what I said about her crazy family full of Lenores. I mean, *really*, my mother and Mimi?

"Oh. Dagoberto said you'd be angry." She is patting my hand now. "But there really isn't anything to be angry about. It was all just a mistake. Just like my father always said."

"What?" I'm getting sort of confused.

"Us. You and me. You really shouldn't have tried to make me think I was a lesbian."

"What? We met in a queer bar."

"That's beside the point."

"You were with your girlfriend-of-the-moment who was a prop girl for the show."

"How is that relevant?"

"You were a lesbian, Lenore, long before you met me. That's how it's relevant."

"Don't be ridiculous, BJ. I was simply there with a friend. When you lured me into the bathroom and attacked me."

"Attacked you? What the fuck are you talking about?"

"It was doomed to failure." Lenore seems to swoon. She takes her hand from on top of mine and places the back of it on her forehead.

Cut that move: too melodramatic.

But there is no director-of-the-day to rescue me.

"You can have him," Lenore says.

Which is what Bethany has said about Brad.

I think I know who Lenore means, then think again, thinking I cannot be right. I wait for her next line, holding my head motionless. Only my tongue moves, slightly, against the fence of my teeth.

"Don't you want him?" Lenore asks. She sounds a bit accusing, although perhaps she is only annoyed.

"I'll take him," I try to sound neutral. Neutral as "I'll take half a pound of the low-salt ham, please" for his lunch. Neutral as "I'll take the size twelve jeans, not the size ten," so he has a bit of room to grow. Neutral as an everyday exchange. Neutral is not easy for me, given the topic, given my training.

Given my worry that I might not be able to see Malcolm except at Lenore's sufferance.

I had thought Lenore would not suffer me very much. I had thought she loved Malcolm. I had thought she had loved Malcolm more than I did. Biology and all that. The same biology she blamed for her breakdown, after Malcolm's birth. But I thought her breakdown only proved how strong the bond was, strong enough to break the bonds of rationality.

And now, with Dagoberto in the picture—or back in the picture, according to Lenore—I thought Lenore had more reasons to love Malcolm. Her son. Their son. Dagoberto the proud daddy, no longer denied. From anonymous sperm donor to dad in twelve easy years, just have the biological mom fall in love with you. The three of them could compose the perfect family tableau. I'd be on another set altogether, probably the bedroom, looking in my mirror and having my thoughts reverberate as whispers.

But Lenore does not want Malcolm. And I'm performing.

"Then, that's settled. What about the house?"

Singular. I'm not sure she remembers the beach house. I'm not sure she knows we—or I—own it. Maybe she thinks we rent it every summer? Maybe she doesn't think?

"I think we should let the lawyers negotiate that," I say. Just like *Episode #567* and my first divorce. Peter, I think.

"I imagine we'll sell and split the proceeds," Lenore presses. "Why wouldn't we?"

"We both like this house?" I try a smile. Because even Lenore knows how much I hate this place. The property listing had said waterfront when we looked at this place—and I suppose the Realtor will choose that description again if we list it for sale—but the water is two hundred feet below, down a cliff without a path. Although Malcolm can scramble down, and I've even done it once or twice with him, it hardly seems worth the effort. There is no shore, no little ledge of rock that could be a wind-carved throne, no place to relax. Nothing to do but climb back up. Up to the house with the beautiful views. The house with its expensive modernist angles, of cedar and glass perched on the palisades overlooking the Hudson River. The house in a town called Grandview. The house with its bedrooms and study and living room and dining room in places other than where the architects had envisioned. The house that Mavis Paige bought.

For Lenore.

Because Lenore had announced that she found the house "safe." And safety seemed important to Lenore, after Malcolm was born. And Lenore's psychiatrist said safety was important to Lenore.

Although it made me dizzy. I'm a bit afraid of heights. Probably because I never took trampoline lessons. I always feel like I could tumble down, into the river, and float downstream. My body washed up on the Upper West Side.

"Don't be silly. It's too big for you to maintain, the way you work."

Can this be Lenore? She sounds so lucid. Lucid, yes that's right word. One of the evil-twin episodes.

"And I just want to start over."

Start over.

Take Two.

"With real love. With Dagoberto."

Take Two.

I want to say something clever, but can't think of anything. So I try to keep my voice level. "Start over? With a man this time?"

"Quit harping on the man thing, BJ. You think that's the issue, but it's not. It's how he makes me feel. Like I'm real. Like I'm important. Life will be hard for all of us, too, you know. It's not like he has a great job like you do."

I clear my throat. What can I say? I'm not going to argue about an unemployed stockbroker or philosophy professor.

"And"—Lenore fingers a new ring on her finger—"it's not like he's white."

"What?"

"It's not like he's white."

"What are you talking about? He's blond, that's seems pretty much like white to me. Or maybe the blue eyes confused me."

Blond. Blue eyes. Like Malcolm.

"Don't be so superficial."

"I can't help it," I mock. Myself.

"Well, at least try. He's from South America. He's Hispanic. And he's been oppressed."

I wonder what Lenore knows about oppression. Before I protected her, her parents did. Daddy a surgeon. Mommy in the garden club, president most years. Until she was replaced by stepmommy. And if all those Lenores seemed just a bit odd in Scarsdale, well . . . eccentricity can be tolerated if there is enough money to insure that the rose bushes win prizes. Scarsdale is very nice in summer, very nice at every time of year. They pay to keep it that way. I wonder what Dad will think about Dagoberto's oppression. Being kicked out of medical school is probably oppressive. But it's certainly a step up from being a lesbian.

"BJ, why don't you think about me and about my life and what I've always wanted? I deserve a chance at that. I'm getting the chance at it; I'm taking it. I deserve to start over. To have a second chance."

Take two.

"I'm starting over," Lenore says, convincing herself.

And then it all makes sense. I know it without her saying it. She's been saying it, although not with precision. With her phrasing: "all of us." With her disinterest in Malcolm. With those gestures of hand spread across stomach and arching back I recognize from twelve years ago.

Starting over. Lenore is pregnant. Or will be. Or is trying desperately.

"I hope you don't flip out this time." I say this kindly, because it is not meant to be.

As if her attempts at killing Malcolm, as if her six months in the psych ward, as if the diagnosis of postpartum depression, as if the continued years of psychotherapy were experiences that had belonged only to her, that had not shaped us both.

"I'm sure I won't," she says pointedly. Pointed-at-me. It is my fault she went crazy. Wouldn't having a dyke lover who played a straight woman on daytime TV do it to any new mother?

110

"Take two," I say. But this time out loud. But this time do it right, Lenore. With a husband. A blond man. And a new baby, one you don't try to kill.

"Take two," Lenore echoes.

"We could move into the city," I tell Malcolm.

He seems unconvinced. "It's dirty."

"True." I am acting as if nothing is wrong. I resist telling him it's temporary, although this is what I tell myself. With Lenore, everything has been temporary, so part of me figures that this will be too. That just as she will get tired of sleeping in the foyer (where she has moved her bed so that it practically blocks the front entrance), she'll get tired of Dagoberto.

And part of me wants to settle things before she changes her mind.

I admit it. I'm relieved.

Sad. But also relieved.

I think Malcolm feels the same way. He's at the age where Lenore is starting to embarrass him. It's hard to bring someone home if you don't know where your room is going to be.

And I'm relieved about Malcolm. I love that kid. Maybe I only stayed with Lenore all these years for him.

That's not true. I stayed with Lenore because I'm a goody-goody. Everyone says so. Lenore was ill and needed me. Or at least needed someone. I wasn't about to send her back to Scarsdale, like she was some stereo system that didn't sound so good once the dampness got in the circuits.

I've called the Realtor. Waterfront.

I've gotten my next thirteen-week contract. I think Brad is going to realize he is in love with me. David and I are definitely getting divorced. He's in love with Patricia.

It's going to be fine.

I tell myself. I tell Malcolm. I tell Evelyn and Mimi. I even tell Lenore.

*   *   *

I tell Malcolm that afterwards we will go have ice cream sodas. Once, such promises were easy bribes. Now it is not so simple.

But I don't want to leave him home alone, meaning with Lenore and Dagoberto. I hate working on Saturday, but I do have certain responsibilities.

Evelyn and Mimi will be there of course. They love these events. I'll invite them along for the sodas. I'll try not to look at them and wonder whether I've been naive all these years, almost all of my childhood and all of my adult life.

As we pull into the parking lot, I fight the urge to cry.

My mascara will run and Malcolm will notice.

I look in the rearview mirror at my hair, my eyes, and that disturbing little black mark that has appeared on my bottom lip. Smooth my melon silk outfit, a casually cut jacket with wide-legged pants. Take my tan suede purse from the back seat.

I do not look at Malcolm. I can't. It seems now I look at him and see Dagoberto. The hair. The eyes. But also some line of jaw. Some gesture I never noticed before.

But then I look again, look for it, and it's gone. As if Dagoberto had never been found.

The building is huge. Much larger than it needs to be, I think. Entering it is like entering a cavern of artificial light.

Just like the cavern where I spend so many days; calling it "the studio" makes it sound different from a factory, but sometimes I wonder. With its perfect little sets in perfect little rows. Everything is arranged in lines. Everything has corners.

Just like the mall where I used to work. With the stores sitting side by side, trying to be different from each other but still seeming all the same. Even the little kiosks in the middle. Even the huge department stores.

Just like this mall. In Philadelphia, but not the one where I worked. I want to slip out of my body and slide down the corridors without being noticed. Changing my name is not enough. It never is. Though people do it all the time. Women, mostly. We change our names as if we could change our lives: It's Elizabeth now, not Libby. Or we refuse to change our names as if it would not change our lives: It's still Ms. Jones, not Mrs. Fizthugh. (Will Lenore become Mrs. Luz?) We pretend it is not about faces and bodies, about paint and plastic surgeries, about diets and costumes.

"Over there."

I'm hardly through the doors and I hear the whisper. Pointing at me. My face. My body. I'm close enough to see the confusion flit across her face. The eyebrows pull toward each other, magnetized by effort. To see the hand raise from the body, unsure whether to wave or point.

It makes me feel lonely.

Stupid, I know. For how can I be lonely when the new department store, excuse me, "shopping environment," has invited me to its "opening extravaganza"?

They put me in Home Furnishings. In the middle of the white sale, in which nothing is white. Ecru, maybe. Natural. Winter. Angel. But nothing white.

Malcolm wanders to electronics. And then to a couch in a sea of other couches, little living room sets arranged as if on tiny stages. I watch him, even as I look for Mimi and Evelyn.

"Are you really going to marry Brad? I think he really loves you."

"I don't know," I answer honestly.

"Well, I hope you get the better of Bethany. She's such a brat!"

"Thank you," I say.

"You know, maybe if you gave up trying to be a lawyer, you'd be more attractive to Brad."

"I'll think about that," Jill Willis says. Mavis Paige would say a sentence or two about her career as a lawyer, helping the less fortunate. BJ would say. . . ? What would BJ say?

I'm not sure I know.

I'm not sure it matters.

Mostly, they talk to me as if I am Mavis Paige. Although a few talk to me as if I am Jill Willis, asking me about my acting career and my home in Connecticut.

"I'm such a fan of yours. You could be on regular television."

"Thanks so much," I say. And I am sincere. When I started, I didn't have the acting ambitions that some of the others did, but I'm not immune to them. Or immune to the way in which we aren't taken seriously. For some of us, the myth was that doing daytime drama was temporary, or would actually provide a track into movies or nighttime television. Which did happen to a few of us, just enough to maintain the myth.

We believe we should be acting in what we call "real theater." Right. From *In the Name of Love* to *King Lear*. Not that *King Lear* was on Broadway. Would Lenore love me if I played Cordelia? But unlike many of the others, I didn't have the time or talent for summer stock. Cordelia does the Catskills.

I like to tell myself that we, the soap actors, are the true professionals. That we get up every day, day after day, and do our jobs with skill and talent. And we're not hacks, at least not more so than anybody else, including Vanessa Redgrave. And at least we have steady jobs. Thirteen weeks at a time.

And if this wasn't enough for the ones who persisted in auditioning for TV movie specials or some off-Broadway experiment, it was enough for me. After all, I measured my career against working in Bloomingdale's.

"You're really sweet," someone says.

"Too sweet, if you ask me," another woman says.

I see Mimi join Malcolm on a couch. He gives her a hug. She pulls out something from her shiny black purse. He smiles.

I look for Evelyn, my mother. I don't see her. Then I do. Talking to some other woman. I think the one who told me I should give up being a lawyer so I could please Brad. Pointing toward me. They both look old and overweight.

No one is talking to me now. I stand. Like a mannequin.

And then it is over. My two-hour gig. Surrounded by sheets and towels. The publicity person from the department store thanks me.

She is thin, with little wrinkles around her eyes when she smiles. She seems pleased, but I know she is paid to seem that way.

And then we are leaving. Malcolm and Mimi and my mother and me. Walking toward the escalator. Past the child moving her hands along the rubber handrail as if she believes she is operating the steep and long trail of moving stairs.

As I step on the first stair, hiding any twinge of my fear of heights, voices drift up to me.

"She's a lot heavier than I thought she would be."

"Really. I guess TV makes you look thinner."

"Nah. It adds ten pounds. They must have to be really careful with the cameras."

"Maybe it was the outfit."

"That color! Hideous."

"I guess they don't dress them off of the show. But you'd think she'd know better."

"Wasn't she a model?"

"I don't think so. I heard she came from a horse farm."

"I thought she was from Philadelphia."

"Oh yeah. You're right. Too bad it's not Bethany that's from here. Bethany is much prettier."

"Yes. That Bethany has a certain style. A little bitchy, but . . ."

Mimi interrupts my eavesdropping with a loud reference to the promised sundaes. She must have heard the women, who are disappearing into cosmetics by now. Mimi is protective that way.

Although later, after the sundaes, when Malcolm and my mom are looking at some video games in which I'm sure my mother has no interest, Mimi says pretty much the same thing, which makes me think she couldn't have heard those women's voices. Not about being overweight or pretty or from a horse farm. But about being bitchy.

"This is no time to be nice," Mimi warns.

Not about Bethany or Brad. About Lenore.

I tell her Lenore is being reasonable. I tell her all I want is Malcolm. I tell her I'm prepared to split the assets with Lenore.

I expect Mimi to tell me I was being overly generous. Or compliment me on being civilized. Or give me a little sympathy. But Mimi seems harsh. Angry, almost.

"Don't trust her." Mimi shakes her finger.

I try to look at my mom, Evelyn, but she's acting like she's interested in those stupid little electronic games.

"Get a lawyer." Mimi frowns.

"For once in your life, don't be so goody-goody." Mimi puts her hands out in front of her, palms up, as if she is asking some god for a miracle.

"You tried to kill him."

"You're crazy."

"You can't earn a real living."

"You live in a make-believe world."

Lenore is screaming.

At me.

BJ.

Responsible citizen. Employed as an actor, playing the part of Mavis Paige, a lawyer on the television show *In the Name of Love*. Using the stage name Jill Willis.

Me. BJ. Lover of Lenore. At least until a few weeks ago. Lenore, who is screaming at me now.

Me. BJ. Mother of Malcolm. Still. Although Lenore is saying the impossible. Saying I'm the one who tried to kill Malcolm. That I'm the one who had postpartum depression. Although that would make me the biological mother, which I am not. Which Lenore is saying. Saying that she wants Malcolm now. Saying that she is pregnant, but with a girl.

Pregnant, already? How long? When?

She's punching herself in the stomach.

"He doesn't want a girl. A son. A son. He wants a son. But I've got one. I do."

She is no longer lucid.

I should call the psychiatrist.

I should call someone.

I should know my lines by now. I've had enough time. But I can't find the script.

I stand as still as I can. Waiting for the close-up. Waiting for the scene to end.

part four

Episode

ten

As she unlocks the door, she suppresses the almost involuntary smile of satisfaction that still tempts her lips whenever she sees the name on the flaking gold-colored plate: PROFESSOR GERTRUDE YARNES. Professor. She still likes the way that sounds. More than she likes Gertrude or even Yarnes. Certainly more than Trudi. No one has ever called her Trudi more than twice, except for a teacher or two in grammar school. Her mother named her Gertrude, in the hopes that such a solid name would serve her daughter well in the Detroit factories. But although Gertrude escaped from Detroit as quickly as possible, leaving home for the state university, she knew of no reason to depart from her mother's judgment regarding her name.

Though her lover calls her Bunny. Rather silly, sure. Derived from a shared joke, from a time when she marveled that they "fucked like rabbits." Barbara—called Bobbi by almost everyone except Gertrude, who sometimes calls her Babs just to irritate her and often calls her Baby, especially in bed—had teased Gertrude by calling her Bunny and the name had somehow stuck. And some of their friends, overhearing Bobbi call out "Bunny" from kitchen during a small dinner party and thinking that perhaps the appellation Gertrude was too fussily formal, had started calling her Bunny as well, as if to demonstrate intimacy. But Gertrude would always eventually correct her friends (allowing the first or second "Bunny" to slip by, based in equal measures upon generosity and optimism and a certain dread of conflict), by letting them know that she preferred to be called Gertrude and saying it in such a way that to call her anything else seemed like an insult.

In her office, on the inner side of the door bearing her name, Gertrude prepares for her day. It is early, earlier than one might expect a law professor to arrive at her office, because Gertrude likes at least an hour and a half before other people arrive to ground herself. She knows she seems solid—living up to her mother's choice of name—but she still strives to present herself that way. Even after twenty years as a professor, it is not her nature, even her second nature, perhaps not even her third, to be some cerebral mentor, some knowledgeable expert, some role model to hundreds of women students. Of course, it is easier these days, now that she is not the only female law professor. Although she is still one of not-as-many-as-there-should-be. And still the most senior, in all respects. The most respected. Perhaps.

She reaches for her coffee and thermos, both bestowed by her lover, Bobbi. The thermos is slim and silver, ordered from a catalog. The coffee is hazelnut, well-sugared and generously spiked with half-and-half. She pours some into one of her mugs, most of which were presents from students. Never the students she would have expected would give her a present; after all these years her only clue that a student will bestow a gift is that she would ordinarily assume that this particular student would not. She takes her week's worth of mugs home on each Friday (shaking her head at the firm beige scum on the bottom of each cup and at her own incurable resistance to alleviating this situation by walking down the hall and washing her daily mug in the bathroom sink), letting Bobbi load them in the dishwasher and trusting Bobbi to put them near her briefcase with the thermos each Monday.

While sipping her coffee, she sorts papers and rambles around her office, almost as if she is inspecting it for clues about its occupant. She admires its neatness, its relative spaciousness (one of the perks of seniority), and its personality. Objects—which are not law books or diplomas or plastic crates full of copied cases or file folders brimming with syllabi—are intensified in the office by their incongruity. A small glass bottle of dyed-blue sand labeled as being from the Isle of Lesbos (given to her by a long-ago lover who is now a drama professor). The Indian print bedspread used as a tablecloth (once it had adorned the first bed she owned, the bed in which she had made love with Teddy, the woman who is now the drama professor). *The Three Spirits,* a numbered print she and Bobbi had gotten on a vacation to the island of Vancouver. Such objects are concrete, of course, but they seem less than solid in the office of a law professor. Especially *The Three Spirits,* with its three masked and androgynous faces pressed under glass and bounded by an ebony wood. The six eyes seem to shift with the professor's moods, indicating that perhaps the professor—who writes "solid" on exams and student papers as the highest compliment—also honors a more ethereal attribute, at least occasionally.

Class at two-thirty P.M. Until five. A schedule some of the other professors covet, but Gertrude would prefer to teach in the mornings. The students seem more alert before noon. Their last night's preparation of the cases still fresh in their muddled minds, untrammeled by sitting in other classes (like Tax and Corporations and Secured Transactions), battling with boredom and abstraction. At least Criminal Procedure was interesting; even the students who hated the subject admitted it was interesting. The facts of the cases were always real, so real she could act them out in class, playing the part of the cop while she made an especially conservative student be a suspect. She would stand over the student and ask him questions for a precious fifteen minutes of class time until he became so taut he would make up lies so that she would stop. She would kick open the briefcase on the floor next to his feet and casually sift through the contents, producing a small baggie of sugar. Long after the students forgot the conceptual frameworks for analyzing interrogation under the Fifth Amendment or the plain-view exception in search and seizure doctrine under the Fourth Amendment, she hoped her students remembered the mutability of truth.

Such mutability was not so easily taught in Family Law, her other teaching responsibility, although she taught it less and less since the recent hiring of a new faculty member who specialized in the area. The new professor brought an enthusiasm to the subject that Gertrude knew she never had, not because the subject was not factually real (it was) or doctrinally complex (it could be). And it wasn't that Gertrude found the entire subject alienating, especially now that all the heterosexual professors were focusing on lesbian and gay relationships as the most interesting development in twenty years. Her dislike for the subject was simply because Family Law seemed like a women's area of the law. Gertrude hates to admit such a silly and superficial reason—it was as if she was still in grade school and would not wear lace socks because they were too girly—but it is true. Being a professor of Family Law makes her feel vulnerable in a way that is unreasonable. It violates not only her sense of herself as solid but also some expectation of originality she sees in the six eyes of *The Three Spirits,* or even in the bottle of dyed sand that probably isn't really from Lesbos. So, this semester she is teaching three sections of Criminal Procedure, almost one hundred and fifty students, instead of a single section of Family Law, and a coveted seminar of twenty self-selected students, such as Advanced Family Law or even Sexuality and Law.

With such a large number of students and a reputation for being a harsh grader, Gertrude's office hours are hectic. The sign-up sheets for appointments, taped on her door under her nameplate for the current week and three weeks in advance, are congested with student names. Most of the students have questions about material covered in class. A few students from previous classes request recommendations based upon their good grades. Some students seek career advice (or more accurately, some validation of their career choices). And several students a year schedule an appointment during the last slot of the day to invite Gertrude to coffee (which she declines) and to divulge their sexual orientation, which is lesbian or gay or bisexual or transsexual. Gertrude has been waiting for twenty years for a student to make an appointment to tell her he or she is heterosexual, but although students announce this during the Law and Sexuality Seminar, no one has yet invited Gertrude to coffee over such a disclosure. She believes herself compassionate during these confessions, mostly because she resists the urge to lecture her students about how easy they have it, at least comparatively. But because her own life is the source of her inevitable comparisons, more than a bit of patronizing often seeps through Gertrude's comments. Her condescension was least disguised and most piquant with the women students who came to her office to tell Professor Gertrude Yarnes not only about their lesbianism but about the object of their affections: her. Gertrude found it impossible not to chastise their innocence, not to mention their impertinence, in taking themselves seriously enough to contemplate even the possibility that she would be interested in their fantasies about her. As if she did not have a life of her own, complete with a lover. As if they thought they knew her enough to love her (yes, some of these young women actually uttered the word "love") from her class discussions about the right to a jury trial. Though the protestations of love did not happen as often as they once did. Getting older had its advantages, or so Gertrude thought, although once in a while she would imply to Bobbi that an especially smitten young woman had been to her office. "Make sure you keep your door open," Bobbi advised, in a flat voice that betrayed nothing but confidence. But Gertrude thought she noticed that Bobbi's attentiveness piqued just a degree by some unnecessary jealousy.

What Gertrude is hoping today's appointments will yield is not a student admirer who she can exaggerate for Bobbi's benefit, but a good research assistant. The law review article she has been trying to write for the past year is an outline and introductory paragraph curling on the table underneath *The Three Spirits*. It is a good idea—of that Gertrude is certain—but without external pressures (Gertrude had long ago received tenure and less long ago had somehow shed the compulsion to justify her professorship through publications), her ambition languishes. A smart student, with whom she could discuss ideas as well as footnotes, could breathe some life into the project. She has her eye on someone, of course, someone most professors would overlook, but someone who might bloom with attentive cultivation.

Margaret Smyth. A deceptively simple student, or so Gertrude intuits. Good grades, or so Gertrude discovers. And she seems to have taken Gertrude's hints regarding the position and signed up for another office appointment. Right before Gertrude's scheduled lunch with Jill Willis. "Personal," Jill Willis had said. And Gertrude, who had only before given advice for Mavis Paige (Gertrude taking a certain pride in her role as occasional consultant for *In the Name of Love* about a myriad of legal matters that arise in the scripts), agreed to meet the woman for lunch. A quick bite, Gertrude insisted. Her habits did not include leaving her office for lunch, especially when she had to teach an afternoon class. But she liked the woman she could not help but think of as Mavis Paige. And she wanted to remedy any residual guilt she felt for having missed their last appointment.

Gertrude estimates that there is at least a half of a mug of coffee remaining in her silver thermos by the time she opens the door to allow a student to exit and motions Margaret to enter. Margaret sits down gracefully and deftly, sliding her black leather knapsack under her chair. Gertrude watches as the student quickly assesses the office, Margaret's gaze pausing more than momentarily on *The Three Spirits*.

"Nice print." Margaret offers Professor Gertrude Yarnes a slight smile, almost an apology for scrutinizing the office.

"Thank you. My lover and I got it in Vancouver." Gertrude watches Margaret's face carefully for a reaction, but she can detect none. Not a stray movement of fingers. Not a hint of color on the neck. Not even a flutter around the lips. No discomfort. But no pleasure either.

"Well," Gertrude says finally, "what did you want to see me about?" Making Margaret start the conversation is Gertrude's retribution for Margaret's lack of reaction to her intimate disclosure.

"I'm interested in the research assistant position."

"Oh yes. Do you have a copy of your resumé?"

Gertrude studies the single sheet of beige bond that Margaret hands her. She decides to be blunt: "I don't see anything here that indicates why you might be interested in working on a criminal procedure project. Could you tell me why you are interested in working with me?"

Margaret gives Gertrude all the signs she had missed before. Margaret's index finger rubs a piece of skin at her thumb cuticle. A splotch of red appears at the collar of her shirt. Her lips twitch in an uncomfortable attempt at a smile.

"I like Criminal Procedure," Margaret stutters. "And I'd like to have some practical experience."

"I'm afraid you won't get any practical experience working with me. It's mostly a theoretical project. If you're interested in practical experience, I suggest you look for an internship with the district attorney."

"I might do an internship," Margaret's stammer is still evident. "But I'd like to work for a professor also."

"I need a year's commitment. Until the end of the academic year will do, although I'd prefer some part-time work next summer."

"That would be no problem." Margaret's voice achieves an even tone.

"I suppose I could tell you I'll let you know, but I see no reason to prolong this process." Gertrude's voice is clipped, as if to compensate for her kindness. "If you want the job, you have it. You'll have to fill out some papers, of course. But even if you don't qualify for work-study, I've got some grant funding, so there should be no problems. You'll also need to familiarize yourself with the project. I'm looking at judicial rhetoric regarding perceptions of a defendant's identity and the entrapment defense. We haven't gotten to entrapment in Criminal Procedure yet, but I'm sure you know the basics: Government agents basically set up a suspect. It happens mostly in drug cases, so I'm looking at those, but also sex cases. The sex cases are in many ways the most interesting. With an interesting history, also. The highway rest-stop busts of gay men and the arrest of women on the street after dark as vagrants and prostitutes. What I'm interested in theorizing is how the courts' perception of the defendants' identity—the defendant as a drug dealer or a gay man or a prostitute—is used to defeat the entrapment defense. And on what evidence those conclusions about identity are based. You know, like she was standing on a corner wearing a miniskirt, so she must be a hooker. Anyway, it's all in the outline; I'll give you a copy. Does it sound interesting?"

If Gertrude expects her new research assistant to be enthusiastic, she is disappointed. A disappointment that cannot linger, because her next appointment—her lunch appointment—is knocking at her door. A disappointment that quickly recedes as she observes Margaret squeezing past Mavis Paige in the office doorway. And then Margaret turning back to gaze into the office, or perhaps to gaze at the woman closing the door, who might also be looking at Margaret.

"Thanks for seeing me," the woman in a hot pink dress greets Gertrude. Although it seems to Gertrude as if the woman's attention is absorbed by the door that is now closed behind her. The woman sinks into the chair that Margaret had just vacated. Her purse, an unwieldy affair somewhere between an unlockable briefcase and a beach bag, tips over and its contents scatter around the floor of Gertrude's office. Lots of white papers stapled together. A lipstick or two. A bottle of pills. Pens and rubber bands and blue tissues and a bottle of water. Gertrude does not bend over to assist her, but tries to act as if it is perfectly normal that a person would dump her purse on the rug.

"This is personal," the woman picking up a crumpled tissue from Gertrude's floor says. And for a moment, Gertrude thinks she is referring to the tissue or perhaps the contents of the purse in general, instead of the purpose of her visit. "It's not for the show, I mean. I mean, it's a personal problem. I need a little advice. About the state of the law. It's about my son. Or not really my son, I guess that's the problem."

"Why don't you start at the beginning, Jill."

"BJ. Please call me BJ."

"Oh, sorry."

"No. It's just that Jill Willis is my professional name. Stage name. And this is not a problem Jill Willis would have." BJ sounds a bit hysterical. "This is definitely a BJ problem. It's my lover's son."

Lover. Such a smooth, evocative sound. As Gertrude feels a small smile tug at her upper lip, she wonders how Margaret could fail to react to it. Margaret is a woman who has throttled herself in some effort at self-protection, Gertrude allows herself to think, certainly in contrast to BJ, who seems about to shatter into a million particles, all of them sharp with grief.

Lover. Such a significant term. As Gertrude appreciates. Although she knows that she must not make assumptions and holds some judgment in abeyance. After all, heterosexuals use the word also. And one could not tell the lesbians anymore, if one ever could, although BJ is certainly no surprise. Hadn't Gertrude known this?

The same way BJ had known to come to her about this sort of problem? Although, Gertrude reminded herself, she had published some articles in this area which were mentioned in her biography under her photograph in the law school catalog. One way to let everyone know she was a lesbian. Which is probably why, Gertrude realizes, Margaret did not react. It was such old news.

But didn't the information that she had a lover and they traveled together merit some response? Weren't these younger dykes always looking for role models? Although Margaret seems a little more mature than the average law student. Still, Gertrude was at least a decade—if not the usual two—older than she was. Or maybe Margaret wasn't a lesbian at all. That was possible. Anything was possible. Though not probable.

"My lover is the biological mother, I mean. I think I've been just as much of a mother. And she says she doesn't want him."

"What?"

"She says she doesn't want him. It's kind of crazy actually. Hey, shouldn't we go to lunch?"

Gertrude looks at her watch. "I guess we could. Though we might as well stay here. Would that be suitable? It would probably give us more time to talk."

"Thanks," BJ says simply. And continues her story. Her story of insanity and attempted infanticides and sperm donors and a child who is now eleven years old.

Gertrude has to bite her bottom lip to prevent the words "soap opera" from escaping from her mouth and hovering in the office's electrified air.

eleven

*M*argaret in the doorway. Face to face with her. Close enough to smell a cosmetic. Lipstick, probably. Bright pink and too sweet.

She recognizes her. From the hallway, stealing glances at each other while passing the time. From that odd apparition, that hallucination, at the women's festival. But somewhere else. Someone else.

She prides herself on a good memory, but it seems to be failing.

She could ask Professor Yarnes. Which would probably further diminish her in the professor's opinion. It had felt strange sitting so close to her, after seeing her mostly from the back row of a large classroom. But everything seemed to feel strange these days. Even the professor's attempt to be friendly. Perhaps especially that. The professor mentioning her lover and their trip to Vancouver. And then seeming to expect a response. Some display of envy, perhaps. Or congratulations. Or most likely only a reciprocal revelation.

She could ask that woman herself. Could wait for her right outside the office door. Introduce herself and flirt a bit. Casual and light. Open and amicable. But the law books seem to weigh Margaret Smyth down. Her black knapsack makes her incapable of executing such flighty performances.

Having a lover like that will have to wait. Wait until Toledo or Topeka. Wait until the day she can confide in Professor Yarnes about her own trip to Vancouver with her own lover. Display the lovely print they bought in her office.

Margaret drifts toward the cafeteria, toward a cup of coffee. Cream and sugar. Sits down alone at a long table. Like she always does. Alone. Alone. The other students never seem to join her. The other students walk around her, as if she is not someone to be noticed.

Although she is not as alone as usual. It is almost as if that woman is sitting with her and Margaret is talking to her. Or if not talking, exactly, then somehow communicating. Saying: Look at me. This is my day. This is what I do. This is who I am. Who I really am. Who I want to be. Almost.

She has another cup of coffee. Looks at the forms the professor gave her. Information. Name. Social Security Number. All the usual questions. All the usual lies.

The cafeteria is filling up for lunch. People sit at her table. Faculty secretaries. She should leave. But she spreads her forms out a little further, creating a boundary. She is watching the entrance. Realizes she is watching. For her. Perhaps with the professor? Here for a cup of coffee?

It would be difficult to miss that hot pink dress, even if one were not staring intently at the cafeteria entrance. And a huge purse of some sort slung over the shoulder. She looks simultaneously elegant and disheveled. She glances around until she locates the line for the coffee.

"Yes, I think that's her."

"I recognize her. From one of the best soaps."

"The best?"

"Don't you think? I mean, some have gotten really outlandish."

"I'll say. That's why I like *In the Name of Love.*"

"I don't get to watch it now that the VCR is on the blink. I used to tape every show. She's been on the show forever. Oh shit, I've forgotten her name."

"Mavis Paige."

"That's right. Is she still going to get married to Brad?"

"I don't think it's working out."

"Because of Bethany, right?"

"That bitch. But you know, I don't think Mavis helps herself enough."

"She's kind of wishy-washy, don't you think?"

"Goody-goody."

"Yeah. I wonder why she's in our cafeteria."

"Could be here to see old Gertrude Yarnes."

"Really?"

"Yeah. Didn't you know she does some consulting for the show?"

"No, I didn't."

"I guess on legal stuff. Though you'd think they could get a real lawyer instead of a professor."

One faculty secretary nods her head slightly in the direction of Margaret, as if to quiet her companion.

But Margaret has already heard enough.

The only thing she thinks she knows about soap operas is that Teodesia, her client—her former client—is doing a book on them. Which is more than she wants to know.

And much less.

twelve

BJ in the bathroom. Rinsing off her face. Splashing away the embarrassment. There is very little puffiness in her eyes, thanks to her talent. There are no crying scenes this afternoon. Unfortunately. She could do an excellent job.

Gertrude had been kind, if a bit formal and uncomfortable.

She should never have come.

She should have left the minute she practically got barricaded in the doorway with that woman. That same woman. That woman's legs not moving, as if she were frozen, or as if she were a mermaid with a glimmering tail instead of two legs in plain black jeans. With her penetrating gaze.

She should have a lover like that. Someone stable and normal. Someone who did not rearrange the furniture every ten minutes. Someone who did not take thirteen years to decide she was not a lesbian.

She should have a lover like that woman. A law student probably. Seeing the professor about her grade. Her excellent grade. She would be smart, wouldn't she? A woman who seemed as composed as that. She would be very intelligent.

BJ could ask Gertrude Yarnes about her, couldn't she? Of course she couldn't. She was here begging advice from one of the only lesbians she knew who was an attorney and who might not blab her personal business all over town. And the advice she needed was about an ugly relationship. She wasn't about to jump into another one. No matter how sane the person seemed.

So at least she hadn't made a complete fool out of herself by asking about some student. And Gertrude had been full of practical advice. The law wasn't going to be much help, as BJ had already guessed. What she had to do was pin down Lenore on the decision and then formalize it. So Lenore would be less able to change her mind. Although she'd always, or so it seemed, be able to try to change her mind. That was what worried BJ. She thought she'd take the professor's suggestion to see a practicing lawyer and Gertrude had given her some names.

Though Gertrude had seemed a little uncomfortable about being asked to a taping of the show. BJ meant it as a gesture of gratitude, but the invitation came out garbled and BJ had to repeat it three times before Gertrude understood. But then Gertrude told her about another professor—not a law professor, she had quickly added—who was doing some work on soap operas and would probably love to see the show, so could she "recycle" the invitation? BJ had agreed, although it felt like a slight.

The water does not help her mood. Perhaps coffee. It is easy to find the cafeteria. Just follow the flow of students. Students who might be that woman. But are not. Students who quiver with their own concerns. Although several seem to recognize her, look at her long enough for a wrinkle to form on their foreheads and then dissolve with a sudden recognition.

And after she finally gets a cup, she sees her—sees that woman. Sees her getting up from a long table. BJ walks toward her. Thinking maybe a nod of acknowledgement. Thinking perhaps to even say hello. Thinking that she could feign surprise, one eyebrow raised and a tilt of the head would satisfy the director of the day, and have her lipsticked mouth form an attractive Oh. Not thinking. Just legs that should be sturdier marching toward the spot where she is.

Where she was.

BJ sits at her table. Not exactly where she was. But close.

If she were still here, they would be sitting across from each other. Looking into each other's eyes.

Instead, BJ looks into the brown eye of coffee. Listening to the whispered giggles of the two women closest to her at the table. Women dressed more carefully than most of the others who swirl around the cafeteria.

"I know what you mean, she's even more stuck-up than the usual student. I think she thinks she's beautiful, but she dresses like she's going to a funeral."

"And doesn't hardly talk to anybody. I was the secretary for her section last year, and she barely said hello. I mean, she was polite and everything when she had to pick up assignments, but it was like she couldn't open her mouth."

"Stuck-up."

"Really. And when she does finally say something . . . I mean, what a fake accent. She's supposed to be Australian or something. I don't know who she thinks she's fooling."

"It doesn't sound like she has an accent at all to me."

"I think it comes and goes."

"I don't know how these girls expect to be lawyers."

"Me either. Though she'll probably get a good job researching in some basement."

"Who would hire her?"

"I think she's going to be a research assistant for old Gertrude Yarnes."

"Really?"

"Yeah. Yarnes had me get a copy of her transcript. You know Yarnes: 'That's Margaret Smyth, with a *y*.' Like she couldn't pick up the phone and call the registrar herself."

"But she's better than most, you have to admit. I'll trade you Yarnes for Pederson."

"William 'Could-you-take-these-squiggles-I've-jotted-on-a-paper-napkin-and-type-them-up-so-that-they-look-like-a-law-review-article' Pederson? Thinks he's the damn IRS because he's some famous tax professor. Or supposed to be famous. I mean, have you seen him on television? I sure haven't."

"So you want to trade?"

"Not on your life."

"But I'm kind of surprised about Yarnes. I thought she'd pick someone with a little more pizazz. Though isn't Margaret supposed to be smart?"

"I guess. But you know the dykes around this place, they always stick together."

One faculty secretary nods her head in the direction of BJ, as if to signal her companion.

But BJ has already heard enough.

As BJ gets up to leave, one secretary stands up quickly and greets her as if she is greeting an old friend, which she is: "Aren't you Mavis Paige?"

BJ does not say: No, I'm a dyke.

BJ does think: Margaret Smyth. With a Y. Australian.

BJ does: smile.

part five

Margaret

thirteen

Alone and safe in my back bedroom. A few hazy slats of sunlight shimmer on the foreshortened horizon of the Hudson and flicker through the three graces of my windows. As a dark storm cloud seems to rise from the river, encasing and endangering the city, the sky begins its spitting. I open the windows to feel the dampness, to hear the singular comfort of the rain on the brick. I do not miss Dominique.

I should study, but I am too unfocused.

I wish I really knew how to quilt. I wish I knew how to sip tea and listen to a Mahler symphony, how to act like a lady in a play about the British aristocracy. I wish I had beautiful stationery, scrolled with my initials in the most elegant blue, and a mahogany laptop desk, smoothed from years of use, and a fountain pen, filled with the most permanent of India inks: I wish I could write a letter to someone, anyone.

I could read, but I do not have anything compelling. I like biographies best. Windows into other people's lives. The literary ones are always the most interesting—all those letters from which to quote, all those novels or poems from which to extrapolate—but painters, philosophers, and activists are also usually good. Movie stars are often boring. I prefer women, no surprise. Even better if the subject is a dyke, or if the author at least raises the specter of lesbianism. A little gossip is good for the soul. It's like having friends.

I know I could learn to play chess with the right opponent, but there will never be anyone who I will trust that much. Betty—one of my foster mothers, the only foster mother I can remember clearly, my *last* foster mother—tried to teach me the rules for moving those little white and black figurines from square to square. Her devotion to the game was the one fissure in a life in which sins such as soap operas, novels, and fashionable clothes had been banished, a life devoted to maintaining the elaborate edifice she called God and His Church. As a foster kid, I was part of the Church. And she, I supposed, was like God. At least at home, where she approached the intensity of an Old Testament patriarch when she called out our names for the disciplines that any infractions of her commandments provoked. "Maggie," she would say, and I would come forward for my punishment.

In the world, she was just another overweight and unsophisticated woman who took in kids for money. And at church? Many of the people looked down on her, even us temporary kids could spot that. I doubt her plan to start a Christian Chess Club ever got started, but perhaps it did.

I know when I start to think about Betty, I have got to regain control. I cannot afford such precarious musings. Not now. Not ever.

Perhaps. Perhaps someday. In some companionable solitude. I will play chess with my lover. And I will think of Betty. I will even tell my lover how Betty tried to teach me the game and how I liked the fact that the queen was the most powerful piece on the board. I will even tell my lover how Betty laughed when I said that the pawns made me sad.

I will even tell my lover that I love her.

But I cannot imagine what else I will tell her. What I will have told her.

I cannot imagine that she would love me.

I cannot imagine a me that she could love.

A me that is not sitting in a hidden back bedroom, listening to the rain, trying not to think. Of women other than the woman who will be my lover.

Listen to the rain. It is afternoon. Thursday.

I should be reading the Rules of Professional Responsibility. Yes, Margaret Smyth needs to read the Rules of Professional Responsibility. For her course, Professional Responsibility. Review her notes about a lawyer's duty to protect and preserve the confidences of a client. An ethical duty, but also raised to the level of a rule of evidence. A lawyer need not testify about a privileged communication between himself and his client. Margaret had the words privileged communication underlined. That was the key, at least according to the professor.

The cases in the casebook were about whether the communication was privileged or not. Like if the lawyer and some murderer were at a cocktail party and the murderer confessed, would the confession be protected? The Professional Responsibility professor loved to talk like that, to talk about murder. I wondered if he ever talked to Professor Yarnes, but I doubted he did. He only elaborated on the factors that courts would use to determine whether or not the communication was privileged. The main factor being money, the most incontrovertible indication that the lawyer has been retained and the client is consulting the lawyer in his legal capacity.

"So, if you give someone a dollar at a cocktail party and then confess, does it make it a privileged communication?"

The professor asked this himself, certain that all of us students were thinking it, which I had been.

"Yes." He pronounced triumphantly. "Or at least, probably." Less triumphant. "Or, it's really your best shot."

Best shot. I had written in my class notes. I underlined it now. And went back to the textbook with its rules.

Rules. Rules with numbers. Organized in sections, by topic. Rules to memorize. Rules.

But the rules have just recently become rules. Before then, there was the code: There were rules which were called rules, disciplinary rules. To break one of these rules is to provoke consequences. Disciplines. Disbarment. Suspension. Fines. But there were also rules which were called considerations, ethical considerations. To violate one of these is to provoke what? A guilty conscience? A bad reputation? The displeasure of a mentor?

The Professional Responsibility professor, a shrill sort of man with a bald head and beautifully cut suits, tells us that the main area of testing on the exam is the difference between the disciplinary rules and the ethical considerations, and the difference between the old code and the new rules. Because now, everything is a rule. But only some states have acquiesced to this new way of thinking; this thinking in only rules. The professor prefers the old divisions.

Disciplinary Rule 9-102: A lawyer shall identify and label securities and properties of a client promptly upon receipt and place them in a safe deposit box or other place of safekeeping as soon as practicable.

Ethical Consideration 9-5: Separation of the funds of a client from those of his lawyer not only serves to protect the client but also avoids even the appearance of impropriety.

Appearances are important when considering ethics. So is money.

Disciplinary Rule: Never fantasize about clients.

Ethical Consideration: Plan for forty.

Or is it the other way around?

Which way is it, Dominique? And what does it matter? Who will come to take away my license to practice sex? What mentor will I disappoint?

It is just the rain that makes me feel this way. The rain and Thursday afternoons anticipating Ann-Marie.

I shift my thoughts. This is my talent. I can camouflage my own mind.

But sometimes the camouflage works too well.

Sometimes I am so in control that I am out of control. And so although it seemed to me that I was walking through the closet to go to the kitchen for a glass of water, I stop somewhere in the middle of this long coffin. I stand there. As if I do not know what I am looking for. As if I am going to dig out my tapestry attaché and console myself with my alternate plan, with other possibilities and passports, with Wendy Redfern and Maria Bennett.

As if the idea has just suddenly occurred to me and I have not been toying with it all afternoon. As if I have not looked at my silver watch, checking the time.

As if I am uncertain what I will find in the dark corner, on the floor, wrapped in a once-clean white sheet.

I bring Dominique's television into my back bedroom.

Move some books off a small table. Plug it in. Turn it on. Change the channels.

"There are no witnesses, Mavis."

"There have to be witnesses. There are witnesses to everything." Mavis sounds as determined as the set of her jaw.

She looks the same as the woman in the hallway, in the cafeteria.

She is interrupted by a commercial. Five. Then a bit of program; she is not shown, although her name is mentioned. Then more commercials, all of which are about food: chocolate and baby formula and cookies and prunes and cake frosting and cereal and liquid lunch and more chocolate and cereal and baby formula. Or related to food: antacids and dog food and hemorrhoid treatments and diapers. There is only one about soap. It softens the skin.

She returns. She is wearing the same outfit, something in a subdued blue. She is wearing lipstick. I think I know how it smells. She is looking into a distance that cannot possibly be there. Then she leans back, as if inviting the distance into the view of the cameras. She is now wearing something white and flowing, her lipstick is pale and she looks hazy. This must be a dream. Or a fantasy. She is holding her arms out and a man walks into them. "Brad," she says. "Darling," he says. They hold each other. Her in close-up: eyes closing slowly, face in repose. Him in close-up: eyes open, face in a grimace.

The vision dissolves. The hard edges return. She is back in her subdued blue. Her lipstick is perfect. She says: "I will find the witness. This death was not an accident." The music rises, its attempt to be ominous is obvious and successful.

Her eyes closing. Her smell.

I turn off the television.

Pick up the Rules of Professional Responsibility.

Her eyes closing. Her smell.

Dominique's rule: Never fantasize about clients.

But I am not fantasizing, Dominique. I am only remembering details. I am good with details.

Her eyes closing. Her smell.

I am good at remembering. Although it takes me a few moments to remember that this woman—with her closing eyes and her too-sweet smell—is just a woman, is not a client.

I am good at remembering. The rain.

I am good at remembering. Dominique on the pavement, pointing her finger at the statue of Joan of Arc. Patty in her car, protected only by the door enscripted with her own name. I may have been the last person to see her alive. Or her.

I am good at forgetting. How I could have loved her. Or her.

I am good at remembering. My appointments. Ann-Marie. Soon. Too soon.

But enough time for a few errands until I return to my closet and find something for Tamara to wear to meet Ann-Marie near the cheeses. Enough time to get the laundry. White sheets. Enough time to buy take-out to eat. Thai or Vietnamese? Enough time to stop by my safe deposit box and check the contents. To check the neat bundles of cash, the money that will take me to my new life in the interior of this continent. To check my documents, the papers that prove I am Margaret Smyth, born on a different continent but a U.S. citizen. But no matter how much I worry, I limit my bank visits to once a month when I make my deposits, unless I need to get some of Dominique's jewelry. Like my first date with Patty.

Enough time to telephone Dominic. Or his wife, what was her

name? Didi, yes. To inquire about Patty. To say I was out of the country on some modeling assignment and just heard the news. I am so sorry I missed the funeral. Patty was a wonderful woman, I'll whisper weepily to Didi. I'll try to find out what happened. Did she commingle the funds of a client who needed bullet-proof glass? Did she have a car accident that morning, driving into a ramp while thinking about her mouth on my left breast? Did a security guard—Donna—follow her and pistol whip her to get a ceramic mermaid pin? Did some prostitute she frequented—Melanie, a former centerfold—kill her because she was able to provoke something dangerously close to love?

Enough time to browse a newsstand. To distract myself from my own imagination, overrun by amorphous guilt. Even if there is no news of Patty's death, it is always a good idea to know what is going on in the world. And in the city. Maybe a new show at the Museum of Modern Art for Ann-Marie. I am reaching for *The New Yorker* when I see her. That woman.

Gazing at me.

From a small square on the cover of *Soap Opera Universe*. I leaf through the pages. Find the same photo, only larger. Find her statement.

> *Jill Willis grew up in a suburb of Philadelphia. After a successful New York modeling career, she captured the coveted role of Mavis Paige on* In the Name of Love. *She loves the excitement of New York, but also gardening and raising miniature horses at the Connecticut farm where she lives with her husband, a lawyer, and their daughter.*

So, her name is Jill. And she is married. To a lawyer, no less.

I hurry back home. To become brown for Tamara and Ann-Marie. Deep brown. Chocolate brown. Mahogany and walnut. Clairol French Brunette. Bain De Soilel Tanning Lotion. Clinique Suntan Foundation. Maybelline Cyprus Earth shadow and eyeliner, above and below my almond DuraBright contact lenses. Slacks and a matching shirt in a cocoa-colored rayon heavy enough to feel like washed silk. I roll up the shirt sleeves to my elbows, cuffing them carefully. Then I check Tamara in the mirror glued to one edge of my closet.

Not bad, I suppose. Although I look like a cup of coffee. Perfect! I laugh, wondering if Ann-Marie will have to give me up. Before I ruin her life, like coffee did. Wondering if Ann-Marie will give me up before I give her up, before I disappear without a trace. Because, although I sometimes imagine I will leave a note taped to an imported chèvre in the cheese section for her or even on Sarah Tudor's Riverside Drive apartment door—"gone to Australia"—I know I will vanish without such a courtesy.

Ann-Marie is early. She is already there, hunched over the refrigerated case, inspecting a stolid Edam. She smiles when she sees Tamara. I smile back, ever so slightly. Walk toward her, confidently. She looks down, demure as a minister's wife, a minister's daughter.

"I've got a surprise for you," she says, once we are outside. She pulls an envelope from her purse. "Tickets."

"Terrific," I say.

"To our favorite," she says.

I squeeze her arm, thinking that at least this might mean an easy evening for me. A Broadway show leaves little time before her Connecticut curfew.

"And I've arranged to stay in the city a little later than usual. So we can go to your place afterwards."

"Great," I say. Sincerely, I hope. "I'll get us a cab."

Ann-Marie loves cabs. She loves Midtown. She walks around looking up at the buildings and pointing out landmarks she has pointed out a hundred times before. "This always excites me," she says, as we wait outside the theater on Broadway. "You never know who you'll see. Doesn't Vanessa Redgrave live around here?"

"I think," I say.

"Oh look. Right there." Ann-Marie points. "A famous actress."

"Oh really?" I turn to where Ann-Marie is pointing.

I turn back around quickly.

"I just adore her. Do you think she would mind if I went up to her and asked her for an autograph?"

"Those famous people probably value their privacy," I offer.

"Of course she won't mind. I mean, I'm her biggest fan. I'm one of the people responsible for her fame. Hold our place in line, Tamara. I'm going after Mavis Paige."

I blend into the waiting theater crowd and peer around a woman's complicated hairstyle as Ann-Marie's long strides reach Jill Willis. I can see Jill's weary smile, even from this distance. She does not look like a Jill. Does not look like she has a husband. She looks like a tired dyke going home from work. But she must have a lover. Doesn't everybody? She must have someone waiting for her to come home, someone right this minute preparing a delicious and delicate dinner.

I watch her head tilt as Ann-Marie talks to her. She doesn't move away. She just listens as Ann-Marie's hands illustrate her points. Maybe she is married, after all. She acts so patient. She looks so fatigued, so defeated.

It must be awful. Holding out her arms so that a man named Brad can walk into them. She probably has to kiss him. Again and again for the camera.

And meeting people on the street who think they have a perfect right to walk up and start talking. People like Ann-Marie.

I see Ann-Marie point toward the theater, toward me. I shift my face behind the complicated hair.

I see Jill Willis touch Ann-Marie on the arm, a gesture of departure, but also kindness. Jill Willis walks a few steps and Ann-Marie follows, until Jill's pace becomes more decisive. Ann-Marie flutters her hand good-bye and hurries back to the lump of people outside the theater.

"That was her," Ann-Marie says.

"What is she like?" I say, excitedly.

"Why are you interested?" Ann-Marie turns on me. My curiosity, because it is genuine, must sound false. What I really want to do is turn Ann-Marie upside down and empty her of the last five minutes. I want a transcript of their conversation: What did she say? What did you say? What did she say next? I want Ann-Marie to describe how she smelled. I want Ann-Marie to tell me whether she thinks Jill Willis is married, or whether she is a lesbian, and whether or not she has a lover. I want to know what Ann-Marie said when she pointed back toward the theater. Did she mention me? Tamara, my art teacher. Could Jill Willis have seen me, shaded by another woman's huge hair?

"Isn't she Mavis Paige?" I ask innocently.

"Yes. But I didn't think you were the type. The type to watch those shows."

"I usually don't. But I like *In the Name of Love*."

"That's what everyone says: 'I don't usually watch them, but . . .' " I shrug.

"Though, you do have to admit that it's much better than the other ones. It's more real, don't you think?"

"Yes," I agree.

"And don't you just love her?" Ann-Marie touches my shoulder. I nod.

"Although, she is a bit boring. I mean, you would think she would just get even with Bethany after all that has happened."

"Do you think she really loves Brad?" I ask.

Ann-Marie lifts her one eyebrow, suspiciously like one of the characters from the show, the one who had mentioned the name of Mavis Paige this afternoon. "Of course she does."

I giggle in collusion. "I guess, but it's so disappointing."

"You don't like Brad?" Ann-Marie asks.

I lean toward Ann-Marie's left ear. "It's just that it would be really great if she were a lesbian, don't you think?"

Ann-Marie doesn't laugh. "They couldn't do that." She sounds appalled. Insulted, even.

"I guess not." I retreat.

"They'd lose all their viewers," Ann-Marie pronounces.

"Not the ones like me." I wink at Ann-Marie.

Ann-Marie relaxes into a slight smile. "You are really too much."

"I'd watch the show all the time then." My hand brushes against Ann-Marie's leg.

We are quiet for a few long moments, eavesdropping on other people's conversations, none of which are about Mavis Paige or lesbians.

"So, what else did she say?"

"Nothing much. Just that it had been a long day of taping and that she had to get home."

"She probably has a far drive. Doesn't she live in Connecticut?"

"How do you know that?"

"I read it in one of those soap opera magazines."

"You *are* a fan." Ann-Marie regards me with affinity.

"Hey, maybe she's one of your neighbors."

"Maybe. I could call her and have lunch."

"Be careful," I tease, "she's married."

"So am I," Ann-Marie says bluntly and shrilly. She looks at me—could it be with pity? And she propels a laugh into the space above my head.

It is not until we are ushered into our seats, Tamara in her boring brown and Ann-Marie folding herself into an aisle seat, not until the stage finally dims and the opening music hushes the audience, not until lithe people costumed as animals snake down the aisles, not until I gently take Ann-Marie's hand as I always do when she whispers "I could see this a million times," not until then that I allow myself even the tiniest space to hate Ann-Marie.

"*Cats:* Now and Forever." Ann-Marie announces, loud enough for everyone but seemingly to no one in particular.

The person in front of her, the woman whose complicated hair had hid me from Jill Willis, turns around with her index finger at her mouth and glares at Ann-Marie.

I should feel sorry for Ann-Marie, but I can't.

I can't afford sympathy.

I can afford now, but not forever.

I pass the time contemplating Ann-Marie's demise. I do not dwell on any single method of murder, but list every one I can think of, reviewing most of the cases from Criminal Procedure for possibilities I might have missed. But everything strikes me as boring.

As boring as sex with Ann-Marie.

Even dismemberment.

I wonder if she really lives in Connecticut.

fourteen

Alone in the snow. It swirls from the sky, settling on the shoulders of Joan of Arc. I am sometimes unreasonably surprised to see her, still posed in metallic cold, guarding the plot of ground that substitutes for a park, that substitutes for Dominique's grave. I am sometimes surprised that she is still a statue, that she has not slid off the horse and stalked off to a famous delicatessen to get herself some roasted chicken, the kind that Ann-Marie finds so delicious. Just as I am sometimes surprised that it is not Dominique astride the horse. Dominique, changed into some gray steel. Dominique, artfully camouflaged. Dominique, alive.

It could be, couldn't it? Could be that she was taken to the hospital alive and released alive. So scared by her brush with death that she enrolled herself into some drug rehab program. Could be that she turned herself into a success story, accomplished whatever her plan for forty had been. So happy with her triumph that she would not have given a second thought to some kid picked off the street like a kitten. Could be she survived. Could be that the times I think I see her turning some street corner are not apparitions. Could be that at this very moment she is sitting inside the shape of Joan of Arc. There is so much snow that I cannot see very clearly, so it could be possible, couldn't it?

And the moon could be made of green cheese.

I must control my mind. I can. I must.

But what would happen if I did not?

Nothing.

Nothing that matters.

This is the terrible truth. I am no one. I do not really exist.

Except in other people's fantasies. Ann-Marie's fantasy of me as an urbane art teacher. Dominique's fantasy of a pet. Betty's fantasy of a devoted foster daughter. Professor Yarne's fantasy of a research assistant.

Except in my own fantasies. The considerate lover, the competent student, the future lawyer in a nondescript town. The murderer.

My greatest fantasy. That I am important enough to kill people. That I could do it, would do it. That just like I murdered Dominique by tainting her drugs, I murdered Betty by pummeling her with a cast-iron frying pan. Just like I murdered Patty.

Such speculations erect a secure structure: No one dies or leaves me; I murder them.

And even on the days I decide that none of it is true, my delusion serves a purpose. It gives me a limit, a boundary. At least I am not a murderer. Sure, I am a whore and a dyke. In fact, I combine the worst of both, not even separating the whoring from the dyking. What could be worse than a prostitute for lesbians? A killer, that's what. I could be a murderer. No argument about which is worse.

It's so logical I'm certain she will agree.

"At least I'm not a murderer," I'll say to her and she'll fall into my arms. Should I spill my guts on the first date? Or wait until she uses the word "love"?

Or shall I just telephone her now? Ask Professor Yarnes for her number and leave her a message: "You don't really know me, but I've got a crush on you." Is that what it is, a crush? How schoolgirlish. But then again, Margaret Smyth is a schoolgirl. Schoolwoman? No, I won't say crush. I'll be direct: "Hello, my name is Margaret Smyth. We met—well, we almost met—outside Professor Yarnes' office. I was wondering if you'd like to meet for coffee? You can call me back at any of the following numbers, I have quite a few because I . . . because I have a business. I house-sit, yes, I house-sit. I show people around town a bit, some might use the term escort, but that has a lot of negative connotations. And by the way, just in case you're wondering, I'm not a murderer."

I'm sure she'd call me right back.

It must be the snow. Simply the snow and its sharp silence that is responsible for my mind veering toward such tawdriness. Didn't I read somewhere—in one of my precious books—that being alone in the snow drives people crazy? Somewhere on these bookshelves is probably a simply stunning account of some poor bastards lost in a blizzard or stranded in an avalanche in Antarctica. I could back away from my triptych of windows and stop watching Joan of Arc freezing on her stupid horse and look for that book.

Or maybe I could find a different book, a poetry anthology. I could make myself some tea and read aloud a very uplifting poem about snow in the city: Winter white makes everything look just right.

Or maybe I could turn around and tear down these bookshelves, full of their lies and false promises. The biographies of famous people with their pitiful lives, a bunch of alcoholics and whiners. The row of Australia travel guides and histories, as if I could memorize an entire continent. The thin volumes of obfuscated theories, oh aren't you the smart one, Margaret Smyth, reading that?

I could pull the shelves from their anchors and ravage my back bedroom in the apartment of Sarah Tudor. I could. I could.

But then I would have to clean up the mess.

Which proves I am not crazy, snow or no snow. I still think about consequences. It does not even take much exertion of my talent for controlling my mind to realize that wrecking the place means repairing it. Cause and effect, isn't that the hallmark of rationality? As if one could not be rational and crazy, simultaneously.

Dyke-whore. Lesbian-escort.

Law student.

Maybe I should get a cat.

fifteen

*A*lone in the stacks of the library. The graduate school library. The lights go off automatically. As if to signal that the research is taking too long. I walk to the end of the stack and flick the switch. Another fifteen minutes.

I kneel on the floor, spreading the books on the haphazardly vacant spaces on the shelves. I look at indexes. I like indexes. So neat and orderly. So limited. I am not having any success finding what I need. What Professor Gertrude Yarnes needs, or says she needs. In the most imprecise way.

"I need some nineteenth-century texts," she instructed, "that reify identity, especially the legal identity, of certain criminal classes such as vagrants or prostitutes."

So what should I look for in the index, Gertrude? Identity? Criminal? Prostitutes? Texts?

Although I think I have some leads. Phrenology. I don't know whether or not she will be happy when I tell her about this, but it seems perfect to me. The science of measuring the skull. You could tell the kind of person someone was by his forehead size. Murderers have low foreheads.

Luckily, I have a high forehead. Ridiculous, I know. But here I am kneeling on the floor, between stacks of metal bookshelves, measuring my forehead by spreading my fingers. Guessing at the inches.

And what does one measure? From the bridge of the nose to the hairline. What if one has a receding hairline? But I am safely in the high forehead zone.

Not a murderer. I can't be a murderer. It's the one thing that appalls me more than anything. Not one of Dominique's rules. One of my own. Murder is the only unforgivable. Derived from where? Wasn't the husband of one of my foster mothers—Betty, the Christian, I think—in prison for murder? Or was it seeing Dominique die? Not murdered, at least in the classic sense. But killed by a pusher. Or by too many men. Or by life.

Not by me. In my most lucid moments, I know it isn't me. It's just survivor's guilt. There are books on this; I didn't even need a therapist. I didn't kill her. Didn't kill her because she came so close to me. Or I came so close to her. Physically. Though sex is only partially physical. I'm the best proof of that.

And here's a reference to sexual deviance stuff. More measurements, but not the forehead. Did you know lesbians have bigger (or smaller) than average cranial cavities? I'll ask Professor Gertrude Yarnes and after a moment, I hope, she'll laugh at my wit.

Too bad all the sources are on microfiche. I hate those little plastic sheets and the unwieldy machines necessary to interpret them. What the hell is wrong with books? And the copies! White writing on a black background; it just never looks authentic.

I am coming out of the microfiche room, carrying a sheaf of those negative image copies, when I practically collide with her. I am wearing Margaret Smyth's black leather jacket and staring at a loosely wrinkled face I had hoped I would never see again. Too much sun, I judge. But there is no way to avoid her. Sometimes, I just have to improvise.

And hope for the best. So I smile.

"You haven't returned my messages, Cynthia." Phyllis lurches forward as if to hug me.

"Sorry." I act embarrassed. I act as if I don't know she must be lying. After all, I had terminated that message service the day after our date.

"I was worried the way you disappeared."

"Sorry." I act even more embarrassed.

"It's a dangerous city. You could have been kidnapped."

"I wasn't. How come you're still in New York?"

"I'm a graduate student here. In film."

"I thought you said you were from L.A."

"I am. But I'm here to study film. Some people think that's backwards, coming to New York from L.A. to study film, but I think New York is just more real than L.A., you know. And it's easier to get started here. I've met more people since I've been here. . . ."

"How long is that?" Long enough to know your way around the Village?

"A couple of years." Long enough to know your way around the Village.

"You must like it."

"I do. Hey, how about a cup of espresso? I get sleepy in this old dusty library."

"Thanks. But I've got more work to do."

"I guess I offended you, didn't I? Trying to figure out if you were a sex worker. I really do feel awfully bad about that. You should at least let me buy you a cup of coffee to apologize. I can be overbearing, I know. I get all caught up in a project and just go overboard. I mean, I blew this great deal my professor got me through a friend of hers, letting me work with the prosecutors and cops. I was interviewing this woman undercover cop and I thought it was all going really well, like we were getting to be friends and everything, and then she said I was trying to blow her cover. I got called on the carpet for that one! By the Chief Assistant District Attorney himself. Even my professor heard about it. Talk about being humiliated."

"That does sound bad." I give her a sympathetic laugh. "So, the prosecutors kicked you out?"

"Not really. I was done anyway. But I didn't think I was all that obnoxious to you. Was I really that bad?"

"Not that bad." I give her another, softer, laugh. "It's just that. Well. It's just a little difficult."

"What?"

158

"It's just that I put that ad in the paper at the suggestion of a friend. I'm just starting to date. Again. And my friend said it would be a good way just to start to socialize again. After what happened."

"Bad breakup? I can relate."

"Actually my lover died. It's been over a year, but I'm just coming out of it. We were together for a long time. She wasn't exactly my first lover, but pretty close." I look at my shoes.

"That sounds awful. Really awful. I can see why you were so spooked. I mean, just trying to get back into the world and someone thinks you're a sex worker or something."

I nod, but I'm still looking at my shoes.

"Hey. I am sorry."

I nod more. But remain fixated on my shoes. They are black.

"But you know, there is nothing wrong with being a sex worker." Phyllis' tone is rapidly becoming sermonizing. "It's a perfectly honorable profession. You should meet some of these women. Such strength. Such fortitude. And practical. I hope you are not embarrassed to be associated with them. You should be proud."

I look up from my shoes to Phyllis' loose wrinkles and allow three tears to slide down my face.

"Maybe another time," Phyllis says quickly.

I look at her blankly. I can feel my eyes starting to swell, my nose mottle with ugly red.

"I mean, the coffee. Maybe another time." She is already backing away.

"Sure," I say. I watch her go.

And then I follow her. Out into the wide wide world beyond the library.

I follow her for a few blocks. To the subway entrance. I don't know what I was expecting, but everything seems normal. Just an average graduate student in film, fucked up and self-important, going to catch her subway after meeting someone she once thought might be a suitable subject for a minute or two in her documentary but who turned out to be a whining bore. Still, one can never be too careful.

I look at my silver watch. If I hurry, I can intercept Gertrude

Yarnes before she leaves her office for the day and dump off this research. I walk toward the law school, regaining myself as Margaret Smyth. In her jacket. With her copies about phrenology.

I cannot avoid autumn. The jacket feels comforting against the blood of leaves. The city seems brisk. Those of us who are alive are preoccupied with our endless errands. Black is the color we wear. We think it is a testimony to our importance, but it allows us to blend in with each other. Coolness.

Gertrude is still in her office, but she is wearing her jacket. It is neither black nor leather. It is the darkest shade of gray. Woolish. She looks at me sometimes as if she does not know who I am, or cannot believe it is me who is her research assistant. I feel visible, awkward. She is formal as I fish into my black knapsack for the white-on-black copies about skull measurements. It all seems so insignificant.

She puts the copies on her desk. Does not even glance at them. "I'm late," she mumbles. Is fidgeting with her briefcase. I am trying to back out of her office door as unobtrusively as possible when I am caught in the sudden flash of her smile: "Hey, why don't you come with me?"

I am silent.

"It's a book party. At the women's bookstore."

I try to nod. I try to remember whether the Writer has a new book. She does not. I am pretty sure. Then, I am certain. She does not.

And if she did, she would not have her book party at the women's bookstore.

One can never be too careful.

"Don't be so shy, Margaret." She laughs, but it is not a mocking laugh. "I'm not asking you for a date or anything. In fact, my lover Bobbi will be there. Bobbi is not about to let me go hear Teddy speak without making her presence known." Gertrude laughs again. "I'm asking you to accompany me as my research assistant."

"Is it related to the identity project?" I ask. I unclench my fist buried deep in my leather pocket.

She seems to consider this. "In a way. Yes, I guess you could say that."

I wait for her to continue. A composure settles deep in my stomach. I am Margaret Smyth and I am slightly shy.

"Then, you can come?"

I answer with an earnest "I guess."

"Great. Let's go. I'm glad you can make it. BJ will be there."

She acts like I know who she means. A classmate? A famous legal theorist? Not her lover, the one she just mentioned, the one who was named something else. Bobbi? Yes, Bobbi. Maybe she is also called BJ?

We are leaving the building. Together. Entering a labyrinth of streets. "BJ?" I manage an inflection. Inquisitive but disinterested.

"You remember. You've met her in my office. Didn't I introduce you two?" Gertrude is smiling. "She's an actor. Plays the lawyer Mavis Paige on some soap opera."

A catalogue of possible responses crowds my high forehead.

Mavis Paige? I do not watch soap operas.

Jill Willis? She lives in Connecticut with her lawyer husband.

BJ? Sounds like she might possibly be a dyke.

But I do not dare an utterance. Instead, I wrinkle my high forehead in an expression of puzzlement so unmistakable that it would be worthy of the star of *In the Name of Love*.

"You'll recognize her when you see her." Gertrude is definite. But not dismissive. Definitely not dismissive.

I tamp down any suspicions. Gertrude is always on the serious side, even when she laughs. There is nothing sinister about any of this. Perhaps she is just impressed with herself for knowing a television actor. And I must learn to appear in public—outside of school—as Margaret Smyth. Accompanying the professor for whom I am a research assistant to a women's bookstore for a book related to the project on which we are working: What could be more circumspect?

My judgment is corroborated by Gertrude's next question. She is asking me about the research. Have I found anything interesting?

"Phrenology," I say.

"Nice work." Her smile is encouraging, but also equalizing.

I smile back at her.

"Go on," she says, as if she has been waiting for me to speak and my smile is insufficient.

"There are studies of the physical aspects of the head. Mostly using criminals. Trying to theorize 'types.' You know, like murderers have low foreheads. Lots of measurements."

"The scientific method in all of its glory."

"The stuff about lesbians is interesting." I smile at her.

"I can imagine. But I assume they did not stop their measurements at the head."

"The phrenologists did."

She laughs. We are waiting for a green light to cross the street when she looks at me full in the face and says, "So, what do you think of it?"

"It?" I feel like I have been dropped into someone else's conversation.

"Phrenology."

"It's ludicrous."

"Why?" Her tone is professorial. I just look at her until the light changes and we surge off the curb in the swell of other people trying to cross the street.

"Don't you agree?" I resort to answering a question with a question.

"Yes. But then I wonder why. Is it all just fashion? Then, they measured heads. Now, they measure chemicals in the brain."

"I guess." I feel wary, uncertain, and perhaps a little bored.

She stops in the middle of the sidewalk and walks toward a storefront, motioning me to join her under an awning, away from the swell of people marching down the sidewalk.

"You are going to have to do better than that, Margaret. The reason I chose you as my research assistant is because you seem like you can think. I mean, research is fine, but almost anyone can fetch." She laughs, but it is not a generous laugh. "Don't be intimidated. And don't be simplistic. It will make our conversations useless."

"Yes, professor."

"Now, tell me what you really think." She starts to walk again, a little more quickly, and I duplicate her pace.

"I haven't thought much about it. I just found the material this afternoon." I know I am being defensive.

"What lead you to phrenology?"

"I couldn't find anything else."

"In the entire library? I doubt that. Why didn't you bring me a stack of copies about—oh, I don't know—mermaids?"

But she does know; she must know what a jerk she is being. Or maybe I am just not suited to being somebody's research assistant. Maybe I can't be anything other than an escort. Though being a research assistant to some law professor shouldn't be difficult. Not as difficult as being an intern at the District Attorney's Office. I can do the research, even she admitted that. But she wants something else. For me to talk. I can talk. I mean, it's not like I can't hold my own in an intelligent conversation. I date lots of smart women. Jeanine is director of a prestigious organization. The Writer is clever and contemporary and maybe even brilliant. And the drama criticism professor certainly seems esteemed, if the reactions I witnessed to her trendy little presentation were any indication, although I haven't seen her for a while.

"What I'm trying to think through with your help"—she smiles at me again—"is how we think about identity at all. Take the murderer. What do we mean by that?"

"That the person has killed someone."

"Usually. But what about when we know that X has killed someone, but we say, 'X is not a murderer'? We mean something else."

"Maybe, but I don't think we mean the size of their foreheads."

"I agree. We don't. But I'm trying to figure out what we do mean. Or whether what we mean is always just subject to the theoretical fashions of our times."

"I think it is."

"I think I agree." Gertrude's smile seems more introspective now. "But we always think that there is something, some basis by which we can ascertain someone, ascertain how someone *really* is."

"Maybe that's the problem. Maybe there shouldn't be anything. That would make a devastating critique of entrapment, wouldn't it?" I am proud of myself for making the connections, but I try not to smile.

"In many cases, yes. Because although there is some evidence, it's usually not of anything solidly criminal. Otherwise, the entrapment wouldn't be necessary. But think what else goes down the drain with it."

"Human nature?"

"Yes. And love. Attraction." Gertrude seems very serious now.

"Oh."

"You don't believe me? Think about it. When you're attracted to someone across a room, it's because you believe that you have some clues about how someone really is, some intuition, some belief. It isn't the tilt of her nose, it's what that nose conveys. Which you may not be able to articulate, even to yourself. And when you love someone, you can have all the evidence in the world, but you believe they are the person you love."

"But isn't that different from the law?" I'm trying not to be uncomfortable with her talk about love.

"Perhaps. But I don't think it works that way."

We walk for a while in silence.

"Maybe we should have taken a cab. Anyway, speaking of work, I wonder if you're still interested in the District Attorney's Office."

"They haven't called me back after the second interview at their office."

"The place is a rat's nest of red tape! Maybe if a few of them did act on their intuitions more . . ." Gertrude dismisses her own statement with a slight laugh. "But I've another idea. You'd still be my research assistant, of course, but you could do an internship arranged through the school. It would officially be an an independent study, so the grade is pass/fail. I'd grade it based upon an evaluation submitted by your supervising attorney in the office as well as your written work product, probably a paper of some sort—we could decide on that later. So, think about it."

"It sounds really great. Thanks." And I really am pleased. Now that the Phyllis problem no longer looms—a graduate student, really!—it wouldn't be a bad way to get some practical experience. And it would mean I wouldn't have to endure another interview in one of those glass cages.

I don't even stop to speculate about her motives for helping me. I think I can recognize when I have been taken under someone's wing.

"Spring semester," she says.

My sixth semester. My third until final semester. January. It is going to happen. I am going to do this. And every year—no, twice a year—Margaret Smyth will write Professor Gertrude Yarnes a nice letter, a bit formal but also newsy. My career. My lover. My life.

"There's Bobbi." Gertrude exhales. I could swear she sounds excited.

I risk a personal question: "How long have you two been together?"

Gertrude doesn't even flinch. "Almost twenty years. Twenty years in the spring." And then she is hugging her lover and her lover is hugging her back, right there on the sidewalk.

When Bobbi's body pulls away from my professor, I look long and hard at Bobbi. She seems like an excessively average dyke. Jeans and rather trim figure and hair blunt in an unsophisticated cut. A brown leather jacket in a cowboy style that hangs rather than flatters.

Not all that friendly either as Gertrude Yarnes makes the introductions. Though Bobbi does shake my hand and look me in the eyes. Most of her attention is directed at Gertrude Yarnes. I could swear she calls her Bunny. And most of Yarnes' attention is sucked up by Bobbi. But they aren't inconsiderate; they do take the trouble to find three seats together in the crowded women's bookstore.

"We should have saved a seat for BJ," Gertrude says.

"Isn't that her?" Bobbi nods her head.

I look over. She has on a neon green shirt and pants in a print that is obviously supposed to match. She looks a bit like an iridescent lime. And posed. Out of place in this place.

I would like to burrow into myself in this moment. I would like to take out my emotions, one by one, and examine them by the light reflected off the river and through the three graces of my windows. I try to memorize everything. I want to arrest the action.

If only I could have. Could have frozen the frame. With only BJ in it, turning her head to look over in the direction of her friend Gertrude Yarnes. And seeing me. It did seem like our eyes locked. I couldn't look away. I forgot at what instant I should gaze downward, demurely. I forgot how to flirt. And it seemed like she never knew these things, at least without a sappy script to direct her every movement.

Such paralysis could have lasted an eternity. Or been cured only by one of us approaching the other. Standing there. Offering to get the other a drink: "White?" "Mineral water?" Trying to talk but not really needing to say a single word.

Or meeting at some midpoint in our visions. Near the table where the wine and cookies rested. We could have poured each other a glass of something. "White?" "Mineral water?" We could have sipped and attempted a conversation that eddied in small talk.

Or Gertrude could have stood up, bustled me over to BJ, and made her impassioned introductions. Started us out on a topic of great import. One of us could have noticed it was stuffy in the women's bookstore. We could have walked outside. Walked down the street for a drink. "White?" "Mineral water?" We could have sipped and sipped and sipped.

Or anything else. Anything other than me sitting in my chair, next to Gertrude Yarnes, my professor, who is sitting next to Bobbi, her lover. Anything other than me watching a woman come up to BJ and give her a melodramatic kiss on first one cheek and then the other. Anything other than me watching that woman look right at me and theatrically trill her hand in a gesture of greeting and then turn her index finger into a pointer right at my skull and lean into BJ. If I were any closer, I could probably have heard her stage whisper.

Anything other than watching that woman walk toward the front of the crowd to be introduced as tonight's speaker: Teodesia Guivenery, author of *The Postmodern Politics of Daytime Drama.*

part six

BJ

sixteen

*M*alcolm was at another overnight at his best friend Joshua's house, not that I could blame him for being sensible enough to escape. Our house felt ready to topple off the cliff and into the river. Dagoberto seemed to be there all the time, but his presence wasn't steadying Lenore. Her newest adventure in interior decorating had been to put all the mirrors in the house in one room, the master bedroom. It was a little overdone and tacky, but I figured she had her reasons. I assumed that the odd angles at which the mirrors hung on the walls were caused by her sloppiness. But when she busted her credit card limit to buy even more mirrors—one with an ornate gold frame instead of the simple wood I thought she favored—I knew this wasn't simply about romance. Besides, she had moved all the other furniture out of the master bedroom.

She is having an episode, I said to myself. That's what her psychiatrist calls them, episodes.

Maybe the whole fling with Dagoberto is just an episode. I'm not sure how to tell. Maybe everything could be resolved and things could get back to normal, meaning like things were before Lenore found Dagoberto. Maybe Dagoberto will see how crazy Lenore acts and just vanish.

I guess I was feeling the slightest bit of hope when I walked into the master bedroom to tell Lenore I was leaving for work. She was sitting on the floor of course, since there was nowhere else to sit. It was still dark outside; the ceiling light was on. Lenore was nearly naked. Actually, she was in her underwear, but it was so lacy that she looked nearly naked. Her swollen stomach increased her nakedness.

I kissed her on the forehead. "I'm leaving for work."

"Before you go," Lenore says in the most normal of tones, "could you do me a favor?"

"What's up?"

"Could you look in that mirror right there . . . No. Not that mirror, that one."

"Yes?"

"And tell me who that is?"

Not only am I not sure which mirror she means—as if it would make a difference—but I am not sure whether she means her or me. Or some third person who I cannot see.

So I just say, "You."

And she repeats, "You."

This could be an episode or it could be sharing a family joke. When Malcolm was around two, or maybe three, I was trying to teach him how to use the word "me." I'd point at him and say "me" and then he'd point at me and say "me." Then I'd point at me and say "me" and again he'd point at me and say "me." I thought it might help if I switched to "you," but it didn't. I'd point at him and say "you" and he'd point at himself at say "you." I'd point at myself and say "you" and he'd point at himself and say "you."

So I took him to a mirror, a wood framed one we had bought at a craft show, and kneeled down next to him. I'd point at my image in the mirror and say "me" and he'd point at my image in the mirror and say "me." By this time, I was laughing in confusion and already thinking about how funny it would be when I told my mom and Mimi about it. When I pointed at my image in the mirror and said "me" and he pointed at me and said "me," I considered this enough of a breakthrough to stop.

The entire time, Lenore had stood there, unsmiling and seeming sort of numb. But later, when she was a little better, she enjoyed telling the story. In her telling, though, she was me. She told the story so much that Malcolm got pretty sick of it and would groan every time she started. But I thought I could tell it also made him happy to hear it. Like everything was normal. Like funny things happened at our house—funny things that weren't odd funny or sick funny. Or pathetic.

Only once, in all these years, did I ever correct Lenore's version. Malcolm and I were alone, shopping for jeans for him. He was between sizes, as he always seemed to be, so I had to drag him to a mall to try on the pants. "How do they feel?" I asked as he looked in the mirror.

"Good."

"How do you think they look?" I was trying to get him to notice how he looked. He was only nine or ten then, but I thought he should take a little more care with his appearance.

"Fine."

Then he started giggling.

"What's wrong?"

"Nothing. I'm just glad she didn't want to come with us. Or she'd be telling the me-me mirror story right now."

"You know," I said without my usual pause to think about the consequences, "that was me." My words bubbled up from some pool of resentment I didn't realize I had.

He looked at me for a long moment. Standing there outside a department store dressing room, his new jeans slightly big and stiff, despite the fact that they were the expensive stonewashed type. And he said, "Of course it was you. I remember it. I remember everything that happened."

"Get your regular clothes back on," I said too quickly. He had spooked me. I was pleased that he thought he remembered us laughing in front of the mirror, though I was convinced he couldn't have. He was too young. Too young, I always told myself. Too young to remember. Everything. Anything.

But he wasn't old enough to see Lenore like this. Not the lacy underwear, but the vacant expression on her face. I didn't feel old enough myself, or maybe too old. Like going to the restroom alone on the New Jersey Turnpike, there was never a good age for it. After all these years, I hadn't gotten used to it.

"You see me? You really do?"

"Yes," I answer.

"Then you're a fool." Lenore stands up, suddenly, seeming to leave her vacant expression near the floor and acquiring a sneer. "I'm no longer me. I'm somebody now. Do you hear me? Somebody. A man loves me. Do you hear that? A man. A real man. Not you, BJ. And if you think you're going to ruin that. If you think you're going to try to take Malcolm away from his father, you should think again. I'll fight you to the death on this one. And you'll never win. Because you're just a dyke, BJ. Admit it. You're just a dyke and you'll never win."

It would be so much easier if I could feel sorry for her.

I closed the door of the master bedroom as quietly as I could. I could still hear her yelling through the closed door. I left for work, after checking on Malcolm's plans to have dinner and sleep over at Joshua's house. Joshua's mother is a social worker. I try not to wonder what Malcolm tells her. Or what Malcolm tells Joshua, who might tell his mother.

But without Malcolm waiting for me, there was no reason to go home. Lenore might still be in the mirrored master bedroom waiting to scream at me. Or Dagoberto might be with her. He is there more and more. At the house. At my house. I am going to have to deal with this, I know. But not tonight.

One of the prop girls at work had been telling me I should get out more. I didn't ask whether she had heard about what a disaster my life had become, just decided to follow her advice. Thought I would be as sensible as Malcolm.

So, I fished in my purse for the hot pink postcard announcement. My first catch was a half-eaten Snickers bar—my lunch—so I finished that. I also caught a bunch of gum and some diet pills. Then I found it, only slightly ripped. *You are invited to a book party.* It seemed like it happened pretty fast to me, but she had said she was almost done with it before "our mutual friend Trudy" connected us. At first, I didn't know who she meant, but then I remembered Professor Gertrude Yarnes. I just never thought of her as a Trudy, but I guess we aren't good friends or anything.

Anyway, I thought that I wouldn't mind seeing the book. Maybe I was mentioned, maybe even quoted. Maybe she wrote something about how hard it was for me to come out, how no one wanted to hear it. I did talk to her for hours. Not that she was especially easy to talk to. She mostly talked about herself. Her book. Her projects. How important she was and was going to be. Not that obvious, but not much more subtle.

And she kept calling me Mavis.

"Please call me BJ," I said as insistently as I could.

"It's better to call you Mavis," she answered very matter-of-factly. "This way, people will know that I am talking to a soap opera character for my forthcoming book."

I didn't know what people she meant. I looked around the coffee shop and didn't see anyone noticing us.

I invited her to the show, to see a blocking. I introduced her around and I think she interviewed some of the other people from *In the Name of Love*. She said everyone was very helpful. I think she insulted one of the writers, but I wasn't sure exactly what happened. I just made sure I let him know that she wasn't really a friend of mine, just a drama professor friend of the law professor consultant for the show.

She invited me to lunch. At the same place Lenore had made reservations for Dagoberto and me. She had been waiting for me, like Lenore had been, only she stood up and walked toward me when she saw me. It all felt so normal, even if she did kiss me on both cheeks as she did every time we met. And this time, I didn't have to pay for everything. She had Light Curried Crab Salad with Lemon Couscous. I had Prince Edward Island Mussels in Tomato

Vodka Broth. She had three glasses of white wine. I had mineral water. We split the check.

So, what the hell, I might as well go to the book party. I hail a cab and give the driver the address of the women's bookstore. I didn't have to work too late since I've got really small parts in this week's scripts, so maybe I'll be on time. I think I look pretty good, wearing a Carol Little outfit I bought with the clothing allowance for Mavis Paige at Bloomingdales. It's a glowing green, solid on top and tight print pants in a modified Indian design. A little bright for autumn, perhaps, but I think that just adds to its allure. Not that I want to make an entrance or anything.

Though in the back—the very, very back—of my mind, maybe I did think that woman would be there. Her.

It wasn't Teodesia I was thinking about; of course she would be there. And anyway, she had practically asked me for a date, or what seemed like it might be a date. It's been such a long time since I've done anything like this, I'm not sure I'd be able to figure out what was going on even if the woman said, "I'm asking you for a date."

It was Gertrude. After all, she was the one who had arranged for me to meet Teodesia.

Not really Gertrude. But who might be with Gertrude.

I knew even then it was far-fetched. Thought that maybe I had lived for too long in the small town of *In the Name of Love,* in which a character cannot go out to dinner without running into someone she knows.

So I was stunned when I saw her. Her. She was wearing a black leather jacket and some dark pants, maybe black jeans, and she was sitting next to Gertrude. She looked smaller than I remembered. More plain.

More approachable. Like I could walk right up to where she was sitting on those uncomfortable folding chairs, and say hello to Gertrude, and sit next to her. Right next to her.

But she saw me before I had a chance to go over to her. She saw me and she looked at me and I could feel her looking at me and I could feel myself looking back and I couldn't see anything else in the room.

Didn't see Teodesia working the room; didn't see her walk toward me and kiss me on both cheeks. She was flushed and excited. I congratulated her on the book. I hadn't seen it yet, but I knew that was the thing to do. And I told her I thought the book party was nice and so crowded. I thought that was the thing to do.

"It is wonderful, isn't it? Amazing who will turn up—and with whom!"

I think I nodded.

"I mean, who would have ever thought old Gertrude would have such predilections. Though Bobbi is here also. I suppose they've hired her for a ménage à trois."

I think I noticed the glass of white wine in Teodesia's hand.

"Though perhaps they've taken the poor girl under their wing. Trudy is such a maternal type. The woman sitting next to her is a sex worker, you know."

"What?" I whisper.

"A prostitute. I interviewed her for a previous project."

I think I followed the invisible arc of Teodesia's index finger, straight into her head. That woman. Her.

I think I listened while Teodesia was introduced. I think I watched Teodesia walk away from me.

I know I ran, or practically ran, out the only door of the women's bookstore.

I am walking. And walking. Drawn by the Hudson River, its night mist making me feel more and more unreal. Drawn by the Hudson River, as if it is the ocean. I am walking on the beach. Walking fast. Walking north, towards the women's beach. Walking toward a world of mermaids. In a world of mermaids, there are no prostitutes. In a world of mermaids, you just see a woman and decide you love her and you walk up to her and say some code word like "glp" and she answers whether or not she loves you and if she does, you start to kiss right then and there.

I wish it were so simple.

If that wish is too much—I try to be reasonable, even in my fantasies—I wish I was walking on the beach. I wish the sun was shining brightly on a summer evening rather than a dark night in autumn. I wish my life were normal, my normal girlfriend waiting a simple dinner for me in our normal house, a house not perched on a cliff overlooking this same river, a house with the bedroom furniture always in the bedroom. I wish I were real. I wish she was not what Teodesia said.

Perhaps Teodesia meant someone else. No. There was no one else. Perhaps Teodesia was only kidding, lying even. Yes. That must be it.

She is a law student and her name is Margaret Smyth. With a Y. Probably from Australia. And she is working for Gertrude Yarnes. I heard those women talking.

I walk parallel to the dirty river. The street is wide. Is it the West Side Highway this far south? Or only Twelfth Avenue? I could follow it north and get to Grandview, get to my house. After crossing the Hudson. Sooner or later.

I could walk back to Midtown. Get my car from the garage. Go home. Or drive somewhere. Where? South to Philadelphia? Run home to Mommy and Mimi. I've been gone too long for that.

I could go back to the bookstore. I should. Go back and talk to her. But what would I expect her to say? And what would I say? Just ask her if she is a sex worker? "Glad to meet you, are you a whore?"

So what if I am, she might reply.

So what if she is?

It's not like I care about her. Or even know her. It's not like she's lied to me.

It's not like I'm some Connecticut housewife raising miniature horses. It's not like I didn't come to New York to model and learn the ropes. It's not like I'm as goody-goody as everyone always thinks.

It's only . . . what?

What I am not. What I didn't become. What I avoided.

Mavis Paige would walk back to the bookstore and confront the situation. She would look Teodesia right in the eyes and dare her to assault the purity of her feeling. She would sit right next to Margaret Smyth with a Y and be understanding. The viewers, most of them sitting alone on their needing-to-be-reupholstered couches, would root for true love. As if they could recognize it on a TV screen even if they couldn't recognize it in real life.

I turn inland, back toward the lights of Manhattan. I shouldn't be out near the river alone anyway. It is too dangerous. I feel cheered by the small bundle of people who loom ahead. I feel safest in the city in a small crowd.

The traffic is milder on this side street. Cars are careful, respectful. One slows, as if to allow a pedestrian to cross the street. But then I see the figure lean into the window. The driver must be asking for directions. This part of the city can be confusing.

A car pulls over just ahead of me, just ahead of the street light. I feel a little uneasy, but keep walking, acting as if nothing is wrong. The driver juts his head out the window. "How much?" I blink back at him. I walk past the car, giving it a wide berth. He mumbles something. Could it be "sorry"? Then he pulls away.

I am still walking. Only more quickly now. Approaching the people I saw from a distance. Approaching the jumble of bright colors. Hot pink hot pants. A canary miniskirt. Something orange. Winter white tied at the breasts. Purple thigh-high boots. The more subdued colors achieve outlines. Fishnet stockings. Black high heels. A jacket flung over a shoulder.

I suck in my breath. I become unflappable. I am a former model, a well-regarded television actress, a dyke.

"You undercover?" Canary miniskirt says this.

"Dressed like this?" I point at the tasteful lines of my lime green designer outfit. The women laugh. At least, I think most of them are women and most of them are laughing.

"You a social worker?" Canary miniskirt persists.

"Working so late?" They are all laughing now.

"You're a lawyer. I recognize you," purple thigh-high boots says.

I shake my head. I am almost motionless now.

"I never forget a face," purple thigh-high boots replies.

"You're sort of right and sort of wrong." I smile.

"I don't like riddles." Another car pulls up. "And I don't have time for a bunch of shit." The boots approach the car.

I try to walk more quickly. But I feel like I'm caught in slow motion.

"Are you lost?" someone says.

"I'm just going for a walk." I think I sound less shaky than I feel. But I am already past the women. Already almost to the next wide avenue. Eleventh or Tenth? Where are the fucking street signs?

"Be careful," a small voice calls from behind me.

It is then that I can feel the tears threatening the corner of my eyes. I am a good crier. Everyone on *In the Name of Love* says so. I can cry without my nose getting red. I can cry and look sympathetic rather than pathetic. We all have our talents. I wish mine were not such a trivial one.

But I can feel even my insignificant talent deserting me as I reach Eighth Avenue. My face is wet and could start to swell. A prostitute. A prostitute. I imagine her in the shortest of dresses (black) and wearing high boots (also black) standing on the darkest corner. I imagine a voice from a crawling car asking "How much?" and her answering with a sparkle of smile and a thrust of hips. I imagine her in a parked car giving some sweaty man a blow job. I suppose she charges more to fuck, but I don't want to imagine that.

Why not?

I berate myself for my squeamishness. I berate myself for my desire to imagine it. Like I don't have enough problems with my girlfriend fucking a man that I have to go and start imagining a prostitute. I look in my purse for a tissue, almost spilling the contents right there on the sidewalk.

What's wrong with it anyway?

Not the man part, the money part. She probably really is a student, trying to work her way through school.

Shouldn't she have gotten a job at Bloomingdale's?

Like I would have. If Mavis Paige hadn't have come along. Not everyone is as lucky as me.

But I never would have . . .

That's not what my mom thought. Even she thought I could bargain off bits of my body. She was screaming about it. She said that's what happens to a woman if she doesn't have a plan. Maybe Margaret Smyth didn't have a plan.

As if I had a plan. As if I planned to have a lover who tried to murder our child, a lover who would leave me for our child's sperm donor. As if I planned to live in a house which tilted on a cliff over the Hudson River; a house in which the living room furniture was crowded into a tiny bedroom and the master bedroom looked like a funhouse hall of mirrors.

I am afraid of heights.

I like predictability in my surroundings, not constant variety.

I hate mirrors: They make me look heavier than I am, like television cameras.

I did not plan to sell myself. I did not plan to sell myself as myself, sell myself as Jill Willis, sell myself as Mavis Paige.

I did not plan.

Maybe I should. Maybe that's what I need. A plan.

A perfect plan. One that would solve all my problems.

No, let me reasonable. Maybe not all of my problems, but at least the major ones.

Let me start with my most pressing problem: Malcolm. I need to get custody.

I can worry about everything else later. After I have custody. Maybe Margaret Smyth with a Y doesn't even like children. Then her occupation wouldn't matter.

A plan.

I don't have one by the time I walk back to my usual garage. But somewhere on the West Side Highway, before I cross the river to get home, a plan occurs to me.

It's not foolproof. Nothing is foolproof. But I've got the old documents making me a guardian. I can work out the details.

But it's good. Yes, pretty good.

And I know how to do it. I've done it before.

I am going to institutionalize Lenore.

seventeen

*M*alcolm in the snow. Snow falling like the fake flakes sprinkled in the studio, confetti but cold. It swirls around the eruptions of hot breath from our mouths. Malcolm smacks smoke rings from his lips as he walks toward the bluffs that drop down to the river. I look back at the house, knowing Lenore and Dagoberto are up there, knowing that Malcolm knows it, too. We don't really talk about it. I can't imagine what we would say, how the script would read.

What could I say if he asked me why I couldn't make Dagoberto leave? Why I couldn't make Lenore leave? Why I couldn't leave myself? Though I could answer the last question—I wasn't going anywhere without him, my kid who was not my kid, practically not a kid anymore. But why couldn't I leave and take him?

I kept thinking about just taking Malcolm and leaving, but it didn't seem possible. I would be technically kidnaping him, the law professor made that pretty clear. Where could I go? Australia? How would I support us? Unemployed soap opera character seeks commercial work. Or modeling. Or cleaning houses. Or what my mom Evelyn had said, had screamed, that still echoed in my head: prostitution.

And even when it seemed possible, even when I could imagine Malcolm and me walking for miles on some sunny beach in Sydney (if Sydney has sunny beaches—I'd have to find that out), it seemed selfish. Ripping a boy on the verge of adolescence from the only world he has ever known, even if it is a crazy world. A crazy world in a crazy house perched on a cliff inhabited by a crazy mother he knows tried to kill him when he was an infant, and a man who suddenly moves in more than a decade later and says he is his father, and by me—someone who doesn't even seem to know who the hell she is except that she is responsible.

Except that she is a pitiful goody-goody.

Mavis Paige, with a smile for every disadvantaged client who comes her way and with soothing dialogue for every vixen who seduces away her lover.

Jill Willis, always waiting for the next contract renewal, the next tedious costume, the chance to play a part that might even be interesting.

Even BJ, with her basket case of a lover and her mismatched parents, still trying to prove something. Trying to prove to Lenore that I really do love her and she doesn't need to be psychotic. Trying to prove to my mom that I really did become an actor and not some high-priced call girl.

Look, Mom, at least I am not a prostitute. So what if I have a crazy girlfriend and live on a cliff and don't have enough backbone to kick out some low-life guy who says he is my kid's father? Look at me, Mom, I am a rare creature, an actor who has been constantly employed for the last twenty years. Look at me, Mom, my beautiful cry is admired far and wide. Look at me, Mom, I am not a whore.

Although I am attracted to one.

Attracted? Such an adolescent word. I am past that. Way past. I am almost forty. Although I feel as if I am going to be eighty.

"Come on," Malcolm calls, bounding ahead. The snowflakes are like little freckles on his red parka, the reverse image of his face in summer when his freckles blaze sunburnt for a few moments before they turn dark brown against his tan.

"Don't run down there," I scold. These cliffs are steep and the snow makes the rocks slippery. I want to protect him. From falling. From everything. And since I can't protect him from the inside of our house, at least I can try to protect him on the outside. Another reverse image, I guess.

"Come on," he yells. Although he does seem to slow down a bit. His red parka almost neon amid the white snow and gray trees. I congratulate myself on the jacket's purchase, yet again. What a smart shopper I am! To have bought the jacket in summer, at a discount outlet and in a state without sales tax. To have thought so far ahead to this gray ugly frozen day when we were so happy walking on the beach.

I watch him scramble down the haphazard path. He stops at an outcrop of shiny white rock. He likes to chip the quartz from these cliffs. He puts the shimmering white chips on top of his dresser, although they never gleam inside the way they do out here. And when Lenore moves the furniture from room to room, his rocks often get lost.

"Be careful." My toes barely touch the ledge. I am still trying to hide the fact that I am afraid of heights. I am still trying to hide the fact that I hate it here.

Hate it. Hate the bitter cold and the trees empty as death and the river clotted with ice so far below us and the cliffs with their jagged dangers and the view across to Westchester, across to Scarsdale, full of Lenore's relatives who are mostly named Lenore. Hate the house behind me, with its dramatic panoramas and its restless furniture that settles in peculiar places.

Hate it. Hate my life.

My foot, numb inside my boot, pushes a stray stone, which skips down the craggy maze toward Malcolm now far below me. I kick another rock, this time a little more forcefully. It stumbles for a moment on the ledge and then becomes airborne, falling through the blurry space, past Malcolm's red parka, down to the river.

I could follow it.

I could.

A jump instead of a kick.

There would be a close-up on my anguished face. My thoughts

could be whispers and echoes. Maybe even a flashback to a happier scene. My eyes would brim with tears, my face not the least bit blotchy, my only talent conspicuous in my last earthly moments.

Too melodramatic even for a daytime drama.

Malcolm is clambering back up the bluff. He uses his hands to grasp a point of rock, to grab a limb of some dead-looking shrub. I repress the urge to warn him to be careful not to rip his jacket.

"Your nose is bleeding," he says. He is not even breathing hard from his climb.

"It's the cold."

He takes a tissue—bluer than today's gray sky, blue as the box of tissues in the kitchen—from the pocket of his red parka and for a moment I think he is going to reach up and wipe my face as if I am a child and he is an adult, but he hands me the square of crumpled soft blue, which I promptly stain with a smear of red.

From his inner pocket—his pocket within a pocket—he retrieves little chips of the white quartz. They glimmer, but only for an instant. Then they are grey. I tell Malcolm that I think the rocks are wonderful. "I'm going to keep these forever," he says. "In my secret pocket. And I'm going to collect more and more."

"You can't fill up your pockets with rocks. You won't be able to walk."

"I will."

I envy his determination enough to laugh. I wipe my nose a few more times while we stand there, looking out at the pewter-colored horizon. A few more smears of blood blot the blue tissue, but with less red. Malcolm kicks a few rocks over the ledge. We could turn and walk back to the house. We could turn at any moment and walk back, back to Lenore and Dagoberto, back to the living room furniture which is now in one of the bedrooms if Lenore hasn't moved it while we've been gone, but neither of us does. Neither of us has a reason to go back.

Maybe I should get Malcolm a dog.

eighteen

*M*alcolm says: Dagoberto touched me.

Malcolm says: On my private parts.

Malcolm says: Dagoberto. Dagoberto. Dagoberto.

I do what any mother would do in these circumstances. I take my child out of the house immediately and we drive to the mall. Inside, we are assaulted by fake evergreens and red Santas. We pass a group of teenagers posed near the fountain, underneath a placard advertising one of the chain boutiques, in clothes so fashionable one would not dare to wear them on the streets.

"Those look like real people," Malcolm says.

"They are."

"Really? I thought so. But why are they doing that?"

"They're getting paid," I say simply.

"Why would someone pay them when they could use the fake ones that they don't have to pay?"

"You have to buy the fake ones," I argue.

"True." Malcolm sounds so adult. "But wouldn't that be cheaper? If you had to pay the real people by the hour but the plastic people cost what you would pay for twenty hours, then you'd be getting all of the rest for free."

"I can see why you're so good in math," I compliment him. "But maybe the real people are more interesting. Maybe we wouldn't have noticed mannequins, but we did notice these people pretend-ing to be mannequins."

"True," Malcolm says again. True seems to be his favorite word these days. "But I bet you don't get paid very much for just standing there."

"Not much," I agree. "But it's actually very hard work. You know, I once did it."

"You did? Before there was TV?"

"No, there was TV then. I just wasn't on it. I worked in a store in a mall and got paid to model just like that, only it was in front of the store."

"That must have been boring."

"I think I thought it was exciting," I admit. "I had a friend who thought I could be a model."

"I guess I wasn't born yet." Malcolm sighs.

"No. You weren't."

We reach our destination—the food court—and settle down with pizza and french fries and two large Cokes. I put vinegar and lots of salt on the french fries, like I do when we are on the boardwalk, near the beach, smelling the ocean and looking out to see if we can see any lights that must be ships on the dark horizon. Instead of a damp bench, we are sitting at a table under a red and white umbrella, the umbrella ready in case we should require shade from the skylight overhead. We are both eating slowly, using our napkins frequently, dreading the next scene.

Finally, I deliver the opening line: "Tell me everything that hap-pened."

"She doesn't believe me," Malcolm says.

She. Lenore. He has never called her Lenore. He has never called her E, like her father does, like her sisters do, like even her own mother does. Has never called her mother.

She. Her. But not that her, not that woman. What should I call her? Should I call her?

"And do you think I will?" I ask. Me. What does he call me? BJ to my face. BJ to his friends? And in some dark corner of his mind? Mom? Or always BJ?

Malcolm is not interested in answering any questions about me. "She didn't even listen to me. Didn't even listen to what happened."

"Why don't you tell me what happened?"

"I don't want to."

"You don't want to?" I am not prepared for this.

Malcolm shakes his head.

"I will believe whatever you tell me. I know you'll tell me the truth."

Malcolm starts to cry.

I hand him a clean napkin.

Malcolm looks at the skylight.

"Just start at the beginning."

"Joshua . . ." Malcolm blurts out.

Oh, shit. Not only Malcolm, but his friend. And not just any friend, but the one whose mother is a social worker. I see our lives in court. Dagoberto, the molester. Lenore, the mental patient. And me, just as crazy as Lenore for letting all this go on right under my nose while I was away from home pretending to be someone else. I see the state taking Malcolm away. Forget about custody, the kid is going to be in a foster home.

But wait, maybe I can use all this. Maybe it will all work out.

Malcolm says: "I'm sorry."

Malcolm says: "I thought she would . . ."

Malcolm says: "Joshua said . . ."

"Let's start at the beginning. This isn't your fault. You are not the one who did something wrong. That's Dagoberto."

I know it is my role to be calm. I'm not going to smash my fist on the table and say that I'm going to kill that bastard Dagoberto; I'm not going to sob hysterically; I'm not even going to call the authorities and rush us all into therapy. I am going to find out what happened.

Malcolm shakes his head.

Malcolm is still crying.

Malcolm blows his nose in a napkin.

"Want some ice cream?" I ask.

I have rocky road. Malcolm has vanilla. He always has vanilla.

Malcolm says: "Joshua."

Malcolm says: "She would believe me and everything would be better."

Malcolm says: "Dagoberto didn't."

The story falls together from Malcolm's fragments. Joshua, rich with his mother's experiences as a social worker, lent Malcolm some information: Any mother would (should?) immediately kick out any man, including a father, who sexually abused her child. Malcolm already possessed the facts about sexual abuse; he is one of the generation of children who have been educated—at home and at school—that his private parts are private. So Malcolm had concocted a scheme, with Joshua acting as consultant. Only Lenore had not believed him. Had screamed and called him a liar and told him that he was just jealous because she had found a man.

And I had taken him to the mall.

What a pitiful set of parents the kid has.

"How long are you going to ground me for?" Malcolm asks.

"You know that not telling the truth is very serious, don't you?"

"Yeah."

"But you know, sometimes there are extenuating circumstances." I sound like Mavis Paige advising a client.

"I guess." From his tone, I realize that Malcolm does not have a firm grasp on "extenuating." It sounds like it could make things worse.

"One hour."

"Really?"

"Yes. But only if you promise me you'll never lie to me again." I don't include Lenore.

"I do. I really do."

"And I promise you something, too."

"What?"

"I promise everything will be better very soon. So you don't have to try any more tricks."

I have a few tricks of my own, Malcolm. But I don't say this out loud. Why should he believe me, anyway? It's almost Christmas and I'm living in my house—a house that is legally only mine—with my lover and our child. And my lover's boyfriend, and she's pregnant with his child. And although she wanted to get pregnant, now she's decided to get an abortion—or at least she has been screaming about that—although I think it must be too late. Did I mention she's a former mental patient?

Maybe I should become a writer for *In the Name of Love.*

Since I don't know how much longer I can be Mavis Paige. It isn't just the rumors I hear about developing a lesbian story line, one that doesn't include me. One that must mean that I'll be phased out. Or I'll act badly that my character isn't getting to be the lesbian that I've always said belongs on the show, and they'll punish me by writing me silly parts without the opportunity to cry.

My real worry is the Mob. They are after me. This is not a good sign. Although the words "the Mob" or even "the Syndicate" have not appeared in the scripts for years, the implication is obvious. What is not obvious is what this means for me. After all these years, I'm still nervous as the end of each thirteen-week contract cycle draws near. Will I be killed off? Really, or just seeming to be dead and then brought back to life? I did hear a confession of murder from Brad's brother, who has been blackmailed into working for "them," but I'm not going to tell whatever I know, even if I'm subpoenaed before the grand jury, because I'm such a scrupulous attorney I would never violate attorney-client privilege, even Brad told Bethany as much. We are taping Christmas episodes; Christmas Day lasts almost a week. Surely, I won't be killed around the holidays.

"Don't worry, they're not going to kill you," Mimi says. We are talking on the phone. I called her after Malcolm and I got home from the mall. I called her instead of calling the psychiatrist.

"I'm not sure. I hear gossip about cutting costs at the show."

"No. Those Mob guys aren't all that smart." Mimi has no reservations about using the word "mob" or giving advice: "Just don't go out to any restaurants."

"I've got another problem."

"Brad, I know."

"No. Dagoberto."

"He's not still living with you, is he?"

"Yeah."

"Have you asked him to leave?"

"I've talked to Lenore."

"Lenore? I'm not talking about Lenore. Have you asked Dagoberto face-to-face to get the hell out of your house?"

"No. I guess I haven't."

"Well, do it. Don't be so wishy-washy. Face him down, man-to-man."

"I guess."

"And you haven't done anything stupid with the house and the beach place and your money, have you? Like put Lenore's name back on anything?"

"No."

"Good. Then there's no problem."

"There's Malcolm."

"No judge in the world would give Lenore custody. She's crazy as a bedbug."

"I'm not so sure that's true. I'm not the real mother."

Mimi is silent.

"And now there's a real father."

"Have you seen a real lawyer?" Mimi's voice has her tough comforting edge.

"Yes."

"That same lawyer who helped you with all the papers before? I thought you were the guardian in case Lenore got sick again."

"I am. But if she's not sick, I'm nothing."

"But you still own everything, right? I'd think she'd want the house more than the kid."

"She keeps changing her mind," I admit.

192

"What about the lawyer? What did he say?"

"She said I've got some problems. The law here is not very good."

"Then you'd better find another solution."

"I'm working on it, Mimi."

I try not to cry as Mimi says good-bye. Try not to keep her on the line forever and forever. Try not to get in the car and drive down to Philadelphia and run into her arms and sob until my ribs feel like they are going to crack.

Try to pick up the phone again. Try to call the psychiatrist. Make an appointment.

Afternoon, after taping. I've only got the smallest part tomorrow. I'm in someone else's memory. I'm missing for the next several episodes. I'm holding my breath for next week's scripts.

Dr. Sidney Henry's office is decorated in mauve. It is supposed to be soothing, in a professional, competent sort of way, but I always find it depressing. His new Westchester office, where Lenore has her appointments on Thursday afternoons, is decorated in a pale mint green, which seems a little more uplifting. I've known this man for more years than I care to remember. I feel like I've bought him at least one car, that chocolate brown Jaguar I've seen in the Westchester parking lot, probably.

"I'm worried about Lenore." I get right to the point. "I think she's getting unstable again. She's incoherent and having delusions. And I'm worried about her being self-destructive."

"Is she threatening suicide?"

"Yes."

"Are you sure?"

"I have a drawer full of suicide notes, Dr. Henry. I'm worried I'm going to get home one day and find her dead. I'm even more worried that Malcolm is going to come home one day and find her dead."

"Can I ask you what makes you keep the suicide notes?" He arches his one eyebrow.

"I thought you might like to see them." I answer without even the slightest hesitation. "Maybe they contain information useful to her treatment."

"What kinds of things do they say?"

"The usual. Her life is ruined. Malcolm is a monster or a leech. I am a bitch."

"Anything about her new boyfriend?"

"No."

"Do you find that odd?"

"Do you?" I retort.

"This is a difficult situation. And I'm sure it's a difficult situation for you. Your lover, for a substantial period of time, in a lesbian but otherwise nurturing relationship, now decides that her own lesbianism was a temporary period in her life and goes on to form a secure attachment to a man. You might understandably feel bereft. And even betrayed. Perhaps you might seek some counseling yourself."

"You think Lenore's attachment to her child's sperm donor, a man she just met, is secure and healthy?"

"I'm not at liberty to discuss my professional opinions. You know that."

"Let me just ask you this, do you believe Lenore is capable of living on her own and not committing suicide, in spite of what I've told you?"

"I won't recommend institutional treatment, if that's what you're asking."

"Thank you for your time, doctor."

"You're welcome."

On my way out of the office, I tell the receptionist to send the monthly bills for Lenore's treatment to Dagoberto Lux. Same address.

Fuck you, Dr. Sidney Henry. I should have known never to trust a man with two first names. I should have known never to trust a man. I should have known. I should have known so much.

It's dark as midnight when I get home, but it isn't late.

Malcolm is in his room, playing a computer game. I sit there for a while with him, killing aliens and retrieving hidden treasures.

I decide right then and there that we are going to my mom's and Mimi's for Christmas. Me and Malcolm. Forget trying to make some sort of holiday here. What am I supposed to do, buy Dagoberto a present? No one will even notice we are gone, I say to myself, with a little pity but also some determination. It may be a small plan, but at least it's a plan.

When we come back, to the house that seems too big and too alone on the cliffs, it does seem like no one even noticed we were gone. And it seems like we weren't. It seems like Christmas morning and the artificial tree in the Roxborough duplex never happened, like all those new computer games and CD-ROM diskettes and CDs of music and the sweaters and scarves, and the turkey with the greasy gravy that I love, none of it ever existed.

Lenore is in the hospital, having a second-trimester abortion authorized by Dr. Henry. At least according to Lenore's sister Lenore, who is on the other end of the phone line, on the other side of the river. I wonder if she twists and twirls the telephone cord like I do. I wonder if she is looking out the window, at the deep blue sky. The view past the kitchen sink is my favorite in this house, not just because the kitchen sink is stationary, but because it is one of the few views from any window that makes this house seem sensibly sea level.

"You want my advice?" Lenore's sister Lenore is asking, although she doesn't wait for me to answer. "Get rid of that Nazi while you still have the chance. Making my crazy sister get an abortion is the last straw. Even I know it will just make her even more crazy."

"Nazi? That's a little harsh." I recognize my good-girl Mavis voice. "Dr. Henry isn't even German, is he?"

"Jesus Christ, BJ. Not the fucking psychiatrist. Dagoberto. Dagoberto's a real Nazi."

"He's a creep, I agree. But I think he's too young to be a real Nazi. Aren't they all dead? I mean, the guy is not over forty, too young for World War Two, don't you think?"

"It's in his blood. That stuff is passed on from father to son."

I don't mention Malcolm. I just shake my head, looking through the window toward the sky. "He isn't even from Germany. He's from South America."

"Jesus, BJ. That's just more proof. That's where all the Nazis went after they lost the war. I mean, I know everybody doesn't go to college . . ." She lets her insult hover in the telephone lines strung under the river for a moment. "But I thought *everybody* knew that the Nazis fled to South America."

"Yeah, I guess I knew that." Didn't know it. Didn't go to college. Didn't have some surgeon daddy to send me to school.

"And even if you didn't know that, his hair should have tipped you off. I mean, how many blond South Americans do you know?"

"There are quite a few," I argue. "And anyway, so what if his parents came from Germany? I'm not sure what it has to do with anything."

"Just be careful," Lenore's sister Lenore says.

As Dagoberto comes into the kitchen.

I hang up and start making myself a cup of coffee, adding a few drops more of the newest artificial sweetener.

"How was your holiday?" he asks politely. His accent is clipped and sharp. I wonder where he is from, but I don't even consider asking him. I just look at him. He looks taller and blonder than ever. I see a trace of Malcolm's jaw line in his, so I turn back to my coffee, stirring it with great concentration.

"I don't know that's any of your business." I try to sound stern and determined. A woman with a plan.

"I think you've misunderstood me," Dagoberto says.

I notice his wrist. The red Swiss Army watch has been replaced by something more expensive. Not a Rolex, but expensive.

"I think you had better move out." I finally say what Mimi said to say. Maybe the Nazi label has given me courage.

"I don't think that would be best."

"It would be best for me."

"You are not a selfish woman, BJ. I know you cannot think only of yourself. Lenore needs you."

196

"You must have gotten the psychiatrist's bills."

"I am not talking about money. I am talking about love. And loyalty."

"If you don't move out voluntarily, I'll call the police."

"I think we can work this out. If you listen to me for a little while. And then, if you don't like what I say, if you don't agree with me, I will go without any fuss. But I will take the boy."

"You're trying to bargain?" I wonder if I could call the police for kidnaping.

"Why do you always think everyone is after your money? I don't want things from you. Although I think that the beach house would be a good place to raise the boy."

I don't ask how he knows about the beach house, just wait for him to go on.

"Or we could sell it."

"My mother owns it," I lie.

"No matter. All I want is for the three of us to be together." He puts his large hand on my shoulder. "And I don't mean Lenore."

"Excuse me?"

"Don't make this any more difficult than it is." His hand touches my chin. "It's you who I love, BJ. Always. Yes, for a confused moment I thought it was Lenore. She seemed so vulnerable and I responded to that. But it's been you right from the beginning. I just haven't known how to tell you."

"I have to think about this," I say, stalling for time.

I haven't spent the last twenty years in a soap opera without learning a few things. Isn't this exactly the kind of thing that Brad would say to me about Bethany? But I should be more Bethany and less Mavis. Goody-goody Mavis would be indignant: You haven't loved me at all; you are a scheming gold-digger. Bethany would be more crafty: This certainly comes as a surprise.

"This certainly comes as a surprise," I say.

"I should have told you this before. I have been very stupid. I have let my love for you be buried by my pity for Lenore. You know as well as I do that she belongs in an institution, where people can take care of her."

"That's not what her psychiatrist thinks," I venture.

"I'm afraid he does now. He certified the abortion, past the second trimester, on the basis of her mental condition. Said having another child was a danger to her life."

"Oh."

"I know it's been difficult for you. When we settle Lenore in a suitable place, we could take a vacation. A trip somewhere. Anywhere you'd like. Where have you always wanted to go?"

"Australia." I say the first place that pops into my head.

"We could go to Brisbane," he says. "And up to the Great Barrier Reef. Miles and miles of beautiful ocean. And the scuba diving! Tropical fish of the most vibrant colors. You would just love it there!"

How the fuck do you know what I would love?

But I follow Bethany's example and simply smile off into a distance that isn't there.

I follow Bethany's example and glide toward the window, looking out past the cliffs and down to the river.

I follow Bethany's example and do not punch him in the face, or even flinch, when he steps behind me and puts his long arms around me. I simply slip away. I simply go into the bathroom—the one room Lenore has never been able to rearrange—and shut the door. He follows me. Opens the door and walks in, as if he has never heard of privacy.

"It's you that I love," Dagoberto says. We are standing close to the bathtub. "It's always been you."

"This is sick. Truly sick." I say this to myself more than to him, but he takes it as a challenge.

"There's nothing sick about it, BJ. Nothing at all. I knew I loved you from the first moment I laid eyes on you."

And my house and my kid and my bank account, I think.

Dagoberto steps closer.

The bathroom seems smaller.

"Think about it. That's all I ask."

198

"There's nothing to think about." I study the tropical fish imprinted on the shower curtain.

"You think *you* are nothing? Think about yourself for a change."

The tropical fish seem to swim. Toward a future. Toward a barrier reef in Australia. Or even toward Connecticut. I could live there. With my husband, the lawyer. Dagoberto could go to law school. It must not be too hard; that woman was doing it, wasn't she? And Dagoberto was once in medical school, wasn't he? He must be pretty smart. I could live with him, not some crazy woman. Not some prostitute.

We could raise miniature horses.

"I do think about myself," I protest.

"Not enough." He reaches for my hand. "We could be happy. Do you know what that is? Happiness? Do you know what it means to be loved? I don't think you do. What do you think?"

"I think you watch too many soap operas." I push past him, almost stumbling into the bathtub. Breathing normally only when I am safely on the other side of the bathroom door.

part seven

Margaret

nineteen

I am wearing a red suit made of a quality merino wool. A little brighter than usual for Margaret Smyth, but if she can't wear red on Valentine's Day, then when? And a white blouse with a tucked front, a popularization of the tuxedo shirt and as much of a costume. The outfit will be completed by my beautiful black leather briefcase, purchased in a regular department store now that I need a level of professionalism that my black leather knapsack cannot provide. And stockings, by which I mean pantyhose, but I never think pantyhose because then I think hose and then I think Betty. It's what Betty always said: "hose." What I always expected was to see her legs encased in green plastic, water spraying from around her ankles.

I wonder if Betty is dead. By now.

I never wonder about the other foster mothers. I can't even remember their names. They are shadows. I only remember Betty. My last foster mother.

The one I may have murdered.

Like a dream, I left Betty on the floor after I hit her on the side of the face with a frying pan. Cast iron, the frying pan was, and it was—had been—her mother's, or so she said. Said again and again and again. Said it for the millionth time that evening, yelled it really, as if my transgression was magnified by her mother's previous possession of the frying pan I had failed to dry adequately after washing. Though I meant to. Dry it. I remember I meant to. I meant to light the burner and put the frying pan on the stove; I meant to do it just the way Betty liked, so that Betty would leave me alone. But I forgot. Or maybe I hadn't forgotten, but was still putting off lighting the match and turning on the gas and quickly sliding the match to the gas and hoping the flame would be round and controlled enough so that it didn't crawl up my sleeve and into my hair, the way it did to one of Betty's other foster daughters, so that the ambulance came and she never came back. Maybe I was just screwing up my courage when Betty came toward me, her face getting redder—as red as that girl's face after the fire had left it—as she lifted her left arm higher than her head. Her left hand floated there a moment, like half of a halo, and she laughed through her teeth. "You're not as pretty as everyone thinks you are."

Everyone thinks I'm pretty? It was like being slapped awake in the morning, like another foster mother had done. Although Betty was also known for an open palm that could redden a cheek (face or ass) with a stunning efficiency. I thought she was going to slap me now, until I saw the cup of her hand twisted into a fist. I picked up the frying pan. Maybe I wanted to protect my newly acknowledged pretty face from becoming any less pretty. The cast iron was a kind of convenient armor. Until I used the frying pan less like a shield and more like a bludgeon.

I remember her face, tilted toward the floor and red. Like the setting sun. It was redder than before and the red was on the outside now, not just showing through the skin, but gushing from a rupture. I left her there and walked out the door. Down the road. I hitchhiked. To New York.

I remember her phone number. Still. Mulberry Eight, it begins. I rehearse the call.

I will recognize her voice and I will say, "Betty."

She will say, "Yes. Who's this?"

And I freeze in my fantasy. Because for a moment I can't remember what she called me. Peggy? Margie? Not Margot, surely. Rita? Greta? Madge? Maisie? Even Daisy?

My forgetfulness does not last long enough. I cannot forget that she called me Maggie. Maggie, so that it sounded like "Maggot." Maggot, what the other foster kids in the house would call me sometimes. Maggot. Maggot. Maggot.

"Who's this?" she will repeat.

I will not answer Maggot. Or Maggie. Or even Margaret.

This is what I will say: "I'm the one who hit you on the side of the head with a cast-iron frying pan."

But she will already know that. The cops will be on their way to arrest me. Never mind that the statute of limitations for assault has long since expired. Or maybe the voice wouldn't be Betty's after all, but the voice of her daughter—didn't she have a daughter, a real daughter?—who has been waiting for me to call for all these years so that she could avenge the murder of her adorable mother, and we both know the statute of limitations for murder is eternity.

So, I never call.

I never think of her. I can control my mind. Camouflage any anxiety. One of my talents, practiced under her roof if not tutelage.

I just go on with my day. Every day. Even Valentine's Day. Classes. Or my internship at the District Attorney's Office. Or dates.

Dates. I try to keep to my newest rule: no new clients. But it is getting difficult. I lost Ann-Marie. In a Christmas card: *Dearest Tamara: I hope this card finds you happy, and that you find a place in your heart for change.* She wrote she could no longer be unfaithful to her husband; she wrote she had found faith again. She did not write, *Dearest Tamara: Fuck you,* but she might as well have. *Dearest Tamara: You fucked me and now I'm fucking you. Dearest Tamara: My husband has decided to fuck me. Dearest Tamara: I'm giving up you just like I gave up coffee.*

I found the card on the bedroom chair after she left, the Thursday before Christmas. I was hoping for a present; I was hoping for a check. But my only present was that I could now retire Tamara. I never liked the name anyway, too much like tomorrow. I never liked brown either, too much like beige. Tamara could go off into oblivion wearing her brown outfits now that Ann-Marie had found God. What I found was free Thursdays; what I had to find was Sarah Tudor's rent.

Luckily, the Writer has been needy lately. Needing to be admired. And the Musician has also been needy. Needing to not be admired. And Jeanine gave me some cash to lay low in New York while she was on her two week sojourn to Sumatra, supposedly with me, her devoted lover from the East Coast; I assume she went with some guy.

But soon it will really be spring. And spring makes my clients less desperate than winter. Perhaps in June I will take out one last advertisement. Rules are made to be broken. That is, if by May I don't have a lucrative job with some Wall Street law firm. I've been haunting the law school placement office and going on interviews for positions as summer associate. The money is filthy, of course, and the work is repugnant, but I can hardly complain about whoring.

And it would only be for a summer.

And it might give me enough for the last year of law school.

If I even get an offer, that is.

That's the ultimate insult: One decides to sell oneself, but there are no buyers.

One takes it day by day. Trite but true, I suppose. Day by day. Sounds like a soap opera: *Day by Day*. Starring the star-crossed lovers. Jill Willis and Margaret Smyth. Although perhaps I would have a stage name. Something sexy but sympathetic. Something that would make the viewers root for the two of us to live happily ever after.

Day by Day.

What bullshit.

Bullshit or not, it's the only hope I have for the future. To try to direct each day toward the inevitable escape, to do what each day directs one to do. Today what my day demands is the District Attorney's Office. Another day at the internship procured by Professor Yarnes. Another day closer to graduation. Finish this semester, and then two more. And then freedom. Or if not freedom, a life.

Red suit. Merino wool. White tuxedo shirt.

Another Thursday morning.

The District Attorney's Office is always dusty. There is something dilapidated about it, something dated. Or maybe my expectations are too grandiose, too law firm with too much sparkling plate glass, bullet-proof, of course. On my desk, a vase of peonies, pink and huge and out of season.

Only the costumes satisfy; all attorneys wear uniforms. White shirts or blouses, blue pants or skirts, the cut of the clothes varies with gender but the colors remain predictable. As does the attitude. No one smiles at me or even nods in some vague acknowledgment of my existence. Not even the attorneys who I have interviewed about their notions of entrapment for my project with Professor Yarnes deign to glance toward the blaze of my red suit. Not even the one who asked me for coffee afterwards. I told her that I couldn't; I told her that I had to study; now she turns her head away from me.

I act as if I belong, as if I do not need to be welcomed, as if the "good mornings" intended for other targets never pierce me. My shield is my briefcase, so professionally black. It is a good grade of leather and has long straps; I sling it over my left shoulder and it bangs against the hipbone that hides underneath layers of merino wool. My briefcase is full of files, manila, which are full of sheets of paper, yellow. In my closet, my knapsack rests, temporarily empty of schoolbooks and purpose. Although not as far back in the corner as my tapestry attaché. I will need the knapsack. Tomorrow. For classes. I will not need the attaché. Or so I pray.

I am not sure what I should be doing here. Everyday, I wait for someone to send me on an errand or to give me a bit of research to do. Meanwhile, I give myself tasks that seem related to the project for Professor Yarnes. Reviewing the entrapment appeals. Watching the prosecutors at trial prove the defendants' identity. Eyewitness testimony is always best. The scientific evidence—fingerprints, DNA, blood—is unusual. The number of confessions startles. I take copious notes, filling my yellow legal pads, filling my manila file folders, filling my beautiful black leather briefcase.

In the hallway, there is a desk someone told me I can use. Not really a desk, more like a student's table from an underfunded school district. I sit on the metal chair. It is unsteady. I keep both feet on the floor. I place my beautiful black briefcase on the water-warped veneer of the desk. I want to push my face into the leather and inhale its promise, but I simply pull it open and tilt my nose toward it, hoping for a sniff. I slip out the files, unfolding them to reveal the sheets of yellow paper which I spread in a pattern that might indicate order. I reread my notes, holding my pen poised to add a word or two, although I never do. I snatch glances of people who pass by me in the hallway; they walk quickly and I do not raise my eyes; none of us can be distracted from our important tasks.

After what seems like an appropriate amount of time, plus the ten minutes I add for insurance, I give myself permission to pack up my beautiful black leather briefcase. I go downstairs and treat myself to a cup of coffee from a little stand inside the building. The coffee is delivered with a flourish, although it is not an espresso or a latte or an au lait. I lift the cup towards her, as if my subtle toast is for her and not Ann-Marie. The woman behind the counter smiles at me; she must think I am an important attorney. Or perhaps she is just friendly. I smile back. I am practicing being friendly. I take my first sip of the coffee.

"Thanks, it's great. Just what I needed."

The smile returns to her face. "You should try the latte," she advises.

"I might."

"We have decaf."

"I'm not a decaf person," I say.

She laughs, as if I have said something incredibly amusing.

I prolong the coffee. Deciding what to do next. I might as well go to the Clerk's Office. It's all public records there and since I'm "with" the District Attorney's Office, I have free rein to look at the files. There is even a rather nice clerk there—as nice as this coffee counter person—who once showed me the room of closed case files. And who once winked at me, or perhaps it was just a blink to get the hair out of her eyes.

The clerk I like isn't at her usual spot, so I wander toward the closed case file room. I suppose I'll do some statistical work on the entrapment defense. I'm planning to pick a year and count the number of entrapment defenses raised, the number of those that actually went to trial, and then the number of those that were successful. I think I can already approximate the last number.

I'm trying to decide on the year, leaning towards several years so that I'll be able to make some sort of comparison in my notes, when I see the clerk I like, wheeling a filing cart down the corridor.

"What's up?" She waves.

"Not much. What's up with you?" I hope I sound casual, yet professional.

"The usual. More work."

"I know the feeling."

"It's the damn reports." She is stopped now, leaning closer to me. I wonder if she is a dyke. It occurs to me that I could ask her out, for lunch, or better yet for coffee. In a casual sort of way. Though the idea drags no desire after it; she isn't Jill—or is it BJ?—Willis.

I know I am being ridiculous, thinking about BJ.

I know I need to be realistic. So I focus on the clerk's face, listen to her every word. Some obtuse insult to bureaucracy. Some indifferent reference to the lottery.

"It's time for my morning coffee break." She lifts her eyebrows so high they disappear into her bangs. "As soon as I get all these John Does back to their bin."

"What are John Does?" I ask her. I'm being polite, but I'm also thinking of my project for Professor Yarnes.

"You know," she says. "John Doe indictments. Though sometimes it's Jane Doe. Mostly it's John. Poor John. Such a lot of trouble that poor guy gets into. Usually the indictments sit a while and then the

D.A. amends them with the person's real name. After they figure it out."

"I thought the police department did all that."

"Well, if you ask me—which no one does—the cops *should* be doing this. But the prosecutors like to keep their numbers up. You'd think they got paid by the indictment. And it keeps the grand jury busy. The John Does usually go to the grand jury; it makes those grand jurors feel important, I guess. All it really does is make more paperwork."

"But how can they indict someone if they don't know who it is?"

"It isn't that they don't know." She raises her eyebrows past the horizon of her bangs again and boosts her voice into a womanly falsetto. "It's that they just don't know the person's name. You know, John Doe a/k/a The Wing is some drug courier, and John Doe a/k/a The Boss is some organized crime figure, and John Doe a/k/a Mack the Knife is some adolescent selling crack to other adolescents. You wouldn't believe the names these criminals choose. You'd think they could be a little more original. I mean, if you'd think you'd want your also known as to have a little style."

"Like?"

"Like Cleopatra." She giggles a little.

I don't point out that Cleopatra is hardly more innovative than Mack the Knife, maybe even be less so.

"You know," she continues, her eyebrows reaching toward each other conspiratorially, her voice a collusive whisper, "Cleopatra was bisexual."

"I think I've heard that," I say. I notice her bangs, a straight fringe of hair across her forehead.

"I thought you might have. You seem like you would know." She looks down the hallway, suddenly seeming embarrassed. "I mean, you seem studious and everything."

There are moments of fissure, when the world seems as if it will split open, revealing another world perhaps, some parallel universe in which this moment is significant. Or revealing an abyss so deep that light is not possible, even as a memory. But those moments quickly pass, as does this one. I blink Cleopatra away, she probably never existed anyway, but even if she did she is just another ancient crack on the wall that supports this ill-kept government building.

"You know, I'd like to look at these John Does," I say. "Speaking of being studious, my pro—"

She interrupts my attempt at an explanation. "Sure can, ma'am. Public records." She mimics an officious bow. "Just get the cart back to me? Or, why don't you take it over to my desk and sit there. I'll be back in a while. I'm going to get some coffee."

I barely notice she does not offer to get me a cup. I am thinking about her bangs, how the hair is so straight above her eyebrows. I am thinking about Cleopatra, or more accurately, Cleopatra images in museums. I am thinking about how the John Doe indictments can be transformed into an interesting segment of my project for Professor Yarnes.

I need to concentrate. I start to leaf through the papers and start in the middle of the cart of indictments.

The People of the State of New York
v.
John Doe
a/k/a
Jersey Jim
For conspiracy to distribute a controlled substance, to wit: cocaine.

Is his name really Jim? Or James? Is he really from New Jersey? Maybe I should do some work on the John Doe indictments after the John Doe has been replaced. I'll have to ask the clerk how to find those.

I leaf through more of the skinny files on the cart. The offenses are mostly drugs. Although I do see an indictment for a well-publicized murder in Central Park. With an unconvincing alias: Spotted Shirt Man. I doubt anyone really calls himself Spotted Shirt Man. I guess that's what the clerk meant about the politics of all of this. I take out my pad and prop it against the wall and take some notes. I can already hear myself presenting this to Professor Yarnes; I am witty and intelligent and she is fascinated and impressed.

The name on one of the next indictments does not strike me as noteworthy: John Doe a/k/a Sunshine. It's the name of the victim, buried in paragraph 8, after the offense of manslaughter and a description of the venue and the averment of jurisdiction. The name of the victim is Patricia. Patricia Surace. Patty. My Patty. Patty, CEO of Protective Products. Patty, cousin of Dominic. Patty, who disappeared and turned up dead in the obituary column. Patty, who I may have been the last person to see alive. The very last person.

Patty. Victim. Victim of a hit and run, according to the indictment. Hit and run? I contain a giggle of relief. Hit and run? I couldn't have killed her; I cannot drive. I do not have a car. Not a car with a yellow bumper sticker SUNSHINE according to the indictment, not any car. I cannot drive. I have several driver's licenses, but I have never driven. Not once. Never.

The crack on the wall widens, but this time it isn't Cleopatra or some confused court clerk who is revealed, but my own innocence. Exposed and naked, standing in a chasm that sparkles with uncontrovertible clarity. I never killed Patty. I've never killed anyone. Not Dominique. Not Betty. I could telephone Betty. I could mourn Dominique. I could demand that Patty's cousin Dominic post a reward for the apprehension of Sunshine.

The future gleams at me, a glare through the rupture in the wall of this old building. All I have to do is follow the light. Follow it into the afterlife. Because this life is not my real life; it's after this life that will be real. I feel all religious. Bathed in the truth.

The truth. Tinged with a little triumph, of course. My work for Professor Yarnes will be so brilliant that she will make me a co-author. The law review article will make such waves that we will turn it into a book. The book becomes a bestseller. I become a professor. My lover, a former soap opera actress, wears bright colors and goes with me to faculty parties. We love the Midwest. Or the Southwest, yes, the Southwest. We like to go on long walks in the desert. The air has such clarity it could cut through any wall of any dingy government building. The mesas glimmer like jewels against the horizon.

My enthusiasm and determination swell. I drag the cart of indictments over to the clerk's desk. She isn't back yet; I pull her chair to the side of the desk so that I won't be sitting behind her desk and be mistaken for her. I put my legal pad on my knee, ready to receive more notes about these John Doe indictments. But before I can make any real progress, the clerk with her Cleopatra bangs is standing over me, breathing heavily.

"What a great Valentine's Day," she says. She has a cup of coffee in her hand. There is no coffee in it.

"It is," I agree, suffused with my own predictions of my wonderful future.

"She asked me out."

"She?"

"Yeah. The woman at the coffee counter." The clerk seems embarrassed now, her hand wiping the fringes of hair from her forehead.

"That's great." What else can I say?

"I didn't even know she noticed me."

"Congratulations."

Her eyebrows scowl.

"No really," I say. "I think I know who you mean. She seems quite nice."

Her eyebrows relax.

"Thanks again," I say, gathering my stuff into my briefcase.

"Yeah. See you tomorrow."

"What?" My briefcase drops to the space between my shoes. I catch my stocking on the bottom corner of her desk as I bend down to retrieve my file folders.

"Nothing," she lilts, still effusive with happiness. "Just saying I'll see you tomorrow. What did you think I said?"

Tamara. I thought you called me Tamara.

"I thought you said tomorrow. But I don't work tomorrow."

"Lucky you," she says, waving me off.

"Have a great date." I smile.

"You too," she says, generous in her happiness. "I hope all your dates are really wonderful."

twenty

*T*he yellow soft-as-cashmere sweater clings to my modest breasts and my enviable thighs. The flaxen slacks, tight around my ankles, shimmer in the amber lights from the sunset. I am in a West Village penthouse, a bit west of the West Village I suppose since I can see the ginger-colored ribbon of the river from the buffet table near the transparently clean windows. I am at a benefit reception for a lesbian legal organization. I am with Jeanine. I am Ursula.

I am anxious.

Professor Gertrude Yarnes and her lover are sitting on a couch, balancing petite glass plates on their knees. The professor's lover— Bobbi?—looks decidedly uncomfortable. I've nodded at the professor, hoping it will be enough in case I cannot extricate myself from Jeanine. I hover near the buffet table, pretending to admire the huge polished bivalve filled with caviar. Jeanine grabs my hand as a butchly tailored woman who acts as if she is the owner of the penthouse approaches. I reach for the buffet table with my free hand, pluck a shriveled black olive from a silver bowl and coax it into Jeanine's mouth. Any attempt at introductions interrupted, Jeanine has little choice but to smile as she chews the olive. The woman smiles back at Jeanine, looks me over, and smiles back at Jeanine again.

I can almost hear what the woman will say to some other woman, a bit of gossip to share, another bit of information to quell the persistent rumor that Jeanine is straight and does not deserve to be the West Coast director of a lesbian and gay advocacy organization. Or perhaps there are other rumors? That Jeanine dates a prostitute?

I tell myself not to be paranoid.

I silently repeat all the logical consolations I have provided for Jeanine, the explanations that seemed so convincing then. Somehow, with Professor Yarnes and her lover still sitting on the white couch across the huge room, my rationalizations lack their previous power. What if the professor stands right now and walks over here and greets Jeanine, her old friend, and Margaret Smyth, her student and research assistant?

"Great olives," Jeanine says.

"Greek." The tailored woman answers Jeanine, but she is looking at me.

I glance at her expensive shoes to escape her gaze.

"Have you ever been to Greece?" she asks me. I pretend she is talking to Jeanine. Jeanine must be pretending the same thing, because she answers that she has.

"And how did you like Melitis?" The woman's question is now unambiguously directed at Jeanine.

"Melitis? I don't believe I was there. We stayed mostly in Athens."

"We did?" The woman laughs. "You mean you took your adorable lover to Athens and didn't go to Lesbos?" The woman turns to me. "I'd get a new lover if I were you, darling."

"Thanks for the advice, but I don't like to fly." I turn towards Jeanine. "I didn't even go to Athens with you and your mother, did I?"

"You don't know what you're missing." The woman takes an olive. It flashes dark against her perfect teeth and then disappears. "Excuse me," she says as she wafts away toward another couple.

"Excuse us," I announce to the vacated space. I take Jeanine's elbow and lead her toward the private elevator. I nod toward Professor Yarnes and give her a subtle wave. Bobbi waves back. The elevator door opens and I wave again.

Down two flights, to the apartment's first floor, where we fetch our coats from an oak rack. The empty wooden floor gleams. Jeanine's shoes click on its polished surface.

On the street, I try to cheer Jeanine. "So, what was that all about?" I strive for a lighthearted tone. "I mean, I feel like I was in a Natalie Barney scene."

"Who?"

"Natalie Barney. You know, Paris in the twenties, lesbian salons, a bunch of upper-class expatriates being snotty to each other."

"Oh, right."

Really, Jeanine. If you're going to pass as a dyke, you need to study. You should have gone to Lesbos for goddess' sake. If I were really your girlfriend . . . I stop my thoughts.

"She was something, wasn't she? Do you know her?" I try to resuscitate my sunny tone in the now-dark street.

"Not well. She's on a couple of boards of directors. I just wonder how dykes can afford such places," Jeanine says.

"It was a beautiful apartment, wasn't it?"

Jeanine nods.

"Maybe not for L.A." I smile. "But for Manhattan, it was something. I never knew there were penthouses in the Village."

"You seem awfully impressed," Jeanine's implication is not kind.

"I just liked the apartment."

"But how can she afford it?"

"I don't know, Jeanine." I try to hide my irritation. "I guess it's inherited money or spectacular investments."

"All those trust-fund dykes." Her voice is clouded with resentment. The understandable working woman's resentment of a wealthy woman. Didn't Jeanine tell me about putting herself through college? Didn't Jeanine tell me about her family's loss of their farm? Yes, I remember the weary resignation in her voice.

I remember wanting to tell her to get over it. To appreciate her life, the fact that she even had a family that had lived on a farm, even if they didn't now. But I had controlled the urge. I had listened sympathetically as we ate our dinner at a moderately priced restaurant. I was having shrimp scampi, I remember.

But perhaps another resentment. Could it be that Jeanine believes it is doubly unfair that a dyke could be wealthy? Could it be that Jeanine believes that she herself—straight woman pretending to be gay so that she can keep her job—deserves to be wealthy, or at least deserves it more than the dykey owner of the West Village penthouse we have just left?

"Let's go get a drink," I suggest, more because I would like one than because I think it will please Jeanine. The effort of being an escort seems momentarily beyond me.

But I am lucky because my suggestion does seem to please Jeanine, who quickly agrees. And although there are lesbian bars in this part of town, it seems too early for any of them. So I suggest we go to that lesbian bar that advertises itself for "professional women."

"Oh, right, what's it called?"

"A woman's name," I answer, dismissively. Because I can't remember which one. Which name. Suddenly I can only think of Jill and I know it is not that. I hail a cab and hurry Jeanine into it.

The bar is as cramped as those for nonprofessional women, but the neighborhood and attire are better. The women eye each other the same way, glazing over Jeanine and me because we appear to be coupled. Another striking similarity is the drinks: watered.

"It doesn't even smell like Scotch. Here, sniff." Jeanine holds her glass of clear liquid near my face. "My room is near here," she announces, "and it has a bottle of Johnnie Walker."

"Red or Black?" I ask.

"Black."

"Let's go," I mouth.

It does not take us long to get to the Salisbury Hotel. "I always stay here," she announces somewhere between the street and the door to her room. After the penthouse, the hotel room looks dingy. She roots in her suitcase, open on the chair, and retrieves a bottle of Black.

I stack ice cubes into the water glasses. She pours. We sit on the bed and sip. She takes off her shoes and crosses her legs under her. She sips.

218

I pour.

"More ice?"

She shakes her head from side to side. She sips.

I pour.

"You don't drink very much, do you?" she asks me.

"A nice Scotch deserves to be savored," I answer.

She sips.

"You know," she finally says, "maybe if I get drunk enough, we can . . ." Her voice trails off.

"Can what?"

"Can have sex." Her voice is deep with Scotch. "One doesn't call it fucking, does one?" She rubs her feet, still encased in their thin trouser socks, but wiggling as if to shake off their nylon sheath.

"It depends."

"On what?" Jeanine laughs loud enough for the occupants—if there are any—in either of our neighboring rooms to hear.

"Lots of things. But probably not what you're thinking."

"And what do you think I'm thinking?"

"I think you're thinking the things a straight woman would think." I'm not trying to be cruel, or at least not overly cruel, but I am trying to remind her that she is straight.

"And how do you know what a straight woman would think, Ms. Lesbian?"

"I've dated a few?" I invite her to laugh, but she doesn't, so I try for something more serious. "I guess I don't really know. But then," I look at her rubbing her feet, "I guess I don't know what anyone else really thinks."

"How deep," she mocks, sipping more of her drink. I reach for the bottle to pour her a bit more and she extends her glass. "I can see why you went to law school."

I try not to drop the bottle.

"Surprised?" Her laugh is loud again. "Of course I know. I made it my business to know. You are my lover, after all." She is almost giggling now. "Although it wasn't hard. It's a small world, as they say."

"A law student?" I smile my most disarming smile. "And I suppose you believe the rumors that I am a medical student or a housewife in Connecticut? Product of the same rumor mill that generates all those rumors about you?"

"Maybe you're not suited to be a lawyer; your analytic powers are weak. First of all, I haven't heard any rumors that you are either a medical student or a housewife, although you wouldn't necessarily know what I had heard. And second, and what you do know, my dear, is that the rumors about me are true."

"In that case, I suppose I should apprentice myself to you so that I can learn to become a respected member of the bar."

"Not a bad idea." She laughs again, although her laughter is losing its lightness and sliding into sarcasm. "But you'll never pass the character and fitness investigation."

"Why not? You did."

"Yes, but I am neither a dyke nor a whore."

"Then I guess if I do manage to become a lawyer, I'll be next in line for your job."

"Oh, you are the nasty one." She laughs more loudly than before.

"You seem to be enjoying it." I pour her some more Scotch, trying to blot out her ability to recall this conversation tomorrow, trying to preserve my ability to pay Sarah Tudor's rent.

"I'd enjoy something else more."

"Oh? And what is that?"

"Letting you fuck me." She leans back on the bed in an attempt at a seductive pose. She looks ridiculous. Not just rumpled and almost drunk, but like an imitation of herself playing the part of a seductress in a soap opera.

"That would ruin your reputation." I look toward the hotel room door.

"Or make it."

"Meaning?" I strive to be casual.

"Meaning I could learn a lot from you and your expertise. Meaning one roll in the hay would probably give me enough to talk the dirty girl-to-girl talk that some of the board members insist upon. Meaning, what the hell?"

220

"That's not exactly seductive."

She is quiet. She looks at her drink, or what's left of it. I reach for the bottle again, remembering that I like Jeanine, remembering Sarah Tudor's rent, remembering that I am more than halfway through law school, remembering my plan for a future.

"I'm teasing," I say conciliatorily.

"You want more money, I guess. How much do you usually charge for a fuck? I mean, is there a flat rate or do different activities cost different amounts?"

"I think you should have another drink. And I think you should take off your clothes and get into the bed."

"And then you'll fuck me?"

"Jeanine," I say, "you're drunk."

"I'm not. But I think we should settle on a price before we begin."

"Five hundred," I say.

"For the works?"

"It's not a hot dog stand, Jeanine, but I guess you could call it that."

"What if there's something I don't like. I mean, do we need a safe word or something?"

"How about 'stop'?"

"I thought it had to be something else. Something like 'chocolate' or 'briefcase.' " She is giggling.

"No. 'Stop' will work just fine."

"You'll listen to me?"

"You're the one in control," I try to soothe.

"Sorry. It's just that I haven't . . . and I guess you know that I haven't had sex with men either. Unless you count my father, which I don't." Jeanine's laugh is brittle now.

"I'll be gentle," I say. It is difficult not to feel pity, the most absolute antidote to lust. After Jeanine gets under the covers, I hold her. I am on top of the sheet and hotel bedspread, still wearing my yellow sweater and yellow pants. I stroke her hair. And I think of that woman. BJ or Jill or Mavis Paige.

And when Jeanine's breathing is deeply even, when she does not flinch if my fingers stray toward her face, when she does not wince when I stroke her throat, I get up. I pull the sheets out from their hotel corners. I pick up her underpants, a nice cream color with a wide border of lace, and drape them on the lampshade. I look around the room for the effect, judge the underpants too crass and remove them from the lampshade. Then I use the bathroom and inspect my hair in the hotel mirror.

There is only fifty dollars in Jeanine's wallet, so I leave it there. I guess she expected to write me a check? I look in her appointment book, a good grade of lambskin, and tear out the page with my phone numbers. I make sure the hotel room door, with its fire-escape directions and checkout policies, is locked as I click it closed behind me.

twenty-one

*I*n my coffin of a closet, I pull the red merino wool suit from its wooden hanger. Snow is predicted although spring is imminent; today seems a perfect day to wear wool, given the waning opportunities. Though I hesitate at the red, I do not want to dress flashy too often. I've worn this to the District Attorney's Office before; Valentine's Day, I think.

Perhaps I should know for sure. I remember a girl with whom I shared a bedroom at some foster home or other—I don't think it was at Betty's although it may have been—and she always knew precisely what she had worn and when. She had a little calendar, one of those kinds that one could get for free at any Hallmark card store, and in the little pastel boxes she wrote what she wore every school day. She didn't want to wear the same thing too often, or so she explained to me. She had four outfits.

I hope she has a closet as big as mine—bigger—full of clothes and a huge calendar on which she writes what she wears each day to her important job. Or she is a fashion model, yes, a fashion model who throws her clothes away; no, she donates her expensive outfits to a home for wayward girls. Or maybe she is a surgeon and wears the same things each day. Most likely she is a stripper. Nearing forty by now.

It must have been Valentine's Day that I last wore this suit. Made that clerk's head turn until she got a date with the woman at the coffee shop. Maybe the red suit isn't that impressive; I put it back on its hanger. Pick out a black suit and bring it to the back bedroom. The skirt seems too long and the jacket too short. I don't even try it on before I go back into the closet and trade it for the red. Though in the light of the back bedroom, the red seems too red.

I am being silly. It doesn't matter what I wear this Thursday to the District Attorney's Office. It doesn't matter. It never mattered. Not what I wore or what I didn't wear.

What matters is that I don't have many more times to wear anything at all to the District Attorney's Office. What matters is that it is not too many more days before I take the exams that will end my second year of law school. Not too many more days before I start my summer associate position at a mid-size midtown firm and it will be too warm to wear wool of any color. Not too many more days, months, a little more than a year, before I can start my real life.

The red suit fits well. It clings to me as I walk out of my building, away from the river and the statue of Joan of Arc. Toward the Office of the District Attorney. My briefcase, slung from its long leather strap, bangs against my hips in a satisfying rhythm.

Inside the rundown government building, at the coffee shop, the clerk with her Cleopatra bangs holds a half-empty coffee cup and chats with the counter woman. I greet both of them with a smile I think is very friendly. They scowl at me. I have interrupted their universe of two; I am some stray planet spinning out of orbit, on the brink of splintering into a meteor shower, beautiful only from a distance.

I should walk resolutely into the office and ask a woman attorney to have a cup of coffee with me at this very coffee shop; I should ask the one who had once asked me. I should. But I know I won't. I know I will only sit at the little desk in the hallway and try to continue my research—if I can even call it that—of the John Doe files. I will try not to think of Jill Willis. She is somewhere on this very island called Manhattan, pretending to be someone else, a lawyer named Mavis Paige. I could go home right now and turn on the television and if it is the right time I could find my true love inside a little box. I should laugh at myself, but I don't. I am becoming as pathetic as one of my clients.

Jersey Jim is gone from the John Doe file cart. Which must mean that Jersey Jim is no longer John Doe. Now he's James Benison or Jeremiah Butterworth or Jason Perricelli. Now he's caught. Now he's in jail, probably awaiting trial. Maybe he's plead guilty already and nodded his head when the prosecutor read the indictment in open court. "To wit: cocaine."

When the clerk comes back from her captivating coffee break, I'll ask her how to locate his new indictment and find out what happened to him. Poor guy.

The John Doe with the Sunshine bumper sticker is still in the cart though. I read through the indictment again and think of Patty. Think of possibilities. Perhaps. Perhaps. I could have moved to Staten Island and been a sore spot to Cousin Dominic for the rest of his life. Perhaps. Perhaps. Or I could have convinced Patty to leave her awful family and move across the country with me. We could have taken up residence in San Diego, where there is a nice zoo and it would be too warm to wear this red wool suit. I hope they find John Doe and his stupid car with the yellow bumper sticker and give him the death penalty.

I veer my thoughts back to my project for Professor Yarnes, but it takes more effort than I think it should. My trustworthy talent, controlling my mind, seems less reliable these days. I rummage for a yellow legal pad, sniffing the leather of my black briefcase for motivation. I shift the yellow rectangle on the water-warped veneer of the desk, as if it is a flower—a blocky daffodil—I am arranging on an ancient pedestal. I poise my pen in anticipation of any profound insight which might drift my way, although even the smallest bit of data will suffice. I am eager for anything.

Anything except this.

I hold the indictment in my hand.

Of course, it is a dream. I'm in my back bedroom, the first lights of the morning sifting through my three glass graces. I blink and blink and blink. But I cannot wake myself up. There is a huge crack in the wall and I cannot erase it no matter how I concentrate.

I can only hold the piece of paper, such ordinary paper, although perhaps a little thicker than the cheap sheets of my yellow legal pad. A nice bond. And white. A harsh glare under the flickering fluorescence of the government lights. If I tilt the paper at the right angle, I can make the words disappear. But even the slightest motion makes them reappear.

I re-read it.

> The People of the State of New York
> v.
> Jane Doe
> a/k/a Tamara
> a/k/a Sarah Tudor
> a/k/a Dominique
> a/k/a unknown
> For the offense of prostitution.

Think. Think. It's not me who has been indicted. It's Jane Doe and Tamara and Sarah Tudor and Dominique.

Think more clearly. Move past denial. Confront the situation.

Think. Think. The offense of prostitution. Not such an important crime. Nobody will be spending much time on this.

Think again. Jersey Jim the drug dealer is no longer John Doe but Patty's murderer is still anonymous.

Think. Think. Margaret Smyth's career is over. Everything I worked so hard and so long for . . .

Think. I am under indictment.

Think escape. I will slip this piece of milky treachery under the pages of my daffodil yellow legal pad and into the safety of the black leather of my briefcase and out of this ugly building and into the busy anonymous street.

"How's it going? I really like that bright red suit."

Casual. Casual. I slide the indictment back into the files, nestling it among its crisp companions. Look toward the voice. It's the clerk, back from her romantic interlude at the coffee stand.

I am trying to smile at her. Trying to act indifferent toward the Jane Doe indictments. Trying to be normal.

Think. Think.

I need to think.

"No really," she says, flipping her Cleopatra bangs back from her forehead in a useless motion. "I just love that suit."

I resist the urge to tell her she can have it. To ask her for her clothes in exchange. To ask her for her life. A clerk in a government office having a fling with the clerk in the coffee shop. A regular dyke doing regular dyke things. Working for a living. Going to the movies. A bar on Friday nights. Bringing a huge flower arrangement to her mother on Mother's Day. Along with her new girlfriend. "You'll love her, Mom." And after a while, Mom's reservations do erode and the coffee shop girl is absorbed into the big and happy family.

"Thanks," I say, reaching for my beautiful black leather briefcase. Not the ugly tapestry attaché, the one I wish I had with me right now.

She is smiling, but not at me, not at anybody in this ugly hallway.

"I've got to get to class," I mumble my excuse, walking as slowly as I can manage away from her and the file cart.

I head towards the coffee shop, but veer away. It's too close. Too much of a connection. I will choose a different one. Somewhere anonymous.

I start to walk. But everyplace seems too crowded. Or not crowded enough. That's the whole problem with this city. There's no place that is safe.

Tamara. So, it must have been Ann-Marie who went to the police. Ann-Marie and her Christmas conversion. Probably told her minister husband all about it. And not content to leave it in God's hands, they filed a complaint with the cops. Had to drive all the way into the city. The two of them, holding hands. And then going home and fucking, I suppose. All apologies and coffee. I hope she's started on a coffee binge. And that her liver explodes from the caffeine.

But that doesn't help me.

Tamara. Ann-Marie. Which means they know where I live. Sarah Tudor's apartment, the name on the lease at least. And Dominique. So, there must be some investigation. Some neighbor who confused me with her. You know us whores, we all look alike. And we never age.

We are always under forty. We plan, but our plans unravel at the seams.

What a big mistake. Ann-Marie.

But that doesn't help me.

Think. Think.

Do not panic. Just because I saw a Jane Doe indictment for Tamara and Sarah Tudor and Dominique, doesn't mean anything about me. Doesn't mean I'll be going to jail.

Of course it does. This is exactly the sort of thing that those prosecutors love. Law student prostitute. The lesbian angle makes it all the more titillating. I can already see the newspapers.

A huge coffee shop, near a university. I try to blend in with the academics. But my suit, that stupid red merino wool, is a problem. Unless I imagine myself as a job applicant. An applicant. I need a new job. I need a new life.

I need a plan. A plan to get to Plan B.

I order coffee—a latte—and a spinach salad.

I drink the coffee.

I push around the leaves of spinach.

I need to be sensible. I need not to panic. I need to be careful.

Going home is out of the question. Sarah Tudor lives there with Dominique and Tamara. They are the criminal Jane Doe.

Margaret Smyth is still safe. Maybe. Her name is not on the indictment. No one knows she is an "also known as." At least, not yet. But if they get into the apartment, they will. I've got to get home. And get her stuff out of there.

And get to my tapestry briefcase.

Think money. Think escape.

Pick a passport and start all over.

I am getting closer to a plan.

A carefully dangerous plan. I'll have to go back to the apartment. Get that ugly stupid attaché. Get cash. New ID. The safe deposit key. Why didn't I take at least the key with me this morning? I should have it with me all the time. I should have an extra one.

And why did I wear red? Arrest me red. I'll have to get different clothes. Stop at the same place Patty bought me the black T-shirt. I'll get a pair of Indian print harem pants, like she wore. Like I never wear. Just in case I need to pretend I'm someone else.

Get into the apartment. Destroy Margaret Smyth. The law books and the papers. Not much has her name on it; I've always been careful. But just the books would be a connection. Most people don't have law books hanging around their apartments.

Forget the apartment. Too risky. But the key; I need the key. What happened to that copy? Is it at school? Yes. Yes. My locker.

No. No. I wouldn't have done that. I didn't do that.

I should have done that. Would do it now if I had the chance. But I don't have a chance. No, I do. I do have a chance, just not that chance.

Think. Think.

I could go to the bank and say I lost the key.

No. No. Too much I.D. required for that.

Think. Think.

I probably have some time. No one nabbed me this morning as I sashayed out of my building right past Riverside Drive wearing this fire engine red suit.

I have to go to the apartment. I need new identification. I need cash. I need the safe deposit key. I need my tapestry attaché.

I'll wait until dark. I'll get other clothes first.

I'll go to school. Try to salvage whatever I can of Margaret Smyth. Catch Professor Gertrude Yarnes during lunch and make excuses to her. A sick mother in Australia. In case I need a recommendation later; in case I can resurrect Margaret Smyth at another law school.

In case this is good-bye.

part eight

BJ

twenty-two

*T*he red velvet dress has a wide lace collar, detachable. Brad is spending the day with Bethany, giving her a single white rose. I am beginning to suspect he is involved with the Mob, but I know no one would believe me; they would think I was just jealous.

I am sitting at home, sitting on the couch, watching myself in a red dress on a large screen. I am eating chocolates, given to me by the actor who plays Brad. Dagoberto reaches into the heart-shaped box and takes one.

"I hope it's a caramel," he says.

I do not reply.

"Aren't you glad I tape the show for you?" Dagoberto asks.

I do not reply.

I only look—pointedly, I hope—at the new large screen television set. The two JVC VCRs. The Panasonic edit-controller box, perched precariously on his lap as if it were smaller and cheaper, like some remote control. I know enough about equipment to know this stuff is expensive. I am an actor, after all. This is part of my business.

Certainly more expensive than Lenore's five-hundred-dollar-a-month Visa credit limit.

I should get up off this couch right now and get on the phone and start calling the bank that has Lenore's Visa account; the banks that have my Visa accounts. He must be charging all this stuff on something.

But I don't move.

I am paralyzed.

Paralyzed by being a goody-goody, by other people's inaction. I guess I had expected that Dagoberto would have left for warmer climes by now. His latest project is persuading me that he and Lenore were leaving for Greece, as soon as they saved the money. I'm almost ready to write them out a check. While they were gone, I could spirit Malcolm away. We could start over. Take Two. I'm getting as bad as Lenore.

I am sitting on the couch watching myself, or really watching Mavis Paige in her red velvet dress with its wide lace detachable collar, and feeling sorry for her because I think she still loves Brad. I know that I—BJ Willensky—am much more pitiful than Mavis Paige will ever be. The writers would never allow even Mavis Paige to be pathetic enough to allow a strange man who says he is the sperm donor of her lover's child to move into her house and stay and stay. The cameras would never record Mavis sitting on a couch with him on a winter morning—and not just any winter morning, but Valentine's Day—letting him snatch a piece of chocolate.

It can't get any worse, I think. Unlike daytime drama, real life is boring, even when it's complicated. Nothing will happen. We will go on like this for years and years.

It will snow forever.

I try to convince myself it is the snow that paralyzes me. I do a pretty good job, because as soon as the blizzard is over, Malcolm and I shovel the long driveway. I do think that Dagoberto or even Lenore will come out and help us. But they sit inside, probably still watching television, rewinding me on the television set. Dagoberto probably still has his arm on the back of the couch, behind Lenore, as if they are a normal American couple in a normal house. They are still eating my chocolates.

Neither Malcolm nor I mention Lenore or Dagoberto. What would we say? In the hushed white world, we can pretend that they did not exist. That there is only us and the long driveway and the powdery fine snow.

"This snow is perfect for making snow angels, don't you think, Malcolm?" It is a confetti kind of snow, like the kind that is sprayed from cans on the set during the holiday specials. On *In the Name of Love* it always snows during Christmas.

"I guess," he says, shoveling. He is too old for snow angels, as I knew before I said it, but I like to remind him of the good times we have had. Both of us spread on the ground and waving our arms to make an imprint of wings.

We shovel quickly, along the long driveway to the road. The trees, silhouettes of themselves outlined in white, stand guard. Malcolm's face turns red with the cold and the exertion. Almost as red as his parka.

"Are we done?"

"It looks that way." I try to be cheerful, flushed with accomplishment. But I am sorry that our task—our time—is over. It doesn't matter to me that my ears are cold; I want to shovel this driveway forever.

"Your nose is bleeding," he says. His voice is flat and perhaps embarrassed. I dig in my pocket for a tissue, but can't find one. I wipe my nose on my sleeve.

"It's just the cold," I explain, as if he doesn't know.

"Well, can I go rock hunting and go over to Joshua's?"

"Fine. Have a good time." I do not tell him to be home for dinner. I do not tell him to be careful.

The afternoon sun hesitates and then erupts, making the snow sparkle like the silver of volcanic ash. Icicles hang from the gutters and the snow drifts. By now, the snow has probably turned into slush in the city. But here it is still an obscenely thick comforter, puffed in odd lumps across the frozen ground. Here it is still pristine, except where we have shoveled, except where the deer leave tracks, except where the rocks jut. Except where Malcolm and his friends have blazed trails with their huge boots and their outgrown sleds and their new snowboards.

I spend the time watching television.

I spend the time moving around the room, away from Dagoberto. He is sitting next to me, his arm across the back of the couch behind me when Lenore comes and slides next to me. Her cheeks are red and her breath is short. She takes one of my chocolates. Bites into it.

"We have a small problem."

"What?" I can't understand her through the chocolate.

"Come outside."

"It's cold as hell out there."

"It's important," she says. And because I am who I am, or because I am bored, or because I want to escape Dagoberto on the couch and Mavis on the television, I nod my head in agreement.

But I'm not going to hurry. I stop at the closet for my parka. I follow Lenore outside. Into the bare and ugly world.

The icicles drip from the heat of the house, only to pool and refreeze on the walkways. An awkward lace of bird tracks, a design without a pattern, mars the bed where tulips might bloom if spring ever arrives. The snowplows push huge boulders that block the cave of our driveway, the one Malcolm and I have shoveled. I think Lenore means to tell me that the driveway needs to be reshoveled, but we turn away from the road. Toward the river.

Toward a vast array of gray. The soft gray of the sky, striped with the remnants of clouds. The mud gray of the river, shimmering almost in a certain slant of light. The variegated gray of the trees, poking accusations at the thin air. It is difficult to believe these were the same creatures that stunned all summer with the lushness of an almost-oppressive green.

Even the evergreens have gone gray. Losing their needles to some strange winter infestation, or some disease that has crept up the ravine from the polluted river. The dying shrubs shape themselves into a problem requesting a solution, some strange topiary that suggests I call Annie, the landscaper I consulted haphazardly during the first years we lived here. Until I realized that a real house perched on a cliff could not have the grounds of an English television garden.

Until I realized that a house with Lenore could not have a gardener being paid to fertilize the azaleas who would also not be having sex with Lenore.

Lenore is standing at the rim of our yard. Posing next to a dead yew tree.

"Come closer," Lenore says.

I slide my feet toward the edge. Am I worried that she might push me down the cliff? A little.

"Closer," she whispers.

"Lenore, stop it. You know I'm afraid of heights." I talk to her as if she is a rational person. As if she cares about me.

"Look down."

I do. Or try to. I close my eyes against the dizziness. I could tumble down into the river. Just a ravine, really. Malcolm and I could climb down there, using the path we had forged; Malcolm and I have climbed down there. But from this particular point it feels more like being perched over an abyss. It is how I have always imagined hell would be.

"Look," Lenore commands.

I open my eyes.

I don't see anything.

And then I do.

The red jacket from the Eddie Bauer outlet store. The one I bought last summer at the Ocean Outlets. A good mother thinks ahead, thinks about a goose down parka at the same time as bathing suits. That too-expensive jacket. Even at the discount prices, I wouldn't pay that much for a jacket for myself. But I remember for some reason I was in the mood for indulging my child. And he loved it so, exclaiming about its inside pockets and insisting on its bright color.

He, who never seemed to stumble as he ran up and down the makeshift paths toward the river, was inside the red parka. Crumpled on a small patch of outcropping rock.

I scream his name. The wind swallows my voice.

"I told him not to go down there," Lenore yells at me. "I told him. I told him. It's all your fault. You should never have taught him to climb down there. You killed him. You killed him."

I am already scrambling down toward the red jacket.

"Go call 911," I tell her.

"No." Lenore looks at me as if I have told her to do something bizarre, to take off her clothes and jump.

"Go in the house, Lenore. And dial emergency and give them our address."

"No. I'm not going to do that. You're just concerned about the kid. Not about me. We can have another kid, BJ. I can make everything up to you. You think I don't love you but I do."

I start down the rocks.

Lenore grabs at my parka.

"I'll do anything to make you happy, BJ. Really. This has all been a mistake. I never meant to hurt you. I think we should forget about Malcolm, forget about Dagoberto. It could be just the two of us again."

"Get the hell out of my way." I want to push her. Back toward the house, back to the telephone.

"That's what you think, isn't it? That I hold you back?" Lenore's fists close around my jacket. "Well, maybe I do. My life is such shit. I should just jump off this cliff."

"Then why the fuck don't you?" I yell. Suddenly, that is the only thing that would seem right. It has melodrama; it has justice. She had wanted this house perched on these cliffs, told me my objections were ridiculous, made fun of my fear of heights. She should die here. Die on these rocks.

The episode would be good for a Friday cliff-hanger.

And Malcolm and I could live happily ever after. Except for the scenes in which he has a lover of whom I disapprove, but we will work that out, I'm sure. After some uncertainties and wild days, he will join me in my practice as a do-good lawyer. If it gets a bit monotonous being the boring nice-guy, I'll give him the advice by which I live: Survival is better than top-billing.

I pull away from Lenore. She is crazy, I remind myself. I instruct her to call 911, using my most patient voice. She disappears from my sight, but not because she is running back to the house but because I am scrambling down the cliff. On one of those paths, narrow and haphazard as if for deer, more suited to goats. The way Malcolm always told me to go. The safest route, he said, as if he were a guide on an excursion through unmapped territory and I were some citified pioneer. He was too old to play explorers, so he substituted retellings from his social studies textbook. He told me about Henry Hudson, who stuck his name to the river below us, and about Cortez. He told me about Lewis and Clark. I was a willing student. If I had learned those things in school, I didn't remember them and Malcolm didn't ask me if I did. He seemed to himself the first person in the world to learn these things and it seemed that way to me, too.

It takes me longer than the blazing of the Northwest Passage before I reach the red parka, my Pacific Ocean. Without the roar of a pulse.

I slap his face.

He does not move.

I cannot tell if he feels cold. The wind blows snow into our faces.

I scream his name. Malcolm. The name I gave him. The name that persisted. One of the few things I ever denied Lenore was changing Malcolm's name. After she tried to kill him, she wanted to change his name from Malcolm and call him Bob. Or perhaps Dylan. Or Thaddeus. She said that she didn't want to be reminded of what she had done. And it made a certain sense, I admitted it even then. But for some reason, I wouldn't go along with it.

"I'm not going to humor you about this the way I do the furniture." I was trying the direct approach, which Mimi advised, if not Dr. Henry.

"What's the difference?" Lenore had asked. She seemed like she really didn't know the answer. And I didn't know how to supply one, didn't know how to explain the difference between our child and a couch.

I only knew that if she tried to call him Bob, I'd correct her. I'd say Malcolm. The way I am saying it now. Over and over and over.

Only now he is not smiling. Or making a sound that could be a murmur or a word or a giggle.

I've got to get him back to the house.

How?

I cannot carry him up the cliff. He is not two years old or twenty pounds anymore, even if I am as strong as I was then. Didn't I carry him everywhere? Didn't I hide him from Lenore after she came back from the hospital? Didn't I put him on my back and cart him through the crowds at some parade? Wasn't I strong?

I lift him over my shoulder, as if he doesn't weigh as much as he does, as if every amphetamine I'd ever eaten was still in my bloodstream. Just waiting for this moment.

Steady him with one hand. Steady myself against the sharp rocks with the other hand. I should have gloves, but I don't. Leather gloves, lined with fleece. My parka catches and rips on something, a frozen sticker bush I think. I hold him tighter, protecting his expensive red coat. I don't make it very far up the ravine before I remember that I am terrified of heights. I remind myself not to look down. I look up, up. Up where the house must be waiting for us. Up where the emergency vehicles must be and some firefighters with a rope must already be approaching the edge to hoist us toward the flat ground. Up to the sky, the horizon broken by what must be the ledge of the backyard.

twenty-three

I am sitting on the couch wrapped in my maroon bathrobe. It really isn't maroon, it's a blush-rose color, but we call it maroon because of Malcolm. Malcolm and my suitcase, which is also a blush-rose color. Malcolm, who had to pack for a school overnight trip to an upstate ecological center and didn't want to use my suitcase because it was blush-pink, but all the things he had to take—things like a raincoat and a binder and three sweaters and rainboots and an extra pair of sneakers and three pairs of pants, according to the list sent home from school—would not fit into his usual suitcase, which was a respectable brown. And so, he borrowed my rose-pink suitcase after I told him that it wasn't pink at all. It was maroon, really. The same color as my bathrobe.

Dagoberto is sitting next to me, his arm spread on the back of the couch behind me. He holds the edit-controller for the television and VCRs as if it is a weapon. The television with its huge screen, connected to two VCRs, is his command station in this undeclared war.

I am on the screen. The low-cut maroon sweater reveals the top of my breasts. My hair is swept up in a barrette. My lips are painted a luxurious red and my eyelashes groomed with a thick mascara. I am laughing, pretending to drive across the countryside. If there is a place I am going—a place other than the wild blue yonder—it is not obvious.

Dagoberto clicks.

I am on the screen. The black dress with three small silver buttons at the neck looks wrinkled. My hair is lopsided, hanging around my face. My skin is mottled and my hand presses against my forehead. I am crying, pretending to weep. If there is a reason that I am crying—a reason other than the bad makeup and shoddy camerawork—it is not apparent.

Dagoberto clicks.

Brad is with Bethany. He comes up behind her and puts his hands a little too close to the bottom of her breasts. She turns around to face him and steps back. She perfects her look of fury, the professional close-up revealing her upper lip curled into her trademark seductive snarl. Maybe she will actually slap him this time.

Dagoberto clicks.

Brad is with Mavis Paige. He comes up to me and hugs my wrinkled black dress. He awkwardly attempts a hug, but twists out of focus. The view bumps away from his face and settles on his shoulder. Then his hand goes to my cheek, as if he could smooth away the mottled makeup job. The shot shifts to a flower arrangement, predominantly white.

Dagoberto clicks.

Bethany's mother is walking down the corridor of the hospital. Her crisp emerald green suit becomes her almost as much as her long-suffering smile. Her whispers permeate, as if they are our own thoughts instead of her thoughts. She is afraid that the operation will not be a success. She is afraid the baby will not live. Bethany's sister, Grace, might not make it either. "Dear God," Bethany's mother thinks/prays/whispers.

Dagoberto clicks.

My mom, Evelyn, and Mimi are standing very close together, obviously anxious. They turn, simultaneously, toward Lenore's sister, Lenore. Mimi clasps her hands in front of her dark jacket that doesn't quite close. Lenore's sister Lenore has a weak smile for them. Did I finally get them to come and visit the set? How did I arrange for this fantasy, a bit part for them? And why isn't the camera more kind? Or at least focused on their faces instead of their chests.

Dagoberto clicks.

Bethany is talking to a woman she calls Georgia. Georgia wears a nurse's hat perched on her blond hair. Georgia is gay, or so she tells Bethany in a serious tone that nevertheless maintains its relentless perkiness. Bethany says, "That's nothing to be ashamed of, Georgia. I respect you for who you are—not who you happen to sleep with."

Dagoberto clicks.

My favorite director walks past the white flower arrangement. Malcolm's friend, Joshua, and Joshua's mother, the social worker, walk past the white flower arrangement. Lenore . . .

Dagoberto clicks.

The low-cut maroon sweater reveals the top of my breasts as they almost touch the steering wheel. My mascaraed eyes widen in amazement and terror. There is a sound of screeching. I can hear my own scream. My irises reflect the fire as it threatens to engulf my beautiful red sports car. I frantically tug at my seat belt.

"Wasn't it wonderful of Dagoberto to video the funeral? This way the new baby will see it all." Lenore is sitting on the other side of Dagoberto; I lean around him to see her patting her flat stomach. I don't know how long she has been here, watching. I don't know what she is talking about. Mavis Paige is not dead, that was her evil twin. That was the same damn clip from several hundred episodes ago, when my evil twin died in a fiery car crash. They must be replaying it for some reason. They can't mean to kill off Mavis Paige. And even if they did, they couldn't do it this way. The viewers would protest. I have fans. Loyal fans. Women come up to me and introduce themselves. Lots of women. Like the one who introduced herself as Ann-Marie and told me she was from Connecticut, too, only I saw her with Margaret, Gertrude Yarnes' student or prostitute. They wouldn't replace Mavis Paige. That would never happen.

But they wouldn't have a dyke either. Who the hell is Georgia? And if they are going to have a dyke, that should be me. Everybody thinks so. Even those dykes I met at the women's beach. Nurses, I think. They knew that Mavis Paige was really a lesbian. I've been waiting twenty years for this story line. It has to be me. Me and Bethany, maybe. Or even me and Georgia. Yes, that's it. Georgia is just being introduced so that she can become my lover. Yes. A nurse is simply perfect. I'll lose my memory in the car crash. Georgia's specialty is amnesiacs. She'll nurse me back to health and we'll fall in love.

On the show and in real life.

I'll leave Dagoberto and Lenore sitting on this couch for the rest of their lives, watching episodes of *In the Name of Love*. I'll go call Evelyn and Mimi and tell them their spot on the show was just great, even though it wasn't I don't want to hurt their feelings. I'll invite that woman BJ out for coffee; we'll go to a nice little café. I'll introduce her to Malcolm. I need to check on him soon, shouldn't he be home from Joshua's house by now?

If there was a door to this room, I would close it.

twenty-four

A March morning. A Thursday. I wear a pair of black jeans. A black shirt. No coat, although it is cold on this bluff. Not as cold as it has been.

Not cold enough for Lenore to put back on her clothes. She wanders from room to room, not dragging any furniture behind her. She is pretending she is crazy.

Pretending that nothing happened. Pretending that I still do not remember. But I am starting to remember, to thaw. Like the river below me, I am no longer clogged with ice.

Pretending that she was not waiting at the top of the ledge when I finally dragged Malcolm to the top. Pretending that, when I asked her whether she had called 911, she said that she had, instead of asking whether Malcolm was dead.

"Call emergency," I insisted, but she didn't move. So I hefted Malcolm past her and past the dead evergreens and into the house, putting him on the couch and pushing buttons on the phone, and opening Malcolm's mouth, pinching his nose and blowing my breath into his throat like I had learned on the set.

I called out for Dagoberto; I could hear the television. I yelled into the phone; I kept saying our address.

I cursed myself for not having called emergency before I went down the cliff; I'd have had them waiting for me when I got back to the house. I cursed myself for not paying better attention during the first aid training. I unzipped Malcolm's red parka and pushed my scratched hands against his chest as if I could jump-start his heart.

"Get away from him," Lenore screamed. "You look like a vampire. You're all bloody."

I did taste blood. Mine.

She kept yelling about vampires, but she did not approach me. I would have killed her, I'm sure. I just kept blowing into Malcolm's mouth. Just kept pushing on his adolescent chest. When the rescue squad finally arrived, they quickly assigned one woman to keep Lenore out of the way.

"What's wrong with her?"

"She's not good in emergencies," I remember saying.

I remember acting good in this emergency. Acting calm. Acting.

Someone gave me a tissue to wipe the blood that still flowed from my nose. The tissue was an ugly white.

The sirens roared him away. I was with him. I sat close to the stretcher and the tubes and the hope. I kept the tissue in my fist.

The emergency technicians guarded their speech. I could tell they thought it was hopeless. That they thought he was dead.

Which is what the doctor told Lenore.

Not me. Lenore.

Lenore who got to the hospital later. Lenore who had not been sitting here the past five hours like I had. Lenore who didn't give a damn.

"I'm very sorry," the doctor said to Lenore.

To me he said, "You look pretty banged up. We could give you something."

"I want my son," I said.

He looked at me puzzled. Walked away. Talked to a nurse down the hall who looked at me but did not come over. I sat in the waiting room and waited some more. Waited for some different news.

It was Dagoberto who arranged everything. The flowers. The notices. The memorial service.

It was Dagoberto who videotaped the whole damn thing. Dago-

246

berto who preserved what is better forgotten. I cannot remember what I really saw and what I resaw through the lens of his camcorder.

At the edge of the ravine, I try to piece it together. This is what I remember: Lenore's psychiatrist, Dr. Sidney Henry, came to the funeral. My mom and Mimi came up from Philadelphia. They both looked awful.

The entire cast and most of the directors, prop girls, and costumers of *In the Name of Love* came up from the city. Bethany gave me a hug.

Malcolm's sixth grade class, including Joshua, came to the memorial service. His teacher sobbed into my arms. I comforted her. Joshua's mother kept patting my arm.

I remember waiting for someone to announce it was the end of the day's taping. I was taking care not to further wrinkle the black dress I must have borrowed from another actor. I don't look good in black.

I was crying my beautiful cry, with my eyes brimming but my nose staying flawless. Although Brad was critical: "You look really bad. Let me know if there's anything I can do."

Dagoberto's video has a close-up shot of the headstone. It is the best focused shot, although the angle distorts. Still, one can read the text quite clearly. The headstone is engraved: BELOVED SON OF LENORE AND DAGOBERTO LUX. More proof that it is not my Malcolm buried there. Buried anywhere.

Every morning I come out to this bluff and look down the jagged path which juts down to the river. Every morning I look for him.

He must be at Joshua's house, sleeping over again. Trying to get away from this house that has become a crypt. I need to do something so that Malcolm can come home. I need to have a plan.

I should talk to Lenore. She seems too lucid, too logical, as if nothing has changed. She is always naked, but other than that, she seems very normal except that she is always talking about getting pregnant.

I stand at the rim of the cliff. Almost half of my foot hangs over the empty air. I stand there and stand there.

A lot.

Every morning.

When it is dark and when it is not.

If I had a psychiatrist, she would come and rescue me.

If I had friends who hadn't abandoned me before this, they would abandon me now.

If Dagoberto wasn't always sitting on the couch, in a room that could be a den, watching the giant screen he controls with his remote, even he might be someone I would talk to. Instead, I walk by and see him watching me on television, rewinding me and playing me again. Sometimes, he invites me to sit down next to him, but that seems like something that I shouldn't do.

It is only ever Lenore who comes and stands next to me on this outcropping of rock, hanging over the river. When she is not here, I sometimes think that she is all that I have left and that we have been through so much together. I should feel compassion. I know I should. Instead of emptiness.

Which changes into something else when she is standing next to me. She is naked and it is cold and it is early morning. She is not eating a chocolate, but she could be.

She killed him, I think.

She killed him.

She is screaming this morning. There are words in her screams, but I don't care enough about her to excavate them from the sound.

"Shut up," I say.

"Is that what I should do? What should I do? Just tell me what to do."

The arch of her foot is only half on the ground. She looks down the cliff, like the bottom has eyes, the eyes of a lover who returns her gaze. Once, she must have looked at me like that. Once, but I don't remember. I only remember the chocolate. And the weight of Malcolm's body as I carried him back up the rocks. My red velvet dress must have been ripping on every frozen bush.

I am wearing black. Black jeans. Black sweater. Black boots.

I will always be wearing red velvet. I will always hear Lenore screaming about Malcolm's blood on my mouth. But it wasn't his blood. It was my blood. My nose always bleeds in the cold. It was cold then.

I will always wonder. A little faster. If I had not have stopped to get my parka. A little more careful. If I had been out here with him, instead of inside an empty house pretending everything was fine.

A grayness beyond gray. Even the small patches of shining quartz cannot relieve the grayness. Malcolm loves the quartz. He tries to chip it out with a sharpened stick. He has a little collection. It's in a box in his room in the house behind us. His room. His collection.

I move my foot back and forth on the edge. I am no longer afraid to look down. I am no longer afraid of heights. There is nothing left to fear. I am right on the ledge. Where Malcolm must have fallen. Chipping quartz underneath the snow. The sharp stick no protection against gravity.

The path is over to our left. I think about scrambling down that path sometimes. I think about taking Lenore down there. Make her walk back up, carrying something. A stone the size of a child. Anything. It wouldn't make a difference to her.

Almost blue, the river shimmers. Beneath us both. Far beneath us both. I think it calls my name, but I can't tell what name it is calling me. BJ? Beverley Jane? Jill? Mavis? What name will I be called by, when I am called?

Lenore. The name echoes up from the water, through the palisades. Weren't these cliffs formed by glaciers? Didn't I learn that in school? Or did she tell me that?

Lenore. Her name. Her sisters' name. Her mother's name. Her father's other wives' name. My voice. My voice inflected with the voice of my junior high school English teacher, reciting some creepy poem about a bird. A hawk flies by, below us, deep in the ravine, far above the river.

"Jump," I say.

At first in my own head.

And then out loud. To her.

"Jump," I say. I look at Lenore, look at her as deep as I can, as if her eyes were at the bottom of these bluffs which lead to a river which flows downstream past a city and into an ocean.

"Jump," I say. "Right here. Over the edge."

Her foot caresses the farthest outcropping of rock.

Then she takes a step; it isn't a jump. Just a casual movement. Like children closing their eyes and walking off a diving board, pretending to be shocked when their feet find nothing solid waiting beneath them.

Or I push her.

Either way, it doesn't matter.

Either way, I murdered her.

Either way, Lenore does not scream.

I have to get very close to the edge to see her naked body down on the rocks. Looking down makes me dizzy.

I think I'll go to the kitchen and make some breakfast.

Toast. Yes. And more coffee.

I put the coffee cup into the microwave so that the liquid will be hot. I want my throat to scald. To sterilize.

"I saw everything." The voice is Dagoberto's.

I look at him and see Malcolm's jawline.

"I want everything."

"Everything?" Does he think I have something left to lose? I have already lost everything.

"Or you go to jail. For a very long time."

"You've been watching too much television," I say, sipping my steaming coffee. Noticing his hair, so blond it looks like a white halo. Was it always so blond? It is lighter than Malcolm's. Much lighter.

"I'm learning how to get what I want."

"What is it you want?"

"What you have."

"You must be joking." Maybe he thinks I mean that his request is unreasonable. What I mean is that I don't have anything. Not anything that matters.

"I'm not. I could live a very fine life. The problem with you is that you don't know how to enjoy the things you have. I want this house. And the beach house. And all that cash you have snookered away." His accent is less sharp and his diction more sloppy.

"What are you talking about?" How much cash do I have? And what does he know about? He can't know too much, since his only source would be Lenore.

"Simple. You provide me with a comfortable life. I don't tell the police."

"They wouldn't believe anything you said. Lenore jumped. She's been threatening to kill herself for twenty years. I have a drawer full of her suicide notes."

"Not anymore, darling. I've taken care of that."

"Her psychiatrist knows."

"If you think Dr. Sid is going to save you, then you can take your chances. He'd probably be more likely to believe me that you killed Lenore because she was leaving you for me."

"I'm not sure your testimony could hold up in court. Who are you anyway? Some New Age Nazi war criminal? Some flimflam man? You probably have a record as long as my arm."

"Really, BJ. Just because you're a lawyer on a television program, don't think you know anything about the law."

"What I do know is that you're just some lowlife."

"It doesn't matter, BJ. It won't matter if you ultimately win. You'll be ruined anyway. You'll lose this house paying off your lawyers. And you'll never get back your job—or any job—with this kind of scandal. They won't want you if you're suspected of being a murderer. What will they say in *Soap Opera Universe*? And what about your parents? What about them?"

Mimi would punch you right in the mouth, I think.

"We'll have to do it slowly," I say. I am starting to bargain. I want to live. To save what's left of my life. If I'm capable of murder, I'm capable of calculation. I'm a late-bloomer, but I have the advantage of twenty years of listening to people deliver the right lines.

"Fine." Dagoberto smiles. "But I want all the legalities taken care of right away. And money."

"I don't have much money."

"I've seen your contracts, BJ. You make a lot of money."

"Lenore costs a great deal."

"Yes, but you're the frugal type. This is the rainy day you've been saving for. You need to get your hands on lots of cash."

"I don't keep cash around."

"You can liquidate some of those bank accounts. And use your charge cards. Cash advances. Very handy. And I think you still have some cash available." He laughs. "You have very good credit, you know."

"Or did." I realize how he's been buying his watches and video equipment. "Anyway, I'll need money to buy an apartment in the city."

"You can rent. Like the peons."

"I'll make an appointment with my lawyer."

"No. You can go to the bank today, BJ. We can worry about the papers later."

"While I'm gone, you take care of Lenore."

"I'll call 911. And I'll arrange a nice funeral for her, BJ."

Maybe it's the last comment. Or the memory of Malcolm.

But something strange settles in me. I go inside to change my clothes. A different pair of black jeans. A black shirt. My costume these days. I rummage through the closet, looking for something else, although I am not sure what. Some vinyl attaché full of passports? One for Wilhelm Heinrich, or some other suitably Nazi name? Something I could use to blackmail Dagoberto, as if anybody cared any more about a bunch of war criminals and their children who have grown up to be vaguer sorts of criminals.

In the bathroom, I wonder about makeup. Some eyeliner? Black, of course. No. My eyes are too puffy to support the sleek lines of dark chemicals; my hands too unsteady to manipulate the brush with any accuracy. Is there anything else in the cabinet? Among the towels and shampoo I spot an unfamiliar bottle. Ah, peroxide. Dagoberto lightens his hair. He probably isn't really a Nazi. Just like he probably isn't really Malcolm's sperm donor. Not that it matters. Nothing matters. I laugh out loud.

Check the medicine cabinet—perhaps some aspirin?—but it is filled with Lenore's tranquilizers and my diet pills. I laugh again, more quietly. Wherever I'm going, I won't need either of them. If I grow out of these jeans, I'll buy more. Black ones.

I look in the hall closet for a suitcase.

I find something in black leather. I don't remember buying it. I don't remember what it's called. Too small for a suitcase. Too large for a briefcase.

"Going somewhere?" Dagoberto stands in the doorway now. His hair looks less blond since I found the bottle.

"You should use less Clairoxide," I say. "Streak it more. It looks a little fake."

"I don't need your beauty advice. Where are you going?" He is standing very close to me now. The sharp protrusion of his Adam's apple is pointing right at my nose. From this angle, his face is not like Malcolm's.

"To the bank."

"Ah. For the money." He has a sparkling laugh as he steps back, bringing his jawline into my view again. Malcolm's jawline. Maybe.

"Money," I repeat.

"You know, Lenore was wrong about you. She always said you were such a goody-goody. But you are just a whore, like the rest of us."

"Whore?" When I repeat it, the word sounds hollow. The word sounds like something my mother Evelyn would say—did say—and Mimi would—did—say was too extreme. The word sounds like some meaningless worry, left over from my adolescence.

"Yes. Just a prostitute. Willing to sell yourself. High-priced, of course, as fits your station in life." He waves his arm across the horizon of the house as if he is a dancer and this is a tragic ballet. "But the price always requires negotiation, I suppose."

I wipe some lint off my jeans. Wearing black is so high maintenance. She was wearing black the last time I saw that woman. Her.

When I heard she was a prostitute. That's what that drama profes-sor said. After she said sex worker. Then prostitute, as if I didn't know what a sex worker was. Pronouncing the word "prostitute" like it was from a foreign language, like it was exotic. Like it could shock. Like I didn't see those women all the time, didn't walk past them that very night.

Like I wasn't one, too. At least according to Dagoberto.

I should tell him that Lenore was wrong about him, too. She had told me he was so smart, "brilliant" I think she said. But he must be stupid not to see that I am not a prostitute, I am a murderer. Or that even if this is prostitution, he's the whore selling something and I am the one who is buying.

Otherwise I would not be off to the bank for the money.

He tries to kiss me good-bye as we walk outside. Away from the cliffs, towards my little car in the driveway.

"You know," he says, "it doesn't have to be this way. You have an-other choice."

"Oh?" I notice the darkness of his hair near the roots. He really should be more careful.

"We could be together. Go off together. It's always been you who I really loved, not Lenore. I've confessed that before. It's still true. I still love you. Only you."

"Still? Knowing everything you know?" My eyes tilt up toward his. It is a perfect gesture of devotion. Angle closer. The morning sun-light is too diffuse, too damp with the struggle of spring. The light should be more intense. We shouldn't be doing this outside. I knew I should have worn some eyeliner for emphasis.

"You were in a terrible situation. And I feel bad that I couldn't help you more. But we could start over. Just the two of us."

I let him kiss the side of my face.

It is difficult not to be curious. This plot will twist and turn. What can the diabolical Dagoberto have up his sleeve? He is already going to get everything he wants—all my money—why should he want me?

254

I pull out of the driveway, such a terrible incline, and drive through the winding narrow streets through this perfect little hamlet.

At the bank, I sit on the wrong side of one of those little desks, like I have done so many times before. Luckily, my usual banker is there. She has been so helpful over the years. Advising this or that. Assisting me with my particular problems. A crazy lover. Although I may not have ever mentioned Lenore was crazy. May have just pretended that I was uncertain and cautious. I was simply being sane to protect myself from some transient lover. Even after all these years. After all, weren't these lesbian relationships sort of unstable by nature?

Of course, I always remember the bank advisor at Christmas. Last year, I gave her . . . something. I don't remember, but I'm sure it was something suitable. Maybe even that lovely scarf she is wearing.

The scarf that looks rather sophisticated as she is advising me against what I am doing. She tells me that I'll have to pay penalties and lose interest.

"If you can just wait," she says.

I shake my head and insist on cashing in the certificates. I wonder if she has heard about what happened with Malcolm. I am grateful that she doesn't mention it, but I think she looks at me with a sad slant to her expression.

I transfer the money to my Bahamian bank account. Opened years ago as protection against Lenore and Lenore's creditors. Now it is protection against Lenore's boyfriend.

At my safe deposit box, I take out the cash and put it in my black overnight bag. Leather. That's what they call it, an overnighter.

Blackmail, that's what they call it.

Or maybe it is just my excuse to escape.

An escape he tried to prevent with the promise of love. What do they call that?

Another sort of blackmail? I love you. Always a form of blackmail. Always?

I take my documents. My passport.

The deeds to the houses. I need to take care of Evelyn and Mimi. Not all love is ugly. Some love is simple.

Or at least it seems that way.

I drive toward the city. Stop at an office supply store. The deeds are in a rack, at the back of the store. I don't know which kind I need—I guess I thought there was only one kind—so I buy one of every type: fee simple and life estate and quit claim. I know I'll need help figuring out which one to use, figuring out how to fill it out. I haven't needed anyone named Lenore to tell me I'm not all that smart. But I'm smart enough to know when I need help. Just a bit of advice with the final arrangements.

I head for her office.

part nine

Coda

twenty-five

*T*his Thursday morning in that sodden middle-of-the-semester month of March, she puts the key in the lock in the doorknob, having to force it a little and jiggle it a great deal. It seems as if the lock is getting more and more temperamental, as if everything is lurching toward disrepair in these days of budget cuts. Even her name on the door is flaking off, deteriorating into specks of gold glitter. For some reason, the capitals were the first to crumble: The door announces ROFESSOR ERTRUDE ARNES. She considers bringing in some Krazy Glue and glitter, but she never does, just as she never brings in the WD-40 for the lock.

Or maybe she should ask Bobbi to make her a different nameplate. In silver this time, rather than gold. Or a sign that she could simply adhere to her door, like a bumper sticker. Something permanent, or at least semipermanent. Bobbi would know what would work best; that was her business after all. "Signage," Bobbi sometimes said when one of Gertrude's acquaintances asked Bobbi what she "did." People always seem to ask Bobbi what she "does," never what her favorite color might be (green) or what books she likes to read (mysteries). Never what they really want to know: How have you and Gertrude managed to be together so long when you seem so different from each other?

If anyone had asked that, Bobbi would not have said anything profound. She would have said that love was a gift. She would have said that quarrels should be kept in perspective. She would have said that we try to be honest without using honesty as a substitute for cruelty. She would have said we still have hot sex and romantic sex and we still reach for each other's hands in our sleep.

All of which would have been unsatisfactory. Because what they really wanted to know, especially Gertrude's academic friends like that silly Teodesia (Gertrude's former lover, as Teddy always reminded Bobbi) was what Gertrude the law professor found interesting about Bobbi the printer.

Bobbi did not even print books or pamphlets. She did print letterhead (although she didn't like that much) and business cards (which she liked even less). Mostly now she did posters and stickers. Lots of fluorescent colors and seven-color print jobs. She liked a technical challenge. Even when she had been an apprentice, as she had called herself, although no one else had been looking at it that way, she enjoyed the technical aspects. She was still in her apprentice stage, taking classes at the community college and working for one of the big chains—a few years away from realizing her hope to have her own shop—when she met Gertrude. Bobbi was delivering name tags to a women's law symposium; Gertrude was a nervous student getting everything ready for the important speakers.

They never described it as love at first sight.

Because it wasn't first sight, strictly speaking. They had seen each other at women's night at a gay bar. Had looked at each other across the small smoky space, unable—and unwilling—to make eye contact. Each had gone back the next week and looked for the other, had spotted her and watched her, had thought about maybe asking her to dance, had watched her dance with other women, any of whom could have been her lover, it was so difficult to tell.

Seeing each other here, in the foyer of the law school building, well, it seemed like fate. Although neither of them would say fate any more than she would say love at first sight.

Fate was something for blind old men in Greek myths and characters in soap operas. It would not do for a woman like Gertrude, who believed in free will. It would not do for a woman like Bobbi, who took pride in her judgment of herself as practical.

So they didn't say anything. Not when the first night they were together (that night) turned into the first week and then the first month. Finally, one woman uttered the word "love" and the other answered. The first months turned into the first year and then another. Gertrude graduated and went to work for a judge. Bobbi bought a shop that was going under. Sometimes they argued about money: Gertrude was still paying back her school loans and Bobbi was paying a hefty mortgage on the shop and machines. Sometimes they argued about food or cleaning the house or some former lover. But mostly, they thought everything was idyllic. And it did not change. Not even when Gertrude got a job she hated with a law firm and then a job she loved as a professor. Not even when Bobbi got a huge contract from a guy she had known in elementary school who was now a rock concert promoter and then she hired an employee who was arrested for distributing amphetamines.

Not even now. It was still rather idyllic.

It was almost like fate. Almost like love at first sight.

Though to say this was to court disaster. It was difficult not to take each other for granted, not to take their relationship for granted. That was the danger. They talked about it sometimes. The danger and how to avoid it. They resisted becoming too smug about their love. They got each other little gifts. They took showers together on Sundays. They both knew it wasn't the little attentions that worked, however, it was simply that they liked being together.

Simply.

Or maybe there was something to that lesbian merger theory, Gertrude sometimes thought with a pang of disloyalty. Because the truth was, she couldn't imagine her own life without Bobbi. Being Bobbi's lover was as much of a part of her identity as being a professor, probably more. Sometimes she thought that's how the name plate on her door should really read: PROFESSOR & LOVER GERTRUDE YARNES. Though, of course, she wouldn't want "lover" on her law

261

school office door. And given the present sorry state of her sign, the capital L would be gone by now, leaving only "over." No, that didn't sound good at all: ROFESSOR & OVER. Rather military, she thought. She'd have to remember to tell Bobbi. And to ask her about making a proper sign. One that could weather the budget cuts.

Inside her office, she tosses her two totebags full of papers on one of the chairs and hangs up her jacket. Puts her thermos on her desk. Before she forgets, writes herself a note to remind herself to ask Bobbi about the sign. Checks her calendar for the day. Marred by an afternoon appointment with the vice-chancellor to talk about the budget. Maybe she can run to the coffee shop and get some lunch before the meeting, something good (sweet and yeasty), a reward for being so responsible, a talisman against being tactless.

Compared with enduring meetings with university administrators who seem more like businessmen than academics, teaching is easy. Not only because she has taught Criminal Procedure before—and in fact, is using the same casebook and syllabus as she did last semester—but because teaching is not boring. There is always some new insight, some flash of a student's intellect, some unforeseen development in the law.

Today's class goes well. Seventy-five minutes on one case, such is the luxury of law school pedagogy. Yet this case deserves such devotion. The multiple opinions of the Supreme Court Justices take at least a half hour to untangle. The facts, always both complicated and intriguing in Criminal Procedure cases, are even more complicated and intriguing than usual. There are two confessions. The defendant, incarcerated on a firearms charge, admits the murder of his eleven-year-old stepdaughter to a fellow prisoner, incarcerated for extortion and now a government informant, after the prisoner/informant makes veiled threats and promises of protection. Was it entrapment? Was it truly voluntary? The professor guides and goads the students through the maze of legal doctrine.

The Court suppresses the first confession. Which makes the real question in the case whether the second—and now only admissible—confession was credible enough to support the conviction. At trial, the wife of the prisoner/informant testified that when the defendant was released from prison, she and her previously released husband picked him up. She asked the defendant a casual question about where he was heading. In response, the defendant made detailed incriminating statements concerning the murder of his eleven-year-old stepdaughter.

Gertrude puts the question like this: If you were on the jury, would you believe that the defendant would confess in detail—to a woman he had never before met—the brutal murder of his eleven-year-old stepdaughter after just being released from prison?

The class divides. Half of the students argue that confession is not only good for the soul, it is inevitable, that a man who has just been released from prison would want to unburden his conscience or perhaps even brag about a murder for which he has not been charged. The other half of the students argue that confession is not only stupid, it is not spontaneous, that a man who has just been released from prison would not want to risk returning to prison by talking to a woman he had no reason to trust.

After she allows the arguments to develop, Gertrude makes the students vote by raising their hands. This way, she hopes, even the students who do not speak in class will be participating. And, of course, she likes to see the way certain students vote, although she pretends to everyone (especially herself) that she is not interested in such things. This semester she watches two students in particular who disagree as she assumed that they would, but who do not take the sides she had predicted to herself that each would. Last semester, she had watched Margaret Smyth, her new research assistant. Margaret had not raised her hand for either choice, but pretended to be taking notes the entire time. It made Professor Gertrude Yarnes smile in spite of herself; even as she encouraged class participation she harbored an absurd respect for anyone who played it so close to the chest.

As if summoned by the memory, Margaret is waiting outside Gertrude's office door when the professor returns after class. For a moment, Gertrude does not recognize her research assistant; Margaret is not a student who would wear a bright red suit. It is Margaret's stance that betrays her to Gertrude: dyke defiance, camouflaged but still definite. In the moments before she greets her research assistant, Gertrude tries to recall several things: whether she has ever seen Margaret in such bright clothing, whether she assigned Margaret a particular task due today, and exactly what Teodesia had said about Margaret at that ridiculous book party for Teddy's new exegesis on soap operas.

Inside Gertrude's office, on the other side of the office door that Margaret had been staring at trying to figure out what to do, Margaret can barely recall the reason for her presence. It had seemed so important to see Professor Gertrude Yarnes, to offer some explanation, to secure some possibility for the continued existence of Margaret Smyth, law student and future attorney in Topeka or Toledo.

"What's up?" Gertrude Yarnes asks, achieving a casual tone.

"I think I'm going to have to withdraw for the semester."

"What's wrong?" Gertrude looks at the print of *The Three Spirits*, the one she had gotten with Bobbi when they went to Vancouver, the one she had mentioned to Margaret.

"I've got to get back home."

"Home?"

"Australia. My mother. My mother in Australia is very ill. I've got to get back."

"I'm sorry to hear that." Gertrude scrutinizes her inscrutable student. Shifting her gaze, as if seeking some wisdom, to the print on her wall. Each of the three spirits looks as implacable as ever.

"I don't see how I can help it." Margaret shakes her head. She looks like she might start to cry. She looks at the little bottle of sand. Lesbos. An island. Wasn't Sappho a prostitute? Didn't she read that somewhere?

"Is there anything I can do to help?" Gertrude is sincere, even if her sincerity is circumscribed by her grasp of her role as professor.

Tears start to seep from Margaret's unremarkable eyes.

"Sorry," Margaret says, reaching for a tissue from her bag.

264

"For what? It's certainly understandable to be upset. Not only for your mother. But also yourself. You've worked very hard."

The tears gather in little rivulets.

Then a river.

This is the thought that flows downstream: What if Gertrude had picked her off the streets that spring? Gertrude instead of Dominique. What if Gertrude had brought her home to some place with a garden and Gertrude's girlfriend had thought it was wonderful that the two of them were suddenly parents to a grimy adolescent who said she was from Australia. What if Gertrude and Bobbi (that was her name) had enrolled her in a solid high school and she had excelled and she got a scholarship to college and she was already through law school, having graduated with honors? What if? Gertrude instead of Dominique.

"I'm an escort," Margaret blurts.

Gertrude does not react.

"I'm a prostitute," Margaret tells Gertrude; tells Dominique; tells her foster mother Betty, tells anyone who might be listening.

"I know that." As she says this, Gertrude realizes that she had not believed Teodesia, that she had dismissed Teodesia's statement as yet another exercise of Teddy's melodramatic streak.

"I'm under indictment."

"I didn't know that. Give me a dollar."

Margaret reaches into her black leather briefcase and retrieves a dollar bill. Puts it on the table.

"Okay, I'm your lawyer. And as your lawyer, anything you say to me is protected by lawyer-client privilege."

"Thanks."

"I don't mean that I'm going to represent you. I . . ."

". . . just want to be protected?" Margaret supplies, remembering her professor in Professional Responsibility.

"Yes. Anyway, you might be able to make a deal. Implicate your clients. Any rich and important men? Political figures? Mobsters? Yes, mobsters would definitely be better." Gertrude is trying to recall some newspaper stories about very advantageous plea bargains.

Knowing that no matter how advantageous the plea bargain, this woman's career was ruined before it even started.

"No. No one important enough. Not even any men."

"I don't think I understand," Gertrude confesses.

"My clients aren't men."

"Then what?"

"Then women." Margaret sounds slightly annoyed.

"Women?" Gertrude struggles not to sound so nonplussed.

"Women."

"I didn't know women . . . did that sort of thing."

"Well, they do." Margaret is both defiant and defeated.

"Apparently." Gertrude regains her composure. "But women or men, I guess it doesn't diminish the problem. Are you sure you're under indictment?"

Margaret can see the Jane Doe indictment as if she is standing in the hallway of the clerk's office. Margaret can see any hope she had of reclaiming Margaret Smyth's legal career fizzle in the stale office air. She shrugs. There is no other option when one has already said too much.

Gertrude does not press for the obvious answer.

Margaret reaches for her black leather briefcase and stands up. "I guess I just wanted to say good-bye. You've been very kind to me. I don't want you to think I don't appreciate it. I always will."

Gertrude tries not to shake her head, in disbelief, in sympathy.

Margaret walks over to the office door and is about to put her hand on the knob, about to twist and turn it, about to stand in the hallway and wonder where to go next.

Gertrude quells a powerful urge to give her student—her soon-to-be-former-student—a crushing hug.

Margaret opens the office door, as if responding to a knock. The knock of a woman wearing black. Black jeans and a black shirt. Dressed like Margaret Smyth used to dress when she was Margaret Smyth.

Gertrude motions the woman inside the office. Closes the door.

Margaret is caught on the wrong side of the door. Inside. Or maybe it is not the wrong side.

The office is suddenly crowded.

BJ is pulling papers out of a pink and shiny office supply store bag. "I have a legal problem. Need to hire you. Deeds."

"Slow down." Gertrude tries to establish some sort of social order. "Mavis, I mean BJ, just hold on a minute. How about a 'hello'?"

BJ doesn't answer for a long time. And then she simply says, "Deeds."

Gertrude says, "I don't do property."

BJ puts the papers back in the bag.

Gertrude struggles for some semblance of civility.

"Do you know Margaret?"

BJ nods.

"BJ, this is Margaret." It is odd making introductions, but Gertrude sees no reason not to be polite.

Margaret mumbles, "I guess I'd better leave."

BJ blocks the door with her body, subtly. Her voice is less subtle, yet it is flattened with resignation. "I need your help. Probably both of you. I kil—"

Gertrude interrupts, "Don't say anything."

Margaret interrupts, "Give her a dollar."

BJ looks in her overnight case for a dollar.

The three women, an accidental triangle on the inside of the office door, could join hands—or at least reach out for each other—and make some sort of circle of solidarity. But they do not. They resist coincidence.

Or try to.

"Let's all sit down," Gertrude says, as if she is hosting an intimate dinner party in the house she shares with Bobbi. She dumps some pens out of a mug and cleans it with a tissue from the box she keeps on her desk. She cleans out her extra mug and does not bother to wipe out the mug she used this morning. Into the three cups, she pours out coffee from her silver thermos. There is about one-third of a mug for each of the women. "I hope you both like it light." Gertrude places a mug in front of each of her two guests, now both seated at the round table in the middle of Gertrude's office. The three women sip their meager coffee.

Gertrude knows she could say something, should say something. It would not have to be profound, an attempt at clarity would be enough. She could act like she was not a professor, a cool academic, a dyke gone soft from a cushy job. She could enter into this drama, rescue the law student who is a whore and the soap opera lawyer who may have killed someone. She could be a hero.

She clears her throat.

She looks at her silver watch.

The vice-chancellor is never late.

"I'm really sorry," Gertrude says, "I've got to get to a meeting. Important stuff about the budget crisis."

BJ stands up quickly.

Margaret rises more hesitantly.

Gertrude flicks her wrist, motioning them to sit back down. "You two stay as long as you like. Just make sure the door is locked when you leave."

Gertrude lets the door close behind her. Then she opens it again. Still standing in the hall, she cranes her head around her own office door. "Take care, you two." Gertrude lets the door slam this time.

It is not any rudeness on the part of Professor Gertrude Yarnes that startles. Or the professor's apparent belief that the law school's budget is more important that the future of either of them; both of them are accustomed to being overlooked. Or even that the professor allows them to stay in her office, which must have all sorts of secrets, or at least one confidential memo, knowing what she knows about their criminality; both of them are habituated to being thought innocent. No. What is remarkable to both women is Gertrude's use of "you two." As if they were some sort of unit. As if both of them could be captured by a single phrase. As if they would be leaving the office together, would be together.

268

Gertrude's singular implication reverberates in the office, ricocheting off *The Three Spirits,* refracted off the crystals of bright blue sand in the bottle marked LESBOS.

Meanwhile, the women exchange words, their first face-to-face words.

What would one say to someone about whom she has been thinking impossible thoughts? What would one say to someone after almost all the possibilities have been foreclosed?

"Did you really kill someone?" Margaret finally asks.

BJ stares at Margaret.

"I mean, are you sure? I've thought I've killed people, but it turned out I didn't. I mean, I was always afraid I had killed someone." Margaret tries to laugh. "A few people actually. But I was just silly and paranoid."

"I'm sure." BJ nods her head.

The two women look everywhere but at each other.

"I'm not sure about what I've heard about you, though." BJ's voice cracks with the silence of the last few minutes.

"And what's that?"

"That you're a prostitute." BJ's voice cracks again, but not from the silence.

"I prefer the term 'escort.' " Margaret's smile is sincere. "I guess Teddy told you that. I was hoping she hadn't."

"It doesn't matter," BJ says.

"But it bothers you?"

"Me? No. Not me. It's just that my mother. Well, she always warned me that I'd wind up a prostitute or something if I wasn't careful."

"Oh."

"Not that I think there's anything wrong with it," BJ quickly adds. "Though, I guess it's dangerous, isn't it?"

"Yes. More than I realized. I'm wanted now."

"Wanted?"

"I mean, I think I've been caught."

"Oh. What are you going to do now? Maybe you can make a deal. You know, turn in important men."

"I don't think . . ."

"Sorry. I guess that's not realistic. It was a story line on *In the Name of Love.*"

"My clients were all women."

"Oh." BJ's sigh of something like relief is involuntary.

"Anyway, I'm not sure what my plans are, but I know I need to go back to my apartment and get a few things and then I'm not sure. Maybe leave."

"And go where?"

"Somewhere. I don't know. How about you?"

"I'm thinking of going somewhere also. I love the ocean. They have beautiful beaches in Australia, don't they?"

"I don't know."

"You don't?"

"I've never been there."

"You . . . ?"

"No, I haven't."

"I thought for some reason, you. . . ."

"No. Although I do hear the Barrier Reef is very beautiful."

"Lots of people seem to think so."

"I think I want some place less . . ."

"Dramatic?"

"Popular?"

The women almost smile.

"I guess. But I'm not sure where else."

"Me either."

Their smiles ripen. Tentative. Hopeful.

Shimmering between them is a possibility. A possibility of stepping out of her life, as if it were a pair of pants that had gone out of style while she was wearing them. Or some color that she wore when she was much younger, almost somebody else. But that can't be possible. Unless it was never her life. Unless her life was just a costume she wore for camouflage.

270

It is BJ who stands up first. Walks over to the professor's bookshelves. Picks up the bottle of sand marked LESBOS. She cannot know who it is from, cannot know that Teodesia gave it to Professor Gertrude Yarnes when they were lovers, many many years ago. Would not care. Cares only that the sand is dyed an iridescent blue. Cares only that she wants it. Cares only that there is no reason not to take it.

She picks it up and holds it up for Margaret to see, before tucking it in her overnight bag.

"Do you need a lift?" BJ asks.

"That would be great."

The two women leave Gertrude's office together. Each of them, in turn, checks that the door is locked behind them. Each of them noticing the sign on the door, its paint flecking off: FESSOR TRUDE ARNES.

twenty-six

*T*here are two beds in the room.

It had been crowded and Italian and dark and in a nondescript part of town. The wine was red. An Australian Merlot. Brown Brothers.

They had suggested food to each other, almost in the same moment, more for some place to rest than to eat. Once inside the restaurant, safety settled around them like an intoxicant and the smell of garlic provoked their hungers. While eating shrimp scampi, the conversation thickened faster than the cooling butter. As if it had been forever since either of them had really spoken. And perhaps it had.

Although they didn't speak about the day's events, the sequence that had led them to this round table in this restaurant. Instead, they traded small stories, anecdotes from the lives each of them had led. BJ told about walking the beach as a child, which led Margaret to talk about something she had wanted once at a carnival, an acrylic box that contained a wave of changing colors. Margaret said a few things about Dominique, which led BJ to talk about her high school crush on Penelope, the girl who had first recommended she model.

They emerged from the restaurant disoriented, blinking against the light as the door squeaked shut behind them. It was as if they had been in a theater all afternoon, watching the matinee of their lives, and now they were surprised to see that the spring sun still slanted toward the horizon. It was too late for some things, like the bank and leaving town, and too early for others, like deciding what to do with the rest of their lives.

Still, there comes a time when one has to go home.

Even if one no longer has a home.

They decided on the Salisbury, at Margaret's suggestion. It was the hotel Jeanine preferred, the hotel in which Margaret had arranged Jeanine's lace-bordered underpants on a lampshade. Margaret had been tempted to sign Jeanine's name as she checked in, but decided to be careful. If it was unusual to pay in cash, leaving a three-hundred-dollar deposit for "incidentals," the clerk at the desk pretended not to notice, as did the doorman who gazed at BJ's one bag, the black overnighter.

There are two beds in the room.

A woman in a red merino wool suit sits on one bed.

A woman in black jeans and a black sweater sits on the other bed.

They glance at each other's clothes.

Neither woman asks: Why are you wearing my clothes?

One woman asks: "Should I turn on the TV?"

"No. Please don't."

There are two beds in the room.

They are very far apart, although the room is small.

A wide and dirty river flows between them.

She is a prostitute, one woman thinks of the other.

She is a murderer, one woman thinks of the other.

Not really, only women.

Not really, probably an accident.

What I was always afraid of most:

the prostitute thinks about the murderer.

the murderer thinks about the prostitute.

Both women stifle a laugh.

The woman on the bed nearer the door wonders how she might swim across the incredible distance and deliver a kiss, a real kiss. A real kiss would be real, like no other kiss she could remember.

The woman on the bed further from the door wonders how she might say what it is she wants, what she desires. It has been so long since she has said what she really wants. Maybe never.

"Well, I guess we'd better get some sleep."

"I guess."

There are two beds in the room.

Each woman pulls the top cover from her bed.

"I wish I had a toothbrush." The woman in the red merino wool suit on the bed further from the door says this.

"I've got one in my bag."

"You do? An extra?" She laughs.

"You can use mine." An invitation. She listens as the other woman brushes her teeth. Spits.

When it is her turn in the bathroom she uses the same toothbrush. Still wet from use.

There are two beds in the room.

There is a woman with clean teeth in each bed. Naked, or nearly so. Clothes spread neatly on a chair. There are two chairs in the room.

Neither woman is sleeping.

Each can hear the sounds of the outside: traffic and sirens.

Each can hear the sounds from the other side of the door, foot-steps and loud talking and once a shout, in the hallway.

Each can hear the other's breath. It calls her closer.

Which woman first slits the envelope of bedcovers and slides into the sterile air? Swims to the little open boat of the other bed, helped aboard by a tangle of arms? Which woman floats to the top of the other one, her elbows shaking as she supports herself? Which woman?

The first kiss is a stumble. The click of clean teeth. After a moment, the kisses deepen, a bottomless ravine.

BJ's tongue traces Margaret's lower lip.

Margaret's left thigh is curved between BJ's legs.

"We can stop if you want to."

"I don't want to. Do you?"

"No."

A kiss on the shoulder unfolds into a bite.

A hand spreads in the hair, at the nape of the neck.

Margaret's fingers circle BJ's wrist.

Jill Willis licks Tamara's throat.

Dominique's thumb traces Penelope's veins.

Lenore's nipples stiffen under Ann-Marie's gaze.

Patty's double tongue opens Mavis Paige and her evil twin, Renée.

The mermaid has legs and they are slick and smooth and they open wide.

The dyke in the literary biography arches her back into a poem.

I never knew; I thought.

I remember the rain, but not like this.

I could die at this moment.

I will live forever.

There is no scream, no words.

There are screams and words and sirens.

Beverley Jane and Maggie curl together, like little girls, one of them crying, both of them wet.

twenty-seven

*T*hat's a beautiful shade of lavender out past those clouds, wouldn't you say?"

There is a splotch of darkness near the horizon, a dark cloud of purple. It does not look like a bruise. Or a huge black bird. Or a swollen clitoris. Or a cliff from a distance. It does not look like New Jersey or Westchester or an interruption of the horizon. It looks like rain. Perhaps. In a few days. Or perhaps not.

"They say you should gaze out at the horizon—or some open spaces—at least once a day, every day. It calms your mind. Clarifies your vision."

"Where did you hear that?"

"I think I read it."

"Did you do that everyday?"

"Read?"

"No. Look at the horizon."

"Not everyday. Not even sometimes. Not ever. Before now."

"I tried. I walked along a beach sometimes."

"What did you think about?"

"Mermaids. You."

"I thought about you once when I was in an open field. The moon was high in the sky."

"And what did you think?"

"It wasn't a thought, really. More like a sensation. More like desire."

And in our conversations, we blend into each other, into the waves and wind. Our voices rise and fall with our feet as they walk.

We risk. Every day is still a risk.

To say "love" is a risk and we say it.

The first time we said "love," but not our first risk, we were near a statue of Joan of Arc. One of us was going into a building owned by the Ridgeway Management Company to a prewar apartment with three long windows and a narrow closet, to retrieve something she had left there, a tapestry attaché with some passports and safe deposit keys. The other waited outside, watching an adolescent boy with a lanky gait and a certain line to the jaw, a boy who was not who she wanted him to be, a boy who would grow up.

To say "fate" is a risk and we do not tempt it.

We do not retrace our escape route. Not the bank, or mailing the deeds to Mimi and Evelyn, or leaving the car in a garage, or the cab with the reckless driver, or looking at the list of departing flights in the airport, armored with our new identities.

We are learning that sometimes silence is better. It cannot be scripted. At least not for very long. If there is an audience.

But there is no audience now. We do not turn each other into spectators. We do not perform. Not for anyone. Not even ourselves.